WHAT HAVE YOU DONE?

www.penguin.co.uk

WHAT HAVE YOU DONE?

Shari Lapena

bantam

TRANSWORLD PUBLISHERS
Penguin Random House, One Embassy Gardens,
8 Viaduct Gardens, London SW11 7BW
www.penguin.co.uk

Transworld is part of the Penguin Random House group of companies
whose addresses can be found at global.penguinrandomhouse.com

First published in Great Britain in 2024 by Bantam
an imprint of Transworld Publishers

A CIP catalogue record for this book
is available from the British Library.

ISBNs
9781787635760 (hb)
9781787635777 (tpb)

Typeset in 12/16.5pt Sabon LT Pro by Jouve (UK), Milton Keynes
Printed and bound in Great Britain by Clays Ltd, Elcograf S.p.A.

The authorized representative in the EEA is Penguin Random House Ireland,
Morrison Chambers, 32 Nassau Street, Dublin D02 YH68.

Penguin Random House is committed to a sustainable
future for our business, our readers and our planet. This book is made from Forest
Stewardship Council® certified paper.

To my readers, with thanks

NOTHING EVER HAPPENS in Fairhill, Vermont. It's a small town, surrounded by farmland, with the Green Mountains in the distance. Cornfields and hay. Covered bridges and ghost stories. Hiking and hayrides. Underage drinking in the graveyard, late at night, leaning up against the headstones. There isn't much else for teenagers to do. Drive around in their parents' trucks once they get their licence. Make out if they're lucky. School and sports and chores and part-time jobs . . .

Nothing ever happens in sleepy little Fairhill, Vermont. Until it does.

Chapter One

EARLY FRIDAY MORNING, Roy Ressler drives his big tractor down the gravel road that borders his fields, his mind on his daughter's upcoming wedding. He's thinking what a beautiful bride Ellen is going to be. It's nearing the end of October; the air is crisp, trees are alive with colour, and the early morning dew sparkles on the ground. All's good with the world.

He glances up at the dark figures circling against the bright blue sky ahead of him, to the right, over one of his fields. They hold his attention for a moment, the way they glide, use the air currents. Turkey vultures. There's more than half a dozen of them. They must have found something. He carries on his way down the road. His dog – a mix of shepherd and black Lab and maybe something else – lopes beside him, keeping clear of the tractor. She stops, sniffs the air.

The birds are massing over one of his fields farther down

the road ahead of him. As he gets closer, he finds himself watching them. He approaches the open gate to the field where the vultures are circling. It must be something big, maybe a deer. They'll pick the carcass clean; there won't be anything left. Nature doing its work. But something makes him stop. He turns off the tractor for a moment at the side of the road near the open gate and scans the field. That's when he notices that some of the birds are already on the ground, three or four of them, hopping and squabbling over something. A carcass of some kind. He can't see what it is from here, but he catches glimpses of something light coloured.

His dog looks up at him, questioning. Roy starts the tractor again and heads across the open hayfield to take a look. The vultures aren't flying away yet at his approach; they're protecting their feast. He knows they won't attack him since they're not predators, and they only feed on the dead. He's curious now, and he keeps driving the tractor toward them, hoping they'll fly off. They're big and ugly as sin. Blackish-brown feathers and hairless, reddish faces – they're made that way because they're carrion feeders, they stick their faces in dead and rotting flesh. That's their job – clean-up crew. Not all of nature is beautiful, Roy knows that well enough, but every part of it has a purpose.

The growth in the field obscures what it is they're perched on. The birds squawk and spread their wings and look even bigger as he rumbles closer; one suddenly flies off with a loud flapping of its wings, but two remain. One stares malevolently at him, face bloodied, but the other is busy feeding, head down, ripping at flesh. The dog sticks closer to the tractor.

When Roy gets within thirty yards of them, the last two take off swiftly with a loud drumming of wings. He still can't quite see what they've been feeding on. He keeps driving closer, the tractor bumping across the field, his body moving familiarly with it. He's high up on the seat, and now he sees. He turns off the tractor and there's an abrupt silence. The quiet seems to underscore his shock. It's not a deer after all.

It's a girl. She's naked and lying on her back. Her stomach has been ripped open by the birds. Even with her eyes gouged out by the vultures he thinks he recognizes her. He retches, turns his head away.

Roy scrambles in the pocket of his overalls. His hands are shaking, and he almost drops his cell phone as he grabs it. He's a volunteer firefighter and he's seen some awful things, but he's never seen anything like this.

And then he stays there, atop his tractor, guarding her, protecting her from those fucking birds, swearing and yelling and waving his arms at them as they swoop and soar overhead, until help arrives.

Paula Acosta hears her alarm go off and gets out of bed. It's 7:30 a.m. on Friday. Her husband, Martin, has been up before her – he's an early riser. He teaches at Dartmouth College, in Hanover, New Hampshire, an almost twenty-minute drive. It takes her under five minutes to get to Fairhill High School, where she teaches English.

She swears it gets harder every year. COVID seems to have made everything worse – especially for the ninth graders. The kids' skills are further behind than ever, their reliance on or addiction to screens and technology even worse. Their social skills seem to be more lacking than before the pandemic, and their attention spans are a fraction of what they once were. Or is it just her? She doesn't think so – all the teachers see it. She sometimes wonders if she could do something else.

Her daughter, Taylor, is one of those ninth graders. Paula knows it's hard for kids to attend the same school where their parents teach. She suspects Taylor sometimes finds it mortifying, although she would never admit it. She must hear what the kids say about Paula – about all the teachers – behind their backs. That's the problem with being in a small community; her daughter doesn't have the option to go to a different high school. The rural kids are all bussed in to Fairhill High. At least she's not the principal – he has three kids in the high school, and she knows it's not easy for them. They act out so they won't be taken for Goody Two-Shoes, or as getting special treatment. They're rebels, all three of them, and the girl is the worst. She feels for Principal Kelly, she really does.

She enters the kitchen. Her daughter is seated at the table having a bowl of cereal, head down, scrolling on her phone. Paula's annoyance at seeing Taylor glued to her phone is always tinged with anxiety. She doesn't like her daughter spending time on social media. They've tried to set limits, but they've had to be careful about it. Paula's done the reading, and she's seen it with her own eyes – she knows what social media does to girls. How it destroys their self-esteem with impossible comparisons. How it distorts their thinking, their expectations, their priorities. She does a unit on media in her English classes to try to combat it, but it feels like she's slamming the lid down on Pandora's box far too late. All the evils of the world are already out there for them to see, to participate in, with the touch of a finger. Even here in their quiet, friendly little town in rural Vermont. It's one of the reasons some of the kids seem to dislike her – she tells them to get off their devices, to read books, to talk to one another, and they don't want to hear it. Plus, she's a hard marker and expects them to actually work. She still has standards.

She leans down and kisses her daughter on top of her smooth brown hair, trying to get a glimpse of her phone screen, but Taylor immediately covers it with her hand. Paula turns away and heads for the coffee, which her husband had made and left warm for her. 'Did you see Dad off?' she asks.

'Yeah.'

'Do you have anything on after school today?' Paula tries to sound casual. She doesn't want to be too nosy – her daughter's at that sensitive age – but she's worried that Taylor isn't fitting in easily this year. Of course, she still has her friends from grade school – they moved to the same high school with her. But it's a new start for all of them and things change.

Paula has one class of particularly unruly grade nines this

year – Taylor isn't among them, admin gets it – but mostly she's doing the upper years, preparing them for college. Still, she knows how kids talk.

'No,' her daughter mumbles.

'Maybe you should join a club?' her mother suggests gently. She doesn't receive an answer.

Chapter Two

ROY HASN'T LEFT his post. They arrive quickly. He sees the police cruiser speed down the gravel road and waves vigorously from atop his tractor. The cruiser comes to a stop at the side of the road. Two men in uniform get out and walk quickly across the field toward him. He'd called the police chief in Fairhill, Mike Hall. With him is Officer Chris Shepherd. Together they make up the town's entire police force. Roy watches them approach. As they get closer, the dog begins to run toward the officers, but Roy calls her back and makes her sit. They come up alongside the big tractor.

Hall glances at him and says, 'Roy,' and he and his officer step closer to the dead girl. The two men stop and stand a few feet away from the body, looking down at it in deep seriousness. Roy climbs down from the tractor and joins them.

'Jesus,' Hall says, rubbing his hand over the lower half of his face.

Shepherd doesn't say anything, just stares. Roy glances at him, thinks he looks like he might throw up.

Hall says, 'That's the Brewer girl.'

'We need to cover her up,' Roy manages. His voice is uneven, and he clears his throat.

'No, we're not touching anything,' Hall says.

'I saw the birds,' Roy says.

Hall nods. He's older than Shepherd, and better able to hide his feelings, but Roy knows Mike Hall well, and he's obviously shaken.

'Best not get any closer,' Hall says, 'and keep the dog back. We don't want to contaminate the scene.'

They stand in silence. Roy notices for the first time the line of deep purple bruising around the dead girl's throat. He focuses on that because he can't bear to look at her face, and it's indecent to look at her naked body, so pale against the ground. Shepherd has turned away and is drawing in deep breaths through his mouth, as if trying to compose himself. Roy and Hall both pretend they don't notice. They give the younger man space. Roy finds he wants to cry, but he won't let himself here. Not until later, when he's alone, or maybe when he's telling his wife. He thinks of his daughter, about to be married. This young girl will never walk down the aisle. That makes him think of her parents, and what they have lost.

'She's been strangled,' Hall says. His voice draws Shepherd's attention back. He seems ready now, to face it.

But the words send a chill up Roy's spine. He can't remember anyone ever getting murdered around here. This is a safe place. People walk around alone at night. Nothing ever happens here.

'With what, though? And where are her clothes?' Shepherd asks, his words brisk now.

It's true. She's lying naked in the field and there's no sign of her clothing, no sign of anything she might have been strangled with.

Hall nods. 'Used a ligature of some kind. That wasn't done manually.' He looks up, away from the body, and surveys the field in all directions, then glances at Roy. 'You notice any tracks from up there on your way in?'

Roy shakes his head. 'No.' He looks behind him and can see only the tracks left by his tractor, imprinted on the field.

Hall follows his gaze. There's no sign of their passage either; the vegetation has sprung back and swallowed it up. 'Someone must have carried her in here,' Hall says. He's silent for a moment. 'We might never have found her if you hadn't taken a look, Roy.'

It doesn't make Roy feel any better.

Hall reaches for his phone. 'I'd better call Vermont State Police – they'll get the Major Crimes Unit folks out here.'

It's early morning, the dew is still sparkling on the grass. The fields are pretty, all laid out in squares, with trees along the fence lines. I'm not sure what I'm doing here, but I'm curious. I watch a farmer in denim overalls climb down from his old red tractor, joining two other men on the ground. They're wearing police uniforms. I recognize them – it's the police chief, Mike Hall, and Officer

11

Shepherd, who does the talks at school about the dangers of drunk driving. I wonder what they're doing here, what they're looking at. The dog is excited about something, but the farmer is holding her back.

There's something in this field, and I want to know what it is. I move closer. I'm above them, looking down. I see what they're looking at, and I don't understand at all. The girl on the ground is naked, and I'm embarrassed for her, with these three men staring at her and not a stitch on. I notice with detachment that her stomach is torn open, and her intestines are spilling out, glistening. She's not in pain, because she's clearly dead. I see where her eyes used to be and feel a muted mix of revulsion and pity. But I'm drawn closer, because despite the mutilation, I definitely recognize her face.

It's me.

But a dead and desecrated me. These men all seem very concerned.

This is a very strange dream. I want to wake up now.

Riley tries again, sending another text message to Diana. R U there? They usually try to meet in the school cafeteria before classes start. She must be running late, but it's not like Diana to ignore a text – she'd be too worried about offending a friend. Diana doesn't like to hurt anybody's feelings. She's basically an angel.

Riley leaves the cafeteria and makes her way to the first-floor girls' bathroom. She checks herself out in the mirror. Good enough. Her mother tells her she's beautiful, but

Riley has no idea, really. Her mother's standards are pretty low. She doesn't know what it's like these days. Riley had to fight tooth and nail for her mother to agree to let her get her brows professionally done, but it was totally worth it. She's lucky to have good skin and hair and perfect teeth, but is she beautiful? She doesn't think so, not even on her very best days. Not beautiful like Diana. Her mom says, *All you young girls are beautiful, you just won't realize it until it's too late*. Her mom also tells her to focus on her brains, which pisses Riley off because it's not like she doesn't get straight As. But it's hard to know what's beautiful. It's not hard to know what's ugly. Everyone agrees on ugly. If you're ugly in high school, there's nowhere to hide. Thank God she's not ugly.

She checks her cell again but there's no message from Diana. She puts her phone in her pocket and heads for her first class – English. Mrs Acosta won't be happy if Diana is late.

Riley takes her assigned seat then waves and smiles at her friend Evan, sitting behind her. The class fills quickly with the sound of bustle and chairs scraping and knapsacks hitting the floor, kids talking. Mrs Acosta arrives and smiles at them and says, 'Good morning,' in a bright, cheery voice, the way she always does.

The teacher looks around the class, noting every single student as she marks attendance. Mrs Acosta is a good teacher, and Riley respects her. All the good students do. The kids who diss her just want a teacher who will let them slack off. Riley doesn't want to slack off; she wants to learn.

She has a brain, and she means to use it. She glances behind her again at Evan, in the back corner. Diana still hasn't arrived. Riley wonders if she's sick. She was fine yesterday. But even sick, Diana would answer her texts, she thinks uneasily.

Mrs Acosta looks over her glasses at Diana's empty seat in the middle row. She glances around the room. 'Has anyone seen Diana this morning?'

'No, ma'am,' Riley says. A few others shake their heads.

The teacher makes a mark on the paper and then sets it aside. But before they can begin, there's a tap on the open classroom door, and Mr Kelly, the principal, is standing there, and he looks odd, as if he's had a shock. From where she sits, Riley can also see a uniformed police officer standing out in the hall, and she feels a spurt of alarm. Mr Kelly gestures to Mrs Acosta to come out to join them. Riley looks back at Evan, and he gives her a questioning look. She turns to look at what's going on in the corridor, but suddenly the door is pulled shut from outside. There's a second of utter silence, then people start to talk. *What's going on? Did you see police out there?*

Riley's stomach does a flip. She's suddenly afraid it's about Diana. Diana hasn't responded to her since last night. Since she was on her way out to see her boyfriend, Cameron.

14

Chapter Three

BRENDA BREWER WORKS nights as a nurse at the hospital in Windsor, Vermont. There's no hospital in Fairhill, it's too small. She doesn't mind the thirty-five-minute commute to and from work, most of the time. She likes living in Fairhill, where everyone knows everybody. There's a grocery store, a feed store, a Home Depot, a main street with lots of shops, some restaurants, and a movie theatre. There's a small park, a couple of churches, a hockey arena, and a library. The farm kids are bussed in to the schools in town. She likes it here; it's enough for her. But she doesn't think it's enough for her daughter. She wants more for Diana.

Brenda's usually home in time to see Diana before she leaves for school. Now that her daughter is older, Brenda has recently switched to the night shift – which is easier and less busy than the day shift. She's been a single mom since Diana's dad left, six years ago, when Diana was eleven. He sends the occasional cheque – not as much as he should, but just enough that she doesn't go after him for what he really owes. Lee has a new family now, with a younger wife and twin boys who seem to absorb all his time and most of his money. Well, what did he expect? On the rare occasions that she sees him, he seems less happy and more stressed than he ever was when they were together. She thinks he has regrets. Serves him right.

Brenda is quite happy, though. Being single suits her. Especially now that Diana is growing up, and parenting doesn't take the time and energy it once did. She's gotten over being left by her husband, and she likes not having to take care of him and his mess. She's proud of how Diana has turned out. Her daughter is strong, smart, and kind. Those are the important things. She's beautiful and popular as well, but Brenda has never been too caught up in that. And neither has her daughter – she has a good head on her shoulders. She wants to do good in the world. Brenda has been lucky – some parents struggle with their children, but she never has. She and Diana get along well. Diana is easy-going and helpful. She's never given her any trouble, but Brenda wonders if that's about to change.

She's thinking about Diana as she drives home from the hospital, passing fields and farms on the familiar route. Her thoughts inevitably turn to Cameron, the boy that Diana's seeing. Her daughter has known him for years; they've been friends for a long time. He's always been there, in the background. It's only this fall, though, that they became a couple. It seems to have become very intense, very suddenly. It has taken Brenda by surprise, even made her a little uneasy. She likes Cameron well enough, but she doesn't want her daughter to settle. She doesn't think Cameron is smart enough, ambitious enough, good enough for her daughter. She doesn't want Diana ending up with her high school sweetheart, like she did. There's a whole wide world out there, beyond Fairhill, Vermont. But the less said at this point the better. She's not one to go looking to create a problem where one may not even exist. Diana is going away to college next year – that will put an end to it.

Brenda is late this morning, as she stayed longer to cover a gap in staffing, so it's almost nine o'clock as she turns into her own street. She loves nursing, but it's hard work, and now her feet and back hurt, and she just wants her bed. She regrets she wasn't home in time this morning to see Diana off to school, but they will catch up later.

Her fatigue evaporates when she notices the police cruiser parked on the street in front of her house. Brenda pulls into the driveway as a uniformed officer turns and watches her from her front step. She recognizes him – it's the police chief, Mike Hall. She suddenly feels her heart pounding, and her hands begin to tremble as she turns off the car. She tries not to give in to her sudden dread. What is he doing here? It can't be anything to do with Diana. Diana's at school.

She gets out of the car and looks at the police chief, who has walked toward her.

He says gently, 'Mrs Brewer?'

'Yes,' she manages to say. 'What's wrong?'

'Can we go inside and talk?' he asks.

17

She doesn't like the look on his face. She feels her centre collapsing, a weakness washing over her. 'What is it?'

'Come inside, please,' he says, taking her arm.

She allows herself to be led to the front door, which she unlocks with unsteady hands. He's going to tell her something she doesn't want to hear. She must prepare herself. But she doesn't want to prepare herself, she wants to send him away. She's angry at him for being here.

And then somehow, they are seated in her living room, and he is telling her that her daughter is dead. Her beautiful, perfect, only daughter. It's all very far away and echoey, as if he's talking at her from another room, but she can see his face swimming in and out of focus and he looks concerned. Well, he should be concerned, coming here and saying such nonsense.

'No,' she says firmly. 'Diana's at school. I think you should leave.' She gets up and moves to show him the door, but her legs give out beneath her. He catches her just in time and eases her back onto the sofa.

'I'm so sorry,' he says, his voice breaking.

She begins to wail.

Cameron has a free first period on Friday. He sleeps in, then gets up and showers and pulls on jeans, a T-shirt and a hoodie. Then he goes downstairs for breakfast. His parents are both already at work. He likes having the house to himself. It's an older house, on the edge of town, with a screened-in front porch and creaky floors. He pours himself some cereal, grabs the milk out of the fridge, and is about to sit down at the kitchen table and check his cell phone when there's a knock at the door. He tenses and glances in the direction of the door. He puts the milk down on the table. The knock comes again, more loudly this time.

He walks down the hall and opens the front door. There are two officers in the tan and olive uniforms of Vermont State Police on the front porch, a strong-looking woman and a younger, taller man. He doesn't recognize them – they're not from around here. He immediately feels a surge of fear.

'Yes?' he says.

'Cameron Farrell?' the female officer says.

'Yes, that's me.'

'Are your parents home?' she asks.

'No, they're at work.' He sees the two officers glance at each other.

She introduces herself and her partner, but the names go right over his head.

'May we come in?'

'Why? What's this about?'

When they don't answer, he gestures them inside. They walk into the living room on the right. It's an old-fashioned room, with slightly dated furniture and some antiques his parents have acquired over the years. He doesn't sit, so they don't either. He folds his arms in front of his chest nervously and waits for them to speak.

'Do you know a girl named Diana Brewer?'

'Yes. She's my girlfriend.'

'Maybe you'd better sit down,' the female officer suggests.

Cameron slumps heavily into the armchair behind him. He doesn't speak now.

'I'm so sorry, but I'm afraid Diana is dead,' she says gently, watching him closely.

'What?' he says.

'Her body was found a short while ago in a farmer's field, not far from here.'

He can hear the blood pounding in his ears. He shakes his head. 'That's impossible. I just saw her—' He stops suddenly.

'When did you last see her?' the officer asks.

He swallows. 'Last night.'

'What time last night?' she asks.

'I don't know exactly. I need to think.'

She waits for him to say more, but he's frightened. 'What happened to her?' he asks, his voice unsteady.

The officer ignores his question, and asks, 'Where did you see her last night?'

Cameron's eyes are filling with tears as he answers. 'I picked her up in my dad's truck. We drove around,' he clears his throat, 'made out.' He looks at the two officers nervously. 'Then I dropped her back at her house and came home – probably just after eleven.'

The female officer is nodding back at him. She says gently, 'I'm so sorry for your loss.' Then she adds, 'We'd like you to come down to the station to talk to us, if that's all right.'

'Okay,' he says. His body is beginning to tremble.

She says, 'You need to call your parents.'

Chapter Four

PAULA ACOSTA CAN'T quite take it in. Diana Brewer is *dead*? She looks back at the familiar police officer in the corridor outside her classroom. 'What?' she says.

The officer, Chris Shepherd, replies, 'Her body was found a short time ago in a field outside of town. Major Crimes is there now.'

Paula turns to Principal Kelly. He looks overwhelmed, like he doesn't know how he's going to cope.

'You mean – she was *murdered*?' Paula asks in disbelief.

'It looks that way.'

'Dear God,' Paula breathes, her right hand moving involuntarily to her heart. 'That lovely girl.' She thinks of her own daughter, Taylor. Then she thinks of Diana's mother, whom she's met, numerous times, in parent–teacher conferences. Her life destroyed, just like that. Paula feels a sudden need to sit down, but there are no chairs in the corridor.

'There are some officers from state police in the principal's

21

office. They want to talk to the students who knew her,' Shepherd says. 'There are detectives and more officers coming in from Major Crimes to handle the investigation.' He glances at Kelly. 'Principal Kelly tells us that two of her best friends are in your class – Riley Mead and Evan Carr. Are they here now?'

'Yes.'

'We'd like to cause as little distress and disruption as possible,' Shepherd says, 'but the news is going to get out very quickly, and it will make its way to the kids' phones. We should get out in front of it and tell them now.'

'She has a boyfriend, Cameron Farrell,' Paula hears herself say.

Shepherd nods. 'There are officers talking to him now. Shall we?' he says, reaching for the classroom door.

Riley watches the door open with dread. Her heart is beating too fast, and she has a terrible premonition of what's going to happen next. Mrs Acosta enters the room first, looking distressed and pale, very different from the cheerful way she'd come in just a few minutes earlier. Principal Kelly looks even worse, accompanied by the police officer she now recognizes, Chris Shepherd, usually so upbeat when seen about town, now wearing a solemn expression. *Someone has died*, Riley thinks. She feels like she might faint.

Principal Kelly clears his throat and says, 'I'm afraid I have some terrible, tragic news.' The class has gone completely quiet, all the teenage energy stilled. 'Your classmate, Diana Brewer, has died.'

Riley gasps so audibly that faces turn toward her. She sees Kelly looking at her too.

He says, directly to her, 'I'm so sorry.'

She can see him choking up as he says it. She's breathing too fast, in short gasps, her eyes blurring with tears.

'Class is dismissed for today,' Kelly says, 'but please don't leave the school just yet. There will be counsellors here very soon for anyone who wants to talk to them. I encourage you all to do so. Also, there are state police here, in my office, and they would like to talk to anyone who knew Diana, to help in their investigation.'

'Investigation?' comes a voice from the back of the room.

Principal Kelly seems at a loss for words, and Shepherd steps forward. 'There's no easy way to say this,' he says, gravely surveying the students in the room. 'Diana was murdered. We're going to need your help.'

Edward Farrell arrives at the Fairhill Police Station at the same time as his wife – his truck follows her car in. They each left work to be here for their son, Cameron. It's a terrible thing – his girlfriend has been *murdered*. It's hard to take in. Such a lovely girl. Their son will need all their support through this.

In the parking lot, Edward hugs his wife, Shelby, tightly. She's been crying. She has a tissue clutched in her hand and her mascara is running. Her blonde hair is in disarray.

'I can't believe it,' she says to him, finally pulling back from his embrace, her face a mask of shock.

'I can't either,' he says.

'And Cameron – how will he cope with this?' she asks in distress.

'I don't know.'

Finally, they brace themselves and turn toward the steps of the small police station. Their son is in there. He needs them.

Inside the redbrick building they are quickly escorted to an interview room, where their son is hunched in a chair. At the sight of him, Edward's heart almost breaks.

Cameron jumps up when he sees them, falls into his mother's arms, and sobs. Edward swallows, watching them. It takes effort not to break down himself, but he wants to be strong for his son. He knows Cameron was serious about Diana. First love. What a way for it to end.

The door opens behind them, and two people appear, distracting Edward from the sight of his son and wife. A tall, well-built man enters – he looks to be in his mid forties, and is dressed in a smart suit and a white shirt open at the neck, and no tie. His brown hair is short and starting to go grey. He's clean-shaven. He carries himself with quiet authority.

'I'm Detective Stone, from Major Crimes, Vermont State Police, and this is Detective Godfrey,' he says, introducing another detective, a woman. She's petite, with dark hair cut short, in a navy trouser suit. 'I'm so sorry for your loss,' Detective Stone says to the three of them. He seems sincere, respectful. 'Please, have a seat.'

They all sit down. 'We'd like to talk to your son about Diana, see if he can help us find out who did this,' Stone explains. 'But as he's a minor, we need to have a parent present. You can both stay.'

Edward nods. 'Okay.' He glances at his wife.

Stone turns to Cameron. 'This is purely voluntary, son. You don't have to answer our questions, but it might be helpful to us. And the sooner we talk, the better.'

Edward watches Cameron nod. His athletic, good-looking son is unusually pale, his face tear-streaked, but he is calm enough now, after his crying jag. He seems relieved that his parents have come.

'My officers said you saw Diana last night. Can we go over that again?'

Cameron glances briefly at his mother and says, 'Okay.' He begins. 'I drove over to her place around ten o'clock. I often go see her around then. Her mom leaves for work just before ten. She works as a nurse on the night shift at the hospital in Windsor.'

'What car did you drive?'

Edward notices that Cameron looks startled at this. Edward is a little taken aback as well. What the hell difference does it make what car he drove?

Cameron says, 'My dad's pickup. He always lets me use it if he doesn't need it, and he was already home for the night.' Edward nods in agreement. 'So I went over to her place and picked her up and we went for a drive.'

'Why did you go for a drive?' Stone asks casually.

Edward sees his son flush crimson, and he knows.

'Sometimes we go for a drive, and park somewhere . . .' He leaves that hanging, as if he doesn't want to spell it out.

'I see. Did you have sex with her last night?' Stone asks. He adds, 'I'm sorry, I have to ask.'

25

Cameron studiously avoids looking at his parents, looks down at the table instead. 'Yes.'

'Okay. Did you use a condom?'

'Yes.'

'If you don't mind my asking, why didn't you stay in the house?' Stone asks.

At that, Cameron looks up from the table at the detective. 'What?'

'The house was empty. Diana's mother was at work. No one else lives there.'

Edward watches his son flush, his eyes directed again to the table. Cameron mumbles, 'Diana didn't like to do it in the house. She thought it was disrespectful to her mother.'

Stone nods, as if he understands perfectly, but Edward is annoyed at the detective. He's being rude and insensitive. His son has just lost someone he cares deeply about. Now he's being embarrassed unnecessarily in front of his parents.

'What was she wearing?' Stone asks next.

'Um, blue jeans, a plaid shirt, and her beige corduroy jacket.'

'What about her underwear?'

Cameron flushes again. 'She had a bra and panties on, but I don't know what colour. It was dark. Socks and sneakers. Why are you asking me this?'

Stone ignores him. 'What time did you bring her home?'

'I'm not sure exactly, but around eleven. And then I went home.'

'Did you accompany her inside, or drop her at the door?'

'I stopped the truck in front of her house and watched her go in. She waved and closed the door behind her, then I left.'

'Did she unlock the door when she went in?'

Cameron pauses. 'I didn't notice.' He adds, 'But I don't think she locked it behind her when we left.'

'Okay,' Stone says. 'Did Diana ever mention that she was worried about someone? Had anyone been bothering her?'

'No. Everybody loved her,' Cameron says.

Chapter Five

SHELBY WATCHES HER son break down after he says, 'Everybody loved her.' She feels her own lower lip wobble, and she reaches for him, seated close beside her, drawing him into a hug, stroking his soft brown hair. She feels his body convulsing in sobs against her. It's true, everybody loved Diana. She was almost too good to be true. They'd been so delighted when their son started dating her. They'd fallen in love with her, too, a little bit. This is all very hard, and she hopes her shattered son can survive it.

She can hardly bear to think of Diana's mother, Brenda. She'll be all alone now, and Diana was everything to her. How bleak her life will be, just like that. Cameron is also an only child; Shelby can't bear to think of what her life would be like if she were to lose him. How fragile life is, she thinks, holding her sobbing son; we should never take it for granted. She still thinks of her son as just a boy – he still seems so young to her. She doesn't like to think of him having sex with Diana in their truck.

Who could have done such an awful thing? She assumes, because she's not naïve and because of the pointed questions the detective just asked, that Diana was sexually assaulted as well as murdered. It all makes her stomach heave.

How could it have happened? Cameron brought her safely home. This is a small town, where everybody knows everybody else – no one gets murdered here. That question about the door – do the police think someone might have already been waiting inside the house for her last night? She supposes it's possible, if Diana hadn't locked the door. People often don't around here. It makes her sick to think of it, to think that her son might have unknowingly delivered Diana to her killer. How else might it have happened? She wouldn't have gone out again at that hour. Maybe someone came to the door later? Or broke in afterward? She was all alone in that house last night.

Shelby fervently hopes they catch the bastard. The death penalty would be too good for him. How desperately awful for her son to lose his first serious girlfriend this way.

And yet Cameron has told the detectives one small lie.

She tries not to worry about it. But after the interview – which seemed to go on and on – as she drives home alone in her own car, Cameron in the truck with his father, Shelby does worry. She knows something that her husband doesn't. Should she tell him? Confront her son? Because she got up last night, when Edward was snoring heavily beside her. She had to pee. On her way down the hall to the bathroom she peeked into Cameron's room, because his door was slightly open. Usually, it was closed. His bed was empty. He wasn't there. She finished in the bathroom and went back to her room, checking the time on the digital clock on her bedside table. It was almost one a.m. She would have to talk to Cameron in the morning, she thought. He was supposed to be home by 11:30 on weeknights. She and Edward were usually asleep before then, so they didn't know when he came in. They didn't police him. They just assumed he was coming in on time.

As she lay there, worried, her earplugs left out, she heard him creep in. She noted the time: 1:11 a.m. She thought about going out and confronting him on the stairs, but she decided it could wait until morning. Reassured to have him safe at home, she fell back asleep.

But now, driving home in her car, she knows he lied to the police. He did not come home shortly after eleven – it was much later than that. She just doesn't know why he lied. Did he leave Diana safely at home at eleven and go do something else and lie because of his curfew? Or did he leave Diana at home much later than he said?

Brenda Brewer is at the police station, in one of the two interview rooms. She's sitting with a female officer who brings her coffee and tissues and speaks in a soft voice. She doesn't know where the police chief has gone. They wanted to get her out of the house while they looked it over as a possible crime scene. She's been told that they think Diana's body was taken to the field, that she was killed – strangled with some kind of ligature – somewhere else. The house is one possibility. It stuns her: the idea that Diana might have been killed inside their house, while she was at work.

A man in a dark suit quietly enters the room, accompanied by a woman, also in plain clothes, and the uniformed officer exits. He introduces himself as Detective Stone and the woman as Detective Godfrey, from Vermont State Police, Major Crimes Unit. They, too, speak softly. Brenda's ex-husband is on his way, but he lives more than a two-hour drive away now. He is the only one who will feel the loss anywhere near as much as she does, she thinks, but he has another family. He has other children. She has no one.

'I know this is unbelievably hard,' Detective Stone says gently, 'but we want to get who did this. Do you think you can answer some questions?'

She nods. She will do her best. But she just wants someone to drug her into sleep and never to wake up.

Stone says, 'We know Diana was in a relationship with Cameron Farrell. But did she ever mention anyone else being interested in her?'

Brenda tries to think, to claw her way through the fog of shock and grief and disbelief. 'Not that I recall.'

'Diana didn't mention anyone who was bothering her, who maybe showed an interest in her that she didn't reciprocate?'

Brenda pauses, remembers. 'She did mention once that there was a customer where she worked who gave her the creeps.'

'Where did she work?'

'At the Home Depot. She had a summer job there, then carried on when school started, doing occasional shifts evenings and weekends.' She answers automatically; she's surprised at how lucid she sounds.

'What did she say about this customer who gave her the creeps?'

'Not much.' Brenda looks down at the tissues crumpled in her hands. 'I didn't like her working evenings, so I was glad she was at the Home Depot because there's always lots of people around. It's a big place. Not like a little corner store where she would have been alone. I wouldn't have let her do that. And I made her promise to always get someone to walk her to her car at the end of her shift, and she always did. They were good that way.' And then she realizes how none of it helped, that her daughter is dead anyway, and she breaks down again.

They let her cry for as long as she needs. Godfrey leaves discreetly and returns with a bottle of water, which she doesn't want. Stone is still waiting patiently; he's not finished. She wants to know who murdered her daughter too. She wants to rip him to shreds with her bare hands. She pulls herself together as best she can.

'Tell us about her boyfriend, Cameron,' Detective Stone says.

She looks at him. 'What about him?'

32

'What's he like?' Stone asks.

She says, 'He's a nice boy. They were friends all through school, but they started dating and became a couple at the end of the summer, just before school started again. It was quite sudden, and very intense.'

'Intense how?'

'I just mean, you know, they were – it seemed like they were in love. They spent every moment they could together. He was always coming over. He was all over her, holding her hand, kissing her, as if he couldn't get enough.' Her disapproval must have shown.

'Did you approve of their relationship?'

She gives him a frank look. 'To be honest, I have nothing against *him*, but I didn't like to see Diana getting so serious about someone so fast, and so young. He was her first real boyfriend. I was glad she planned on going away to college next year.' She stops suddenly, fights back another sob. She adds pointlessly, 'She wanted to be a vet. She loved animals.'

'Did you know they were having sexual relations?' Stone asks.

She lets out a long breath. 'Diana didn't tell me, but I assumed. Did Cameron tell you that? Have you already talked to him?'

'Yes. You understand we had to ask.'

She nods, braces herself. 'Was she – was she sexually assaulted?'

'We're still waiting for an answer on that,' he says. 'Have you ever had a break-in at your house?'

She shakes her head. 'No.'

'Ever notice anyone loitering outside the house, see a car parked there you didn't know?'

'No.'

'Do you keep your house locked?'

She swallows. 'We usually lock the doors at night before we go to bed, but not always during the day. Fairhill isn't the kind of place you have to lock your doors.' She pauses, because she knows now that that isn't true. Brenda used to lock up at night, but now she goes to work and leaves it to her daughter. It never occurred to her that they weren't safe. She knows better now. Now that it's too late. She says, 'The door was locked when I arrived home this morning.'

Stone nods. 'Cameron says he saw your daughter last night, brought her home at around eleven p.m., watched her enter the house, and then went home. Do you remember what she was wearing when you left for work last night, just before ten o'clock?'

Brenda tries to concentrate. 'Jeans and a plaid shirt, sort of red and cream.'

The detective nods. 'Can you think of any reason your daughter might have left the house again of her own volition?'

'No. Have you checked her cell phone?'

Stone says, 'We haven't found it. It wasn't with her, and we haven't found it in the house. Not yet anyway.' He adds, 'And the clothes that Cameron and you both describe her as wearing earlier that night are also missing. Her corduroy jacket and sneakers were found in the house. But we're not releasing this information to the public, so please keep it to yourself.' He adds, 'It's quite possible that it was someone that she knew.'

'I want to go home,' she says, feeling nauseated.

'They're still searching there,' Stone tells her gently.

'I want to go home,' she sobs. 'Please, I just want to go home.'

Chapter Six

AARON BOLDUC IS the manager of the Home Depot in Fair-hill. It's a good job and he's grateful for it most of the time, but now he sits in his office in the back of the enormous store – so big, with ceilings so high that small birds fly among its rafters – and stares down at the tattered blotter on his desk. Diana Brewer is dead, and he must find some-one to take her shift this evening.

The news had come over the radio, which he keeps on low in his office. The story broke around 9:30 a.m. He'd been in his office when he heard that her body had been found in a farmer's field outside Fairhill.

He had sat perfectly still, letting the news break over him.

He liked Diana. Everyone liked Diana. He will have to manage his staff, and their grief, while hiding his own. He wonders if others will now call in 'sick', unable to work. They were all friends of Diana's. But surely they won't leave him in the lurch?

They don't tell you about this kind of thing in management training. Managing people is difficult. *People* are difficult. Managing them has not come naturally to him. He does his best, but the problem is, he is too nice, and people take advantage. It is a constant source of stress for him, that if you're too nice, people will shit all over you. They'll come in a couple of minutes late, leaving him to fret that they might not be coming in at all. Diana wasn't like that; she was always in at least five minutes before her shift started. She was always cheerful and obliging and treated him with respect. Most of his employees need a firm hand, but it's not natural to him. He's a pleaser. He wants to be liked. He grew up in a family riven by conflict; he was the middle child, the peacemaker. And it seems sometimes that managing his staff is a lot like managing his family, only there are a lot more of them, and his job is on the line.

Diana's death will upset everyone. He will do his best to help his staff through it. He's good at giving comfort, at being understanding and sympathetic, at trying to make everyone happy. Surely no one will try to challenge his authority at a time of crisis like this?

But who will comfort *him*? The truth is, he adored Diana. But he must do his best to hide his grief.

Riley is badly shaken as she leaves the principal's office. Being questioned by the police has unnerved her. She sees Evan waiting on a chair outside the office, his face smeared with tears.

'Are you okay?' he asks her, standing up.

She shakes her head numbly. But then a police officer appears at the open door and says, 'Evan Carr, come in please.'

There's no time for them to say anything to each other. She turns away.

Diana has been murdered, her body left in a field. Riley's numb with horror and disbelief. She rushes past the line of students waiting to talk to the officers, to the girls' bathroom located just outside the office, and throws up violently in one of the stalls. Then she remains leaning over the toilet, retching and weeping. She hears one of the secretaries from the office coming in after her and asking if she's all right.

She manages to say, 'I'm fine. I'm going to go home now.'

The secretary hovers near the closed stall, but Riley refuses to open the door or come out. The woman suggests a quiet room in the nurse's office, if she'd like to go there for the time being. She offers to call her mother. But Riley refuses that, too, and eventually the woman leaves, after telling her that there will be grief counsellors she can talk to, and maybe she should stay.

Riley wants to go home. She wants her mother. Riley has already called her and told her the terrible news; she is coming home from work, she'll be there by now.

The loss is overwhelming. She can't register it. Diana is her best friend. They'd met in third grade, when Riley had moved to Fairhill, and kind, friendly Diana had taken her under her wing. They'd been best friends ever since. They'd grown up together – shared everything from summer camp to clothes. Life will be so empty without her. She can't even imagine it. Diana's mother will be devastated. And Cameron, and Evan. How will any of them survive it?

Finally, she exits the stall and quietly leaves the school. She's thinking about the interview as she crosses the parking lot alone and starts walking home, her head down. The officers asked her a lot of questions, but she was trying to process that Diana is dead. It's all a blur, but now she tries to remember it, to pin some of it down. Principal Kelly had been there, at his desk, watching her with great sympathy.

She told them she was Diana's best friend. That Diana shared everything with her, that if anything was wrong in Diana's life, she's sure she would have known about it: Diana would have told her. Things were good with Cameron. They were in love. She's sure she said that. What else did she tell them? She can't remember.

The last communication she had with Diana was when they were texting last night just before ten. The officers had asked to see her cell phone, and they'd looked at the texts. Diana had texted her that she was going to see Cameron at around ten, that he was coming to the house to pick her up. That was the last Riley had heard from her.

She told them she'd started to worry when Diana hadn't answered her texts that morning – it wasn't like her.

They asked her about other students, who Diana hung out with, what she did in her spare time, where she went. But Riley doesn't think she was much help. She told them she doesn't know anyone who'd want to hurt Diana.

How will she deal with this pain? She can't let Diana go. She will never be ready to let Diana go.

She lets herself into the house and her mother immediately engulfs her in a strong, warm hug. Riley collapses into it. She has never needed her mother as much as she needs her now. But her mother can't make this better. No one can.

Chapter Seven

CAMERON FINDS THE short drive home from the police station in his father's truck unbearable. His mother is on her way home separately in her car. He chose to ride with his father; in spite of everything, he's still acutely embarrassed about his mother hearing all that about his sex life. Somehow, he's not as embarrassed about it with his father. He sits beside his dad now in the front passenger seat, his hands clenched on his thighs, staring out the front windshield. He swallows. 'Dad?'

'Yeah?' His father darts a concerned look at him.

Cameron has never seen his dad seem so distressed, even though he can tell he's trying to be strong. It makes Cameron even more anxious about what his father's really thinking. 'Some of those questions – do you think they suspect me of . . .' He can't even say it.

'No!' His dad glances at him. 'Don't even go there, Cameron. They have to ask those questions. You've told them the truth. They can't think you had anything to do with it. You have nothing to worry about.'

He steals a look at his father, now focusing on the road, his face unreadable. But Cameron hasn't told the police the truth. And he doesn't know if his father knows that, or if he's pretending. Cameron told the police he left Diana at her house at eleven. That much is true. She went inside. She slammed the door behind her. She didn't wave.

He squealed the truck's tyres on the street as he left because he was angry. He was furious. Because after they'd had sex, they'd had a nasty argument – their first big blowup. He can't bear to think about it. He'd driven home and parked in the driveway of his parents' house, trying to calm down. He'd gone inside. He felt like slamming things, but he didn't want to wake his parents. He slumped on the couch in the living room for a long while in the dark, thinking things over. He hadn't even taken his jacket off. And then he got up and went out again. He got in the truck and drove back to Diana's house. He didn't know if he wanted to apologize or continue their argument. That would depend on what she did.

What he doesn't know now, sitting in the truck with his dad, is whether his dad heard him come home and go out again, or possibly heard him come back in, much later. He doesn't know whether his dad knows he's lying. He didn't say anything at the police station. But he wouldn't, would he? His mother always sleeps with earplugs in, so he's not worried about her. But his dad might have heard. If he had, he hadn't been able to say anything about it this morning because he was already gone by the time Cameron got up.

You've told them the truth. You have nothing to worry about. Even if his dad knows, he's not going to say anything. He doesn't need to worry about that. But Cameron doesn't know if it's because his dad is complicit, or because he has no idea what his son is hiding.

And there's another thing. What if he was seen?

His overwhelming fear at least blunts his very real grief.

Vultures of another kind, Roy thinks with distaste, standing on the road and watching the reporters milling about on the edge of his property, where they've been kept back by police. He turns away and looks out into the field, which has been marked off by yellow police tape along the fence line. It seems so incongruous, all of it, the police tape against his bright green field, the police cars and crime vans, the people going about their jobs – some in police uniforms, some in white coveralls. A white tent has quickly been erected over where the body is, so they can study her in situ, and in privacy, away from long camera lenses. Near him are the cameramen with their heavy gear and the reporters with their made-up faces, their avidity and lack of respect. They're mostly not from around here. They've arrived from all over pretty damn quickly.

When he'd gone back up to the farmhouse on the tractor to tell his wife what he'd found, into the kitchen where she was making a pie, she'd asked him what he was doing back so soon. Then she turned and saw his face. 'What is it?' she'd asked. Like she knew someone had died.

He'd told her at the kitchen table, the old, scarred pine

43

table where all news, good and bad, seems to be delivered in their house. A girl lay dead in their field. Thank God it wasn't their own daughter. It was shocking, it was terrible, but it didn't affect them, not directly.

His wife hadn't wanted to come down to the field. She shook her head. 'I don't want to see that,' she said, her face grim. But he'd gone back. He didn't want people traipsing all over his field. He wanted them to take the body away and for the crime-scene people and everyone else to get off his property. It was deeply unsettling, and he wanted everything to go back to normal. He had that luxury, that things *could* go back to normal; he knew the Brewer family didn't.

As the morning stretches on, while watching the authorities work, Roy wonders how she ended up in his field. What had he missed, last night, asleep in his bed? Someone must have driven up this isolated road and carried the girl into his field and left her there for the birds.

He tries to think of what kind of person could do that. But his mind stalls. He doesn't know anyone who could do such a thing.

Friday, Oct. 21, 2022, 11:35 a.m.

Diana is dead.

I can't believe it. I must be in shock. I'm home in my bedroom writing on my laptop, trying to process what's happened. I don't know what else to do. I can see my hands shaking as I type. I keep hitting the wrong keys.

If I just keep typing maybe I can hold myself together. If I don't I might just disintegrate.

Diana is dead. She's been murdered. And it's like the world has just stopped.

The police came to our English class and told us. It was like a punch in the gut, and I still can't breathe properly. I saw her yesterday, after school, and she was fine. I can't reconcile that with her not being here anymore. It seems impossible.

They wanted to talk to anybody who knew her, to help in their investigation. They spoke to Riley first, while I waited outside the office, a line of other students behind me. They closed the blinds over the interior glass window so no one could see in. Riley was in there a long time.

A lot of us were crying and hugging one another. Everyone was distraught. They took us in one by one, everyone who knew her well. Riley first, then me. Apparently, they were already talking to Cameron somewhere else, probably at his house, because he has first period free and comes in late on Fridays. He must be out of his mind. I think he really loved her.

How will we live without her? How will *I* live without her? She was such a good friend. Not just to me, to all of us. It doesn't feel real. She had her whole bright life ahead of her and now she's gone, just like that. It's so fucking unfair. I can't stop crying and the tears are falling on my keyboard. Diana was the only one who understood me.

When I went into the office, Principal Kelly was there, sitting behind his desk, and managed to say, *I'm so sorry, Evan.* He looked like he was going to fall apart, but I think we all looked that way. The two police officers asked me to sit down. They introduced themselves but their names went right by me. They asked me my name, and where I lived, and they wrote it all down. I was suddenly weirdly nervous. But I think police officers make a lot of people feel that way.

They asked me what my relationship was with Diana, and I told them we were good friends. They asked if I knew whether Diana was having any problems with anyone, and I told them no, that everyone loved hanging out with her, that she was very popular. I felt like crying again, and it took a real effort not to. Then they asked me if she engaged in any 'risky behaviours,' which I didn't know how to answer. Was having sex with your boyfriend risky behaviour? I wasn't sure. I must have looked confused because they clarified – did she do drugs, or party too hard? They said I could be honest with them, to just tell the truth, that no one was going to get into any trouble for it. I shook my head and told them that Diana would never take drugs, that she drank a bit, that we all did. I figured it was okay to admit that, although we're all under legal drinking age. I told them she was a good student, a good friend, and had a part-time job. She didn't get into trouble.

Then they asked about Cameron, how well I knew him. I said he was a friend of mine, that we'd known each other since we were six. They started asking what their relationship was like. I said it was good. They prodded, asking if there were any problems between them. Privately, I think Cameron was getting too possessive, and that it was starting to bother Diana. But I wasn't going to tell them that. I don't think Cameron murdered Diana, so I said I wasn't aware of any problems, and that they seemed happy together. I told them she would have told Riley more than she told me, that Riley knew everything going on in Diana's life.

Then they asked me if I knew of anyone who was 'interested' in Diana, even though she was already going out with Cameron. I shrugged and told them that she was gorgeous, everyone wanted to date her. And they looked right at me and one of them said *what about you?* But I told them we were just friends and that I wasn't interested in Diana that way.

That was it. They said if I thought of anything, to get in touch, and handed me a card.

After that I came home. I wanted to be alone. There's no one here; both my parents are at work. When I called my mother from the school to tell her about Diana, crying on the phone, she said she'd come right home, but I told her to finish her day at work, that I was going to stick around the school for a while to be with my friends. I didn't bother calling my father.

47

Chapter Eight

This dream seems to be going on for ever. It's changed suddenly, the way dreams do; they're not logical at all. I'm not at the field any more, with the dead girl who looks like me. Now I'm at home with my mother. She's sitting in the living room, weeping, while police and people in white coveralls move around our house. It's so strange, like watching a TV show. I'm here, but I'm not part of it.

I'm worried about my mother. She looks so wretched it almost scares me, like seeing the girl in the field did. I reach out to touch her shoulder. 'Mom, I'm right here.'

But she ignores me. She doesn't see me, she doesn't hear me, she just keeps crying. I sit down beside her for a minute and try to get her attention. It doesn't work. I can't comfort her. I give up and start to follow people from room to room, curious. Obviously, they think I've been murdered. That's what all this is about. I wonder what it means when you dream about your own murder? I want to scream: It's just a dream! *I do scream then, wordlessly, to get someone, anyone, to notice me. But no one seems to hear me. It's like there's a perfectly clean sheet of glass between me and them. I reach out, but there's nothing there.*

I'm frightened now, starting to panic, the dream spilling into nightmare. I shout at them all – Nothing has happened to me! I'm fine. I'm right here! *But they carry on with their tasks, ignoring me. They're dusting everywhere for finger-prints, making a mess of everything with their dark powder. They bend their heads over their work, undisturbed. I'm in my bedroom now, watching them lift up the carpet. I don't want them in here, snooping where they don't belong. It's such an invasion of privacy. I don't like any of this. I'm a private person; I don't share everything. Nobody does. We all have secrets, things we keep to ourselves, that we would never want anyone to know.*

There's something tickling at the back of my mind, some-thing I feel I should remember, something important. But it's just out of reach. I tell myself it doesn't matter. I'll wake up soon, and I probably won't remember any of this anyway. I don't usually remember my dreams.

Paula Acosta has returned to her empty classroom. She couldn't stand being in the staff room any longer, everyone in shock, talking about Diana in hushed tones. She's trying to deal with the news on her own, trying to recover her composure before she goes home and sees Taylor. School for the upper years has already been cancelled for the rest of the day; the lower grades will be dismissed for the afternoon. She will go home then to be with her daughter.

Paula thinks about Diana, how lovely she was, so full of promise, and the horrible, frightening way she must have died. They are a little short on the details, but she knows that she was strangled, left naked in a farmer's field. Who would do that to her? The police will question Cameron. She hopes they aren't too hard on him. He's just a boy, and he clearly doted on Diana. This will utterly derail him. She thinks of everyone else who will be affected by Diana's death, how many lives will be irreversibly changed for the worse. Her mother, her friends, the community – and all the people she would have touched in her life. She was such a positive girl – she would have done good in the world, and God knows the world needs more like her. Why did she have to die? It's so incredibly unjust.

Paula's thoughts grow more agitated as she thinks about who might have done it. Maybe it was a drifter, passing through, someone on parole? A stranger. But what if he wasn't just passing through? What if he's still here? She has a young daughter. The thought of a predator out there makes her afraid.

And what if it wasn't a stranger? She doesn't know if that's better or worse. What if it was someone Diana knew? She sucks in a sudden breath. She's remembered something that makes her heart seize. It's ... disturbing. She leans back in her chair, feeling a little ill. She waits for the feeling to pass, decides what to do.

She knows she is more and more apt to dwell on the awful aspects of the world these days, to assume the worst. It's all going to hell in a handbasket, as far as she can tell. But she must pull herself together now; she can't have her daughter and her students knowing that's what she really thinks. She must maintain some sort of optimism for them.

Riley is in her bedroom in the early afternoon when her mother taps on her door and opens it. 'Riley? Evan is here. Do you want to talk to him?'

Riley looks up at her mother from where she's sitting on the bed with her laptop. Her mom has been supportive, holding her for a long time while she cried. But then when Riley wanted to be alone, her mother gave her some space. Riley considers dully – does she want to see Evan? She doesn't really want to talk to anyone; she wants to be alone with her grief, but he's a good friend and she knows it would be unkind not to see him. He's hurting too. She gets up off the bed. 'Sure.' She follows her mom downstairs.

She and Evan hug the way people do when something terrible has happened, then she leads him into the TV room and closes the door behind them. Evan looks awful. She's sure she doesn't look any better. They stand and stare at each other for a moment.

Finally Riley says, 'I can't believe she's gone. I don't know how we'll go on without her.'

'Me neither,' Evan says.

They sit down in heavy silence. 'What did you tell the police?' Riley asks at last.

He shrugs. 'Nothing much. I don't know anyone who would want to hurt her.' He asks, 'What about you?'

She tries to think. She can hardly remember what she told them. She was in shock. 'Same. I told them I don't know anyone who would want to hurt Diana.' She pauses. 'But I left some things out.'

'What things?'

She looks at him then and asks, 'What did you say about Cameron?'

'What did you say about him?' Evan counters.

'I think I said everything was fine between them.'

'That's what I said.'

They look at each other uneasily. 'But they weren't *completely* fine,' Riley admits now.

'No,' Evan agrees. 'But we know there's no way Cameron killed her, so we don't have to say anything, right?'

But now Riley hesitates. She knows that things weren't that great lately between Diana and Cameron. Cameron had become more and more possessive of Diana, even a bit controlling. Diana had been smiling less, and she'd been quieter. Evan must have noticed it too. Diana had finally confided in Riley last week. She told her that Cameron was getting too serious about her, and she was beginning to pull back. He didn't like it. He was pushing her for more of a commitment.

'I'm seventeen years old,' Diana had complained to Riley. 'How can he want more of a commitment? I'm not going to be a teenage bride. I'm going to be a vet. I'm going away to school.'

'Right,' Riley had agreed. 'He knows that. He's always known that.'

'Yeah. But now he wants us to go to the same college next year. He's insisting.'

'Oh,' Riley had said.

'Exactly. I'm not going to narrow my options to accommodate him. I mean, I love him, but I don't think it's a forever kind of thing for me.' She'd looked troubled. 'I don't want to go to the same college. I'm not ready to settle down. But how do I tell him that? He's so sweet, and he adores me. We're so happy together. And I don't want to hurt him.'

'But you have to tell him, somehow,' Riley had said. 'And maybe the sooner the better.' This was said partly out of selfishness; she didn't really like it that Diana had started spending so much time with Cameron and spending less time with her.

'I don't know. College is still almost a year away,' Diana had said. Then she'd added, her brow furrowing, 'But the longer I let it go on, the harder it's going to be.'

Riley thinks now about the advice she'd given Diana and suddenly feels sick to her stomach. She blurts out, 'Diana was thinking about breaking up with him.'

'What?' Evan looks shocked. 'Why do you think that?'

'Because he was insisting they go to the same college next year, and she didn't want to.' She tells him, 'Diana went out with him last night, after her mother left for work – I told the police that. I showed them her text to me about it. He was going to pick her up. Should I have told them she was thinking of breaking up with him?' She suddenly feels her face go bloodless. 'Maybe she broke up with him last night.'

53

Evan looks back at her, his expression appalled at what she's implying. 'Cameron wouldn't hurt her.'

'But – should they know? Should I tell them?'

He looks at her, uncertain.

She remembers the card the officer at the school gave her, nestled in the pocket of her jeans.

'What are you going to do?' Evan asks her now.

'I don't know.'

Chapter Nine

BRAD TURNER, THE gym teacher, has been sitting in the staff room with the other teachers since the entire school was dismissed at lunchtime. He's trying to hold it together, like everybody else. It's like an impromptu mini wake in the staff room; someone has brought in doughnuts, and they're sitting around talking about Diana, remembering her, speculating about what happened to her, checking the online news on their phones. As Diana's running coach, he probably knew her better than a lot of her other teachers did. He listens to everyone sing her praises.

She was such a good math student.

She wanted to be a vet. She would have made a good one too.

Her poor mother – she's a single mother, and Diana was her only child. She'll be all alone now.

Who could have done such a terrible thing?

I hope they catch the bastard that killed her.

Brad says, 'She was such a talented athlete. The best runner on the cross-country team.'

The others look at him sympathetically and nod.

She was such a nice girl.

So much potential.

He can't listen to any more. He gets up from his chair in the staff lounge and makes his way, for the second time, toward the school office. He wants to talk to Principal Kelly alone, if he can. Last time he checked, there were still some students waiting to talk to the police officers. Now the students are all gone, but the door to the principal's office is closed and the blinds are still pulled down. He wonders if Kelly is in there, and whether he is alone.

Just then, the door opens. Two state police officers emerge, with Kelly trailing behind them. Brad ducks into the corridor to his left before he is seen and makes his way back in the direction of the staff room. On the way he stops at one of the staff bathrooms. He's relieved when he finds it empty. He desperately needs a minute alone, where no one can see him, where he doesn't have to pretend that none of this particularly affects him.

He stands at one of the sinks and stares at himself in the mirror, allows his fear and panic to show for a moment, distorting his usually handsome, confident face. He stares at himself as if mesmerized. Is this really happening? He splashes cold water on his face, over and over. When he straightens up again, he realizes that he is trembling, that he has splashed water on his dark shirt, and it shows. His heart is racing. He must pull himself together.

He dries his face carefully with a paper towel and decides to make his way back to the staff room. But in a minute. He needs a little more time.

Friday, Oct. 21, 2022, 2 p.m.

I'm home again, back in my bedroom, writing on my laptop because I don't know what else to do.

When I left Riley's place earlier, I was really bothered by what she'd told me, that Diana was going to break up with Cameron. That was news to me. I found myself walking to Cameron's house. It's a bit of a hike, to his house on the edge of town, but I wanted some time to think. I certainly didn't think Cameron had murdered Diana, but after what Riley told me, well, it was a lot to take in, and all kind of unsettling. I needed to talk to him, to be reassured.

It disturbs me, what Riley's thinking. It's obviously disturbing her too.

I've known Cameron all my life, from the time we were in grade school. I think I know him pretty well. He's easygoing, most of the time. He's an even-tempered, likeable guy. He's fine until he's pushed too far, and then he explodes. That sounds bad, and it takes a lot to set him off, but if you do, watch out. I tried to imagine him losing his temper with Diana, but I just couldn't see it. He adored her. And she would never provoke him, she wasn't like that.

I remember one time when we were in ninth grade.

There was a kid who was always razzing him, one of the farm kids that was bussed in. Cameron hadn't grown tall and filled out yet, and the other kid was a lot bigger. Cameron put up with it for a long time, pretending it didn't bother him. Then one day at school he lost it and managed to push the bigger kid to the ground and started punching him in the head. A teacher had to pull him off. I thought about that as I walked to Cameron's house. The school would probably have a record of it.

Anyway, by the time I arrived at Cameron's house, I was feeling sick to my stomach. I couldn't believe that he would ever hurt Diana, but I was worried about how things might look for him.

Both the car and the truck were in the driveway. Of course his parents would have come home. I knocked on the door and Cameron's dad answered. He looked awful. I burst into tears again right there on the doorstep. It was embarrassing, but I couldn't help it. Everything just seemed to hit me at once.

Mr Farrell hugged me for a minute. Then he let me go and told me how sorry he was, how tragic it was. I could see tears in his eyes too. I asked if I could talk to Cameron, but he shook his head and told me Cameron didn't want to see anyone, that he was in shock, that he loved her. He choked on *he loved her* and had to fight for composure. I felt less embarrassed then, about crying in front of him.

I asked him if Cameron had spoken to the police,

and he said they'd spoken to him that morning, but Mr Farrell clearly didn't want to talk about it. I really wished I could speak to Cameron, but I didn't ask again.

As I turned away and started to walk home, I remembered how Cameron used to touch Diana all the time, constantly holding her hand, draping his big arm over her shoulder, putting his hand around her waist. And last weekend, at a party, I saw her pull away from him to go talk to someone else, and he frowned, put his beer down, and followed her. It was just a group of girls she wanted to talk to, but Cameron stood there with the girls, looking a bit ridiculous. No one else seemed to notice, but I wonder now if Riley had. We hadn't spoken about it.

On the way home, I was at loose ends. I was feeling so messed up. Upset about Diana, imagining what life would be like now, without her. Our little group would probably fall apart.

So now I'm back in my bedroom, just me and my computer, trying to make sense of something that will never, ever, make sense.

Chapter Ten

RILEY IS NERVOUS. It's early afternoon, and she is at the police station with her mother. It's the worst day of her life, and it already feels like it has lasted for ever, that it will never end. Her mouth is dry as she sits down at the table in the interview room. Her mother sits beside her, clearly concerned about her emotional state, and squeezes her shoulder. Someone places a bottle of water on the table in front of her.

There are two detectives in the room with them. The man introduces himself as Detective Stone. He's about her mother's age, in his mid forties, and seems nice. His female partner, Detective Godfrey, is younger, and smiles at her encouragingly. Riley licks her dry lips, wonders if she's doing the right thing, and tries to prepare herself.

'Riley,' Detective Stone begins, 'this must be very difficult for you. We know you already spoke to the officers at the school this morning. What brings you here now? Do you

60

have something more to tell us?' He looks back at her, waiting. 'You were a close friend of Diana's?'

She finds her voice. 'Yes. Her best friend.' Riley feels her heart begin to race. She looks at her mother for encouragement. She knows she must tell them. She can no longer, in good conscience, keep it to herself.

So she tells them how Diana was being pressured by Cameron to go to the same college, that she was unhappy about it, that she was thinking of breaking up with him. She feels guilty, disloyal, that she's betraying Cameron, and she cries miserably as she tells them. But it's more complicated than that. She also feels guilty because she's the one who urged Diana to break up with him – and what if she did? What if that's why she's dead? She tells herself her first loyalty must be to Diana. She must tell the detectives the truth and let them make sense of it. She finds some small relief when she's done.

Detective Stone hears her out quietly. 'Thank you for sharing this with us. You've done the right thing,' he says, as Riley wipes her eyes with a tissue. He waits for her to recover her composure and adds, 'There's something else we'd like to ask you about.' She looks up at him. 'We spoke to Diana's mother this morning. She told us that Diana worked at the Home Depot, and that Diana had mentioned a customer that she thought was creepy. Did she ever mention anything about that to you?'

Riley had forgotten all about that. How had she forgotten it? 'Yes. She only saw him when she worked nights. She mostly worked Sundays, during the day, but sometimes she worked Friday nights, till ten. He'd come in sometimes. She told me that he always went to her checkout, even if there was already someone at hers and an empty one close by. He'd wait. One time another girl called out to him that she was free, but he said he'd wait and stayed at Diana's checkout. Everybody noticed it.'

'Did she tell you his name?'

'She didn't know his name. He always paid cash, never with a credit card. She thought that was weird. She thought he was weird. He made her uncomfortable.'

The detective nods. 'Do you know if he tried to find out her name, where she lived, anything about her?'

'He knew her first name, it was on her name tag. I don't think he could have found out her last name. She wouldn't have told him and I don't think anyone else would have. They knew she didn't like him. He'd try to flirt with her. She didn't like it.'

'Did he ever accost her outside the store?'

Riley shakes her head. 'I'm sure she never saw him other than at her checkout. She would have told me.' The detective waits for her to say more. She adds, 'People at the Home Depot knew about him. They saw him. The other staff, and the manager. The manager knew he made Diana nervous. They always walked the girls to their cars at the end of the night, for safety. The manager made sure of it.'

The detective nods at her. 'We'll talk to them. Thank you for coming in.'

*

Aaron Bolduc is thinking about staffing problems when one of his employees pokes her head in his office in the afternoon and says, 'There's some people here to see you.'

Her face is red and her eyes are swollen. She's been crying on and off all day about Diana – she's not the only one – but at least she came into work, and he's grateful. 'Thanks, Margaret. Are you doing okay?'

She nods, and turns away, saying, 'I'll bring them to your office.'

Aaron straightens his tie nervously. He's been expecting someone to come. One of his staff has been murdered. They will want to talk to him and the people who worked with her.

When the two arrive at his office, they are not in uniform. They introduce themselves as Detective Stone and Detective Godfrey from Major Crimes, State Police. He doesn't recognize either of them; of course, they're not from here. 'It's a terrible thing,' Aaron says, his eyes welling up. 'Just terrible.' He knows he himself must look terrible as he says it. 'Diana was a wonderful girl. I just can't believe it.' The detectives seem unaffected, but he supposes it's because it's their job. They can't let it bother them personally.

Detective Stone nods. 'We understand that there was a customer who was bothering Diana?'

Aaron breathes out loudly. 'Right. I know who you mean, but I don't know who he is. Big guy. Reddish hair, scruffy beard. Usually wore a red-and-black-plaid flannel shirt with a work jacket over it. He always paid cash, so I don't know his name. He made Diana nervous because he'd hang around her checkout and wait.' He adds, 'Diana was a lovely girl.' He feels himself flush and looks away.

'Do you have CCTV of the cash area?'

'Yes, we do. In fact, I think he was in last Friday night when Diana was working. I can get that for you.'

Aaron sets things up on the computer to review the black-and-white video. He fast-forwards and backtracks, looking for the man in the plaid shirt. Finally, he finds him. They watch as he ambles up to Diana's register. Aaron, watching it for the first time on tape, can see how Diana's face changes as she sees him approach. She's no longer smiling. She starts scanning his items, not looking at him. He's talking to her. Aaron tries to read his lips, but he can't make out what he's saying to her. He's smiling, talking, looking at her. Her answers are monosyllabic. She's trying not to be rude, but she doesn't want to engage. Her movements are stiff. It's busy and another customer comes up behind him, moving forward impatiently, while he continues to talk to Diana, even though his transaction is finished.

'Stop there,' the detective tells him.

The detectives take a good look at the man's face.

'Do you have CCTV of the parking lot?' Stone asks.

Aaron shakes his head. 'I'm afraid not. Just the inside of the store, and the area right outside the doors.'

They switch screens and watch the man carry his purchases out the exit. He disappears into the darkness of the parking lot.

'Would have been good to get his vehicle,' Stone says. 'Anyway, we've got him on film. We'll find out who he is.

Thank you, you've been very helpful,' the detective says.
'We'd like to speak with your staff – anyone who worked
with Diana, especially on Friday evenings.'

Aaron quivers with distress, hoping the detectives don't
notice. 'Of course.'

Chapter Eleven

BEFORE PAULA LEFT the school, she'd gone to speak to Principal Kelly. His door was closed and the blinds were down and she wondered if he'd already gone. She tapped on his door, and he called out for her to enter.

He looked shattered. Graham Kelly was about fifty years of age and in reasonably good shape, but suddenly he looked older. His face was more creased and careworn than usual, and he was a man who looked harried at the best of times. But he seemed relieved to see that it was her. They are friends of sorts; they even confide in each other. She knows details about his problems with his children, things he doesn't share with the rest of the staff. He trusts her. Paula knows some of the other staff don't particularly like him and give him a hard time, but she has always found him good to work with.

'How are you doing?' she asked sympathetically.

He shook his head. He didn't seem to have words.

'You'll get through this,' she told him.

He nodded then and said, 'Thank you, Paula.' He took a deep breath and said, 'School will carry on as usual Monday. The flag will be at half-mast until further notice. There will be grief counsellors in the school for anyone who needs them. I'm not sure yet when the funeral will be, but the school will close for that so that everyone can attend. And we will do our best to support the police in their investigation.'

'About that,' Paula said tentatively.

He gave her a sharp look. 'I'm sorry, Paula, but I can't disclose anything that was said earlier today when the police were here. You know that.'

'Of course I do,' she said. She continued to look at him, waiting for him to bring it up. The elephant in the room. He didn't. So she asked. 'Did you tell them about Brad?'

He gave her a look that was almost cold. 'No, I did not. You can't seriously think that he could have done this?'

She paused for an uncomfortable moment and said, 'Don't you think you should tell them anyway?' He continued to stare back at her. She added, 'For your own sake?'

Kelly had confided in her a few weeks ago – told her in strictest confidence – that Diana Brewer had come to him about Brad Turner, the gym teacher, suggesting that he had been inappropriate with her. Kelly had told Paula that he'd heard them both out and described the whole thing as a 'misunderstanding', and told Paula that Diana hadn't wanted it to go any further. Kelly had seemed certain there was nothing to it, but the whole thing had made Paula uncomfortable. Kelly wouldn't provide any details. She wondered if he'd been too quick to dismiss Diana's concerns. She wished she'd been in the room; she might have handled it quite differently. Ever since, she'd been concerned about the possibility that her daughter – and the other students – might be treated inappropriately by their gym teacher. But Kelly said he'd handled it and told her she had nothing to worry about.

Now Kelly said, 'If I tell the police about this, it will ruin his career, you know that. And quite unnecessarily. He didn't do anything wrong. His fiancée doesn't even know. How do you think he'd feel if she found out?'

Then Paula felt the heat rising in her face. 'Maybe she *should* find out. Maybe she should know that the man she's going to marry has been accused of being inappropriate with one of the teenage girls he teaches.'

Kelly flung himself further back in his leather desk chair, which made a loud creak as if in protest. 'There was nothing to it! I told you. It was all perfectly innocent on his part. He was upset that his actions would be interpreted that way. He was mortified.' Kelly flushed deeply, turned away, and said, 'I think we should give him the benefit of the doubt.'

'But what will you say,' Paula asked, 'if the police find out and you've kept it from them?'

'How will they find out?'

'What if Diana told her mother about it?' Paula said.

'She didn't want her mother to know.'

'What if she confided in one of her friends?' She watched his face cloud over.

'She said she didn't want anyone to know. I don't think she told anyone.' He sighed heavily and considered for a minute, clearly unhappy. 'But I suppose she might have. All right. I guess I'd better tell them.' He looked deeply dismayed. 'But if this gets out – and it probably will – his life will be ruined, and for nothing. There's no way he killed her, if that's what you're thinking.'

Paula left the school feeling uneasy. Kelly seemed certain that there was nothing to Diana's allegations, but maybe he wasn't the best judge. And Diana didn't seem like the kind of girl to make a complaint of that sort – of any sort – that was without foundation. But then, how well did Paula really know Diana? She was her student – bright, friendly, popular. But Paula really had no idea what was going on in Diana's private life. How would she? She doesn't even know what's going on in her own daughter's private life.

When Kelly had first told Paula about Diana's complaint, she'd asked Taylor, without naming Turner, if anyone at school, staff or student, ever made her feel uncomfortable. Taylor had avoided her eyes and said, 'No, Mom,' in that half embarrassed, half rolling her eyes kind of way. But she'd made her daughter promise that if anything like that happened she would tell her, and it allayed her concerns.

Now Paula arrives home and parks in the driveway. She doesn't want to think the well-liked gym teacher had anything to do with what happened to Diana.

Taylor's home already, having walked home with some other girls on the street, at her mother's insistence when they texted earlier. Paula finds her daughter in the kitchen, cutting up an apple. She doesn't normally hug Taylor after school, but today she gives her a swift, firm embrace, and her daughter squirms away.

'Are you okay?' Paula asks anxiously. She has no idea how her daughter will react to the murder of a girl at her school. Taylor has never faced anything like this before. None of them have.

'I'm fine,' Taylor says, taking a bite of apple. 'I didn't even know her, Mom.'

Paula is a little taken aback by her daughter's indifference. Maybe it's just a defence mechanism, an act. Some of the girls were openly weeping at school today. But it's true, Taylor didn't really know Diana; they were years apart. For Paula, a pall of fear seems to have been cast over everything. A girl has been murdered in their small town, and they don't know who did it. He's still out there, and it terrifies her. But Taylor seems unaffected.

'I knew her,' Paula says. 'She was in my class. I've taught her for years. I know her mother.' And she can't help it, she begins to cry, for the first time today, in front of her thirteen-year-old daughter.

'Oh. I'm sorry, Mom. I didn't think—'

Paula says, 'Remember, I don't want you going out alone until they get whoever did this.'

Chapter Twelve

JOE PRIOR GETS in his truck at quitting time and catches his foreman watching him. Joe wonders what the wiry bastard is thinking. Maybe he's thinking it's the last time he'll ever see Joe Prior.

Earlier that afternoon, the foreman had approached Joe from across the dusty construction site with a serious look on his face and showed him something on his phone. It was a photo of Joe, a bit blurry, but it was definitely him. Joe didn't let on, but he'd seen it all already. He has a phone too. He already knew that the police wanted to talk to him in connection with the girl who'd been found earlier that day in a local farmer's field. He was just waiting for somebody to say something. Joe looked down at his foreman's phone and read the story with apparent misgiving. He scrolled further down and saw her picture on the screen too.

Shit.

The picture of him had to be a still from video surveillance from the fucking Home Depot. He looked up at his foreman, who was eyeing him suspiciously. 'I had nothing to do with this,' Joe said.

'Sure,' the other man said. 'But maybe you should go talk to them.'

'Yeah, okay, I'll go now, if that's okay.'

'No, you can go at the end of your shift.' He added, 'Maybe give them a call, though, tell them you're coming.'

His foreman is an asshole. Joe had called the police station and told them he'd be coming in later that day. He noticed the guys at work giving him the side-eye all afternoon.

Now Joe starts his truck and bumps out of the construction site, then turns onto the road into town to the police station. He doesn't bother to go back to his apartment to change first.

They have a picture of him from Home Depot. They know he was flirting with that girl, obviously. No point in denying it. There's no law against that. He'll submit to their questions voluntarily. He doesn't see that he has a choice – people at work know him; they would have found him soon enough.

He parks in the lot of the police station. He gets out of his truck and walks into the station, still wearing his dirty jeans and a flannel shirt that smells of sweat, and his steel-toed boots, but he doesn't think they'll care. He approaches an officer at the front desk, who looks up at him with widened eyes. 'I understand somebody wants to talk to me,' he says. She summons another officer, and he's led into an interview room.

He doesn't have to wait long. Two detectives enter the room and introduce themselves. Joe studies them both carefully. Detective Stone, a man maybe fifteen years older than Joe, looks sharp enough; the other one is a woman called Godfrey, who looks pretty smart too. But Joe doesn't think he has much to worry about here. He sits back in his chair, at ease.

'I understand you've been looking for me,' he says.

'Yes, we have,' Stone says. 'Thank you for coming in.'

'Of course,' Joe says. 'I would have come in earlier, but my foreman wouldn't let me go till the end of my shift.' He adds, 'He can be a bit of a jerk.'

Stone nods. 'Do you mind if we tape this interview?'

'No, not at all,' he says affably.

'Your name?' the detective asks, his voice neutral.

'Joe Prior.'

'Address?'

'One nineteen Division Street, Fairhill. Apartment two fourteen.'

'And what do you do for a living, Joe?'

'Construction, mostly.'

Stone nods. 'Who do you work for?'

'At the moment, Byford Construction. But I move around. Go where the work is. I do general construction – never learned a trade.'

'You quite often go to the Home Depot here in Fairhill,' Stone says.

'Doesn't everybody?' Joe replies, and smiles.

'You know who Diana Brewer is,' the detective says. 'You know why we want to talk to you.'

73

'Yeah. Shit. Shame about what happened to her. Pretty girl.'

'You showed a particular interest in her.'

'I wouldn't say that,' Joe says. 'I was just being friendly.'

'Friendly,' the detective repeats. 'That's not the way we heard it.'

Joe frowns. 'What do you mean?'

'We heard you harassed her. Bothered her at work. Flirted with her. She didn't want your attention.' Joe shrugs, lets this roll off his shoulders. 'Did you ever see Diana outside of the Home Depot?'

Joe shakes his head. 'No.'

'Ever try to contact her? Send her messages?'

'No.' He's had enough of this. He leans forward. 'You're barking up the wrong tree. You're looking for a murderer, and you want it to be me. Sorry to disappoint you. I didn't do it.'

'Where were you last night?' Stone asks, also leaning forward, placing his elbows on the table.

'I was at home.'

'Can anyone confirm that?'

'Yes, actually,' Joe says. 'I had a buddy over after work. We had a few too many beers and he crashed on my couch. Didn't leave till this morning.'

'His name?'

'Rodney Donnelly, goes by Roddy.' He adds, 'If you want to talk to him, I have his number right here.' He shows it to Stone in the contacts on his phone. The detective writes it down. 'Is that all?' Joe says.

'Just one more question. What do you drive?'

'A 2015 Dodge Ram truck. It's in the parking lot.'

'Mind if we take a look?'

'Yes, as a matter of fact I do. Not because I have anything to hide. Just because I think individual rights need to be protected in this country.'

'Okay,' Stone says, nodding. 'That's all we need for now.'

Joe leaves the station and climbs back into his truck. He hits the gas and floors it home.

Chapter Thirteen

BRENDA IS SITTING in her kitchen with her ex-husband, Lee. This whole day has unravelled like a dirty bandage off a wound, revealing unspeakable horror. Every time she thinks of Diana's last moments, she feels a breathless panic as if she, too, will die. But she's still here. Stuck in this awful purgatory, reliving her daughter's death over and over again. She can't wipe it from her mind. What has she done to deserve this? What had her daughter ever done to deserve this? Her life taken from her, before it had hardly begun. How terrified Diana must have been when she realized what was happening. Brenda feels like she's trapped in that moment, with her daughter, feeling her terror. She grips the edge of the kitchen table, tries to breathe through the panic, the crushing pain in her chest.

As she calms, Brenda knows that her life is over now too. Because there's nothing left for her. How will she go on? Diana was her everything. She stares at her ex-husband, slumped in front of her looking down at the kitchen table, not able to meet her eyes. He will at least have someone to go back to. He has two more children, and they will be all the more precious to him now. She remembers how close he was to Diana when she was little, how neglectful of her he'd been these last few years. He hardly knew her, the wonderful young woman she'd become. She wonders if he now regrets that he didn't spend more time with his only daughter while he could. She had wanted him here, but now she almost wishes he would leave.

They sit there together, not talking. The doorbell rings, and they ignore it, letting neighbours leave their dishes of food on the front step unacknowledged. They can't face people, and they certainly can't eat. Why does anyone think that food is the answer to grief? There is no answer to grief.

There are reporters out there too. She doesn't want to talk to them either. Brenda hears the ping of a text from her phone, on the kitchen table next to her. She glances at it. It's Detective Stone. Please let us in. We're outside.

'It's the detectives,' she tells her ex, and gets up to answer the door. She doesn't hurry, because what does it matter? Nothing matters. Nothing will bring Diana back. Her movements are slow and heavy, like she's walking underwater. She would normally have slept after her long night shift, but there was no possibility of sleep today. She's made Lee call and tell them she will be off work indefinitely.

She opens the door. The two detectives she'd met that morning, Stone and Godfrey, are there. 'Can we come in?' Stone asks.

She glances past his shoulder at the crowd gathered on the street. She can see the news vans, the reporters, and the cameramen, but they are standing there quietly, even respectfully. She steps back and lets the detectives in, closing the door quickly. Lee comes out of the kitchen, his face vacant. The detectives introduce themselves to him, and they end up sitting in the living room. Brenda had already told them earlier that morning that her ex-husband had virtually nothing to do with his daughter, had no idea what was going on in her life, that he would be no help. They ask him a few questions anyway, which only confirm how little involvement he'd had with his daughter in the last few years. He has the grace to look ashamed.

Detective Stone still looks fresh and collected, Brenda marvels, observing him. His partner is the same. Of course, this is just a job to them. She wonders how much they actually care. They don't even live around here. This is such a small community, they've had to bring in a team from elsewhere to try to solve her daughter's murder. Maybe that's a good thing, she thinks suddenly. Maybe someone from Fairhill did it.

Stone begins in his quiet voice, 'You said this morning that you weren't aware of any problems between your daughter and her boyfriend, Cameron Farrell.' He pauses. 'We've heard otherwise.'

She looks at him more sharply, nudged out of her stupor. 'What?'

'Riley Mead came to the station with her mother, Patricia, and told us that Cameron was pressuring Diana to agree to go to the same college together next year. Riley said that Diana didn't want to, and that she was going to break up with him.'

Brenda swallows. 'Diana didn't tell me that.' She takes a deep breath. 'If Riley told you then it must be true.' She glances at Lee, beside her, but he's looking at the floor. He has nothing to contribute.

'Did you ever see anything in Cameron's behaviour that made you worry for your daughter's safety?' Stone asks. 'Does he have a temper?'

She shakes her head slowly. 'Not that I ever saw. But he was a bit clingy. Do you think Cameron might have done this?' she asks uneasily.

'We're not ruling anyone out at this time.'

'Oh God,' Brenda murmurs, considering this, covering her mouth with her hand. She hears her ex-husband make a strangled sound beside her, but he doesn't speak.

Detective Stone gives them a moment and says, 'We haven't found any unexplained fingerprints in the house, but any intruder could have worn gloves. We did find some impressions in the grass behind the house. Not enough to get a footprint, unfortunately. There were no obvious signs of a break-in.' He adds carefully, 'Someone might have been watching her. He might have known she was alone in the house when you left for work.'

Brenda's blood chills. The idea sickens her; she can taste the bile rising in the back of her throat.

'Let's assume for a minute that Cameron left Diana back inside the house at around eleven, as he says. We know of no reason for her to have left the house again voluntarily after that, and her jacket and sneakers are in the house. But maybe she answered the door. Maybe someone came in through an unlocked door or window. Maybe someone was already waiting for her inside when she got home last night and took her from the house.' He adds, 'As we mentioned to you earlier, it probably wasn't random. It wasn't opportunistic.'

Brenda can hardly take all this in; she feels numb, disoriented.

'The Home Depot customer came forward,' Stone says. 'His name is Joe Prior.'

She looks sharply at him, snapped to attention.

'He says he didn't do it, of course,' Stone says. 'And his alibi checks out, although we consider it a weak one. He claims a friend was over at his place, drinking all night. They could both be lying. We've looked into him, but he doesn't have a criminal record and everything he said checked out.'

She regards him wearily. She glances once more at Lee; he seems almost catatonic.

'There's something else,' Stone continues. 'We've had officers going door to door, looking for witnesses, to see if anyone saw anything last night, or anything unusual over the past while.'

'And?'

'The neighbour across from you, Helen Payne, said she noticed a truck sitting outside your house last night at around midnight. She'd come back from sitting with a friend at the hospice. She couldn't tell us any more than that it was a truck – a pickup. Its lights were off, but she said someone – a man – was sitting in the driver's seat. She said it was too dark to tell any more than that, and she didn't pay much attention, as she was thinking about her friend. She said she's never noticed a truck sitting outside your place at that hour before, and she often comes back from the hospice at that time. Anyway, she went to bed, so that's all we know.' He adds, 'But she did say it looked like your daughter's boyfriend's truck, which she sees around a lot.'

'Everybody around here drives a truck,' Brenda says bleakly.

Stone nods. 'Including Cameron Farrell and Joe Prior.' He rises to leave, and Godfrey gets up as well. 'We'll be in touch tomorrow,' he says. 'Again, I'm so sorry for your loss.'

Chapter Fourteen

ROY SAYS GRACE with a little more feeling tonight than usual as they gather around the pine table in the farmhouse kitchen for supper. It's just starting to get dark. His wife, Susan, sits across from him, ready to begin spooning out the food as soon as he's finished, before it gets cold. He always keeps it short. *Thank you, Father, for the good things you have put upon our table, and for all the good things you bring us. Amen.* But the dead girl in his field is on his mind.

He looks up, Susan starts serving the food – ham and mashed potatoes and peas – and he passes his plate down. His daughter, Ellen, whose wedding is planned for Christmastime, is on his right. Across from her is where her fiancé should be sitting – he usually joins them for supper on Friday nights – but he's not here. Roy and Susan's other children, both older, have grown up and moved away. They'll all be back for the holidays, for the wedding. Ellen is their last, and the house will seem especially empty when she's gone.

He glances at her now. She's a pretty girl, with lovely skin and thick, chestnut-coloured hair – the apple of her mother's eye after two rambunctious boys. She's lighthearted by nature, but a shadow has been cast over all of them tonight. It has reached even into here, their familiar, homey kitchen, with the checked oilcloth on the table, and the dog lying in her bed in the corner.

Ellen goes past that field every day in her little car on her way into town to work at the bakery. She went by it this morning – she starts very early at the bakery – and the body must have already been there. She drove by it in the dark. It makes him sick to think of it. What if it had been Ellen, instead of the Brewer girl, lying in that field? Susan glances at him and he knows she is thinking the same thing.

She says to her daughter, 'Maybe you shouldn't go out alone at night for a while.'

Ellen nods, pushes her food around her plate. 'Yeah, I was thinking that too.' She looks sombre and says, 'It's so awful. No one can believe it. Brad is really upset about it. Like I said, he knew her pretty well. She was on the cross-country team. No wonder he didn't feel up to coming to supper tonight.'

Of course Brad is upset, Roy thinks. Who wouldn't be? Roy is upset and he'd never even met the girl; he only knew her by sight. Brad must have known her quite well if he was coaching her. They need to catch the bastard who killed her, whoever he is, so they can all go about their lives again, free of fear. Roy knows he won't stop worrying about his own daughter until that happens, and he's sure he's not the only one.

There hasn't been much that's concrete in the news so far, except for the picture earlier of a man, taken from a CCTV video, who has been named a 'person of interest'. Roy, Susan and Ellen have all seen the man's face online. None of them recognized him.

'Maybe he's not from around here,' Susan had said.

'It's good they have a suspect, at least,' Roy had said.

Now Ellen tells them, 'Brad says that the man they're looking for is someone who was a customer at the Home Depot where Diana worked.'

'How does he know that?' Susan asks.

Ellen shrugs. 'That's what they're saying around the school. Some other kids at school worked there too. They're saying that he was harassing her at her job, that's why they're looking for him.'

'Oh,' Susan says. Roy and his wife focus their attention on their daughter.

'Brad says he was probably harassing her because she was such an attractive girl. He says she got a lot of attention.'

Susan says, 'That's like blaming the girl for being beautiful. As if it's her fault somehow. You're beautiful, Ellen; you don't deserve to be murdered.'

Ellen flushes. 'He didn't mean it that way. He says she was a nice girl. Decent. Hardworking. Of course she didn't deserve it. No one does, no matter how they look, or what they wear, or how they behave. This isn't the Dark Ages.'

Ellen is annoyed at her mother. She secretly suspects that she isn't the biggest fan of her fiancé, although she has never said so and they all pretend otherwise. She'd seemed more excited about her brothers' weddings than she does about her only daughter's, and Ellen had kind of expected the opposite. She can't help feeling disappointed. Maybe by the third wedding the novelty wears off. Or maybe it's more worrying for a mother to marry off a daughter than a son. Wives don't make their husbands unhappy as often as husbands make their wives unhappy. That's just simple statistics. She knows it's the woman who's taking the bigger risk in marrying, especially if she has kids. But Ellen graduated from college and is planning a career in early childhood education. The bakery is just temporary. She is not going to be dependent on a man.

Or maybe her mother just isn't quite ready for her last child to leave the nest. So she understands her mom might have reservations. Still, Ellen feels that her last comment was unwarranted. Brad didn't mean anything by it. He was just stating a fact.

She'd seen him after her shift at the bakery. She'd heard the news on the radio while she was in the back, making bread, rolls and pastries. The news shook her – shook all of them working that morning – even though she hadn't known, then, that the girl had been found on their farm.

She had texted Brad, realizing that it was likely that he knew her, that she might have been in one of his gym classes. It took him a while to get back to her, but then he responded. I can't believe it. She was on my cross-country team. Can I see you?

She arranged to come to the high school to meet him as soon as her shift was over, at one o'clock. When she got there, she texted him to find out where he was in the school. He told her not to come into the building; he would come out to her in the parking lot.

She waited for him there, leaning against her car. The two-storey brick school seemed empty – as if they'd sent all the students home. There was a police presence, though – two state police cruisers were parked in front. Brad came out a side door of the school and walked hurriedly toward her, taking her into his arms in a tight hug. She could feel his heart pounding against hers. Finally, she pulled away and looked at him.

'Are you all right?' she asked. Because he didn't look all right. He seemed agitated – his breathing a little disordered, his eyes blinking rapidly. There was water splashed on the front of his shirt. He usually carried himself with an air of good-natured confidence. But now he looked like he was trying not to go to pieces, and he was trembling a little. He wouldn't look her in the eye. It unsettled her. It was shocking news, certainly. She'd never seen him like this. 'It's okay, Brad,' she said, trying to soothe him.

'It's *not* okay – a girl is dead!'

'I'm sorry,' she said immediately, chastened.

He looked at her then. 'No, I'm sorry. I didn't mean to

86

snap at you.' He took her in his arms again and they stood that way for a long while. He whispered into her hair, 'You know I love you, right?'

'I know. I love you too,' she whispered back fiercely. 'Always.'

She would support him through this. Most men, she thought, had trouble expressing grief. They weren't like women, who were allowed to show their emotions, and who had strong support networks, others with whom they could easily and regularly share their feelings. And Brad was a jock, a gym teacher – he wasn't exactly the touchy-feely type. She was the only one he had to confide in. He'd probably been bottling it up inside at school all day until the moment he could be with her.

But then he hadn't wanted to talk about it – he just wanted to hold her and tell her that he loved her. He seemed to need reassurance.

Now she eats her supper with her parents, thinking about her fiancé. She'd understood that he didn't want to eat with them tonight, but she'd thought she would go to his place later, as she usually does on Friday nights. He has his own place, and she doesn't. But he'd told her no, he wanted to be alone.

Chapter Fifteen

RILEY SITS ON her bed, her hands clasped tightly around her drawn-up knees, giving in to her darkest thoughts. She doesn't find it impossible to imagine that Cameron might have murdered Diana. She knows that when a woman is murdered, it's usually the husband or the boyfriend. One part of her thinks this, while another part of her is screaming silently in pain and fear: *This can't be happening.* Less than twenty-four hours ago her world made sense; now it makes no sense at all.

She doesn't know how she will ever get over the loss of Diana, how she will ever be able to let her go. She looks down at the cell phone in her hand. She doesn't know why she does it – she texts Diana even though she knows she's dead.

Hey, Diana. I miss you.

She knows it's stupid and childish, but she does it anyway and then sits there waiting for the ping of an answer that will never come, tears spilling down her face.

I wish you were here. I wish I knew what happened to you.

She scrolls up and stares at the last text she had from Diana, the night before, at 9:52.

Cameron on his way over to pick me up.

She'd shown it to the detectives.

Riley can't bear it. She wants to ask Cameron straight out if he did it, if he lost his temper and did this awful thing. He wouldn't tell her if he did, but maybe she will be able to tell if he's lying.

We'll find out, Diana, she texts. We'll find out who did this to you.

Riley gets up off the bed and goes down the hall to the bathroom and washes her face. Then she goes downstairs and finds her mom in the kitchen. She says, 'I'm going over to Cameron's for a minute.'

'What? No, you're not,' her mother says. She sounds like she means it.

'I need to talk to him,' Riley insists. Her mother knows what she's worried about; she was with her in the police station.

Her mom takes a deep breath and says, 'Do you think that's a good idea?'

'I have to speak to him,' Riley says stubbornly. Riley knows she gets her stubbornness from her mother. For a moment there's a standoff.

'I don't want you out there alone in the dark. I'll drive you,' her mom says finally. Riley starts to say something, but her mom cuts her off. 'You can talk to him as long as his parents are home, and I'm sure they are. Don't worry, I'll wait for you in the car. You can take as long as you need.'

They grab their jackets and leave together for the short drive to Cameron's house. When they get there and her mother parks in the driveway, Riley looks out at the wooden farmhouse with the screened-in porch, so familiar to her from so many get-togethers, and has to steel herself for a moment before she gets out of the car. But then she opens the door. Her mother stays in the car.

When Cameron's mother answers the door, Riley is shocked to see how terrible she looks. But Mrs Farrell loved Diana, too, Riley thinks, and Cameron must be a mess. They probably don't know that Diana was thinking of breaking up with him. 'Can I talk to Cameron?' Riley asks on the doorstep.

'I'm sorry, Riley, but he doesn't want to see anybody,' Mrs Farrell says.

'He'll want to see me,' Riley says, brushing past her, and walking inside the house toward the stairs. She turns back and says over her shoulder, 'Where is he?'

'You can't just barge in here,' Mrs Farrell protests as Cameron's dad appears from the kitchen.

But Riley ignores them both and starts up the stairs, assuming that's where Cameron will be. Riley knows her way around the house. She knocks on Cameron's closed bedroom door at the top of the stairs. 'Cameron, it's Riley. I want to talk.'

Riley holds her breath standing outside Cameron's door, his mom and dad lingering protectively at the bottom of the stairs.

'I don't want to talk to anyone. Leave me alone,' he says from behind the door.

His voice sounds different, full of tears. 'I'm not leaving,' Riley says, her own voice catching on a sob. She waits until he opens the door. Cameron looks utterly miserable. He's been crying a lot, Riley thinks. His handsome face is red and swollen. And his expression – he looks completely desolate, as if his life is over.

The first thing Riley does is hug him. Then Cameron closes the door, and they sit on his bed.

'I can't believe she's gone,' Cameron says finally.

'I know,' Riley says bleakly. They sit in silence. Then she reaches out and grasps his hand, squeezes it. She lets the silence grow. Finally she says, 'Cameron, what happened with the police?'

He looks at her warily. 'What do you mean?'

'They questioned you . . . you're not a suspect, are you?' Riley asks, as if she's worried he might be.

'Of course not. They know I loved her.'

'Good,' Riley says, nodding sadly. 'What did you tell them?'

'I told them the truth. I picked her up in my dad's truck, we drove around, parked, made out. I dropped her back home about eleven and went home. I don't know what happened to her after that.' But he's not looking at her now.

Riley isn't sure she believes him. Why won't he look at her? 'You guys didn't argue or anything?' she asks tentatively.

He glances at her defensively and then looks away again. 'No, of course not. What would we have to argue about?'

Riley gathers herself and says, 'I know Diana didn't want to go to the same college as you next year. She told me.'

'Oh,' he says, glancing at her again. 'What else did she tell you?'

'Nothing. Just that,' Riley says. She doesn't tell him that she knows Diana was thinking of breaking up with him.

'We didn't argue about it,' Cameron says. 'She was happy when I left her at her door last night. That's the last I saw of her.'

Riley stares at him, waiting for more. He still won't meet her eyes.

Shelby Farrell watches Riley leave and turns to her husband. 'That girl is pretty ballsy,' she says tensely.

Edward rests his hand on her shoulder. 'Maybe it was good for him. He needs his friends right now.'

Shelby looks up at him. She's not so sure. She doesn't know what they talked about, what Cameron might have told Riley. She knows kids talk to one another more than they talk to their parents. What if he told her something he shouldn't, and the police get it out of her? Shelby can't carry this on her shoulders alone any longer; she's been doing that all day, and now, as darkness falls, she decides she can't do it any more. She must tell her husband. She pulls him down the stairs to the finished basement where they can't be overheard.

'There's something I have to tell you,' she says.

'What?' He immediately looks concerned.

She says in a low voice, 'Cameron is lying about what time he came home last night.'

His eyes widen. 'What are you talking about?'

She tells him how she woke up and Cameron wasn't there. How she waited for him to come home, which he did, at 1:11 a.m.

'He lied to the police! Why would he lie about that?' she asks her husband in a hushed voice.

He looks stunned, as if he can't absorb it. She helps him. 'Do you think he lied because his curfew is eleven thirty? He probably left her there like he said, only he lied about the time? Remember we grounded him once because he came in past curfew, and he was furious.'

'Yes, but – he wouldn't lie to the police just because of his curfew, would he?' Edward asks doubtfully. He looks alarmed now.

She is not getting the reassurance she was hoping for. It looks like Edward doesn't buy the explanation she's been grasping at. She finds she can't breathe for a minute, because she's afraid she doesn't believe it either.

'We have to ask him,' Edward says.

'No.'

'What do you mean, no?' Edward says.

'Maybe,' she says, feeling sick, 'maybe it's better if we don't ask him. Let's – let's just assume it's because of the curfew. He must be telling the truth about everything else.'

'What? Shelby, we can't just ignore this.'

'Yes, we can. He's lied before about things to avoid getting in trouble. You know that. About where he was, what time he got home. Teenage stuff. I'm sure this is no different.' She turns and flees up the stairs, as if she's running away.

Riley gets into the car beside her mother, closes the door, and says, 'Go.'

Her mother backs out of the driveway, silent. She's obviously waiting for her to tell her how it went. But Riley is churning inside; she suspects Cameron was lying. She's having trouble catching her breath. If only she could talk to Diana. She starts to sob again. Her mother looks over at her anxiously. 'Riley, what happened? What did he say?'

She pulls herself together and says, 'He said he dropped her home at eleven, and everything was fine.' She keeps her suspicions to herself; she doesn't want her mother urging her to go back to the police. She says, 'It's just so fucking sad.'

When they arrive home, Riley goes directly to her bedroom and closes the door. She climbs onto her bed and stares at her cell phone. Finally, she texts Evan.

Chapter Sixteen

Friday, Oct. 21, 2022, 8 p.m.

I've been looking out the window at the moon from my bed. I have a desk where I do my homework, but when I'm writing I like to sit in bed leaning up against the headboard with my laptop, looking out. My room is at the back of the house, so it's quiet out there. If you look out the front, onto the street, you can tell you're in a small town, but when you look out the back, it's like you're already in the country. Just the darkness and the trees and the moon.

I'm trying to process everything, but it feels impossible. Last night at this time, Diana was alive. Now she's dead and I miss her so much it physically hurts. Writing is the only thing that makes me feel better, somehow, when things are bad. I'm good at it; it's my best subject.

Staring out the window at the darkness and the moon makes me think of how we used to hang out in the graveyard at night. We'd go there sometimes after the movies because we're too young to get into bars. Too old to go right home after the movie let out. The last time was a couple of weeks ago. We'd been to see *Bullet Train* – the four of us. We stood around outside in the autumn chill wondering what to do next. It was a Friday night. Nobody was having a party, and we were at loose ends. And there was always that little bit of tension among us – that Cameron and Diana might want to go off on their own. But Diana was too nice to leave me and Riley in the lurch on a Friday night. She would include us until it got late, then she'd go off with Cameron after.

Cameron opened his jacket and showed us a small bottle of whiskey. Diana smiled up at him like he was some kind of hero. I had something too. I'd managed to steal something from my parents' liquor cabinet. I wasn't as lucky as Cameron, who had older friends to buy for him. I didn't have a pint of Jack Daniel's, but I had a water bottle full of stolen vodka that my parents wouldn't notice. So I told them I had some vodka on me and Diana suggested we go to the graveyard.

She was the leader, and we all just automatically followed her. No one minded. She always had the best ideas. If anyone objected, she would have been completely flexible, but no one ever did. That night, we walked away from the bright lights of the movie theatre,

the only one in town, along the sidewalk into the deep-
ening darkness. Diana and Cameron were in front of
me, and I saw how he kept his arm around her, how his
hand would sometimes trail down to touch her bum.

The Fairhill United Church was at the end of the long
main street on a corner, away from the stores and
lights. It's a very old, historic, wooden church, painted
white, with an impressive steeple in the front and large
double doors. There are trees all around and the cemetery is on the right-hand side and sweeps around to the
back. It's where we all went to Sunday school until we
were old enough that our parents stopped making us
go. None of us have parents who are particularly
devout, but we'd go to church for the big occasions.
Christmas, Easter. Weddings and funerals.

The church and graveyard are very old. The church
was built in the late 1700s. The gravestones are interesting, some going back to that time. We used to play
among them after Sunday school sometimes. And once
in grade school we'd gone on a class visit for social
studies when we were learning about the early settlers.
I remember the teacher pointing out all the graves of
very young children. The class was boisterous, a few
of the kids fooling around, not listening, but I was one
of the ones who was interested in what she had to say.
I remember watching her, observing her mounting
frustration.

The graveyard is different at night. It's shrouded in
mystery, and it seems to go on for ever. The trees – tall

old maples, beeches, oaks – rustle in the dark. There was never anyone there at night, so it was our favourite place to drink.

That night two weeks ago was our last time there all together. It's almost as if we had some feeling about what was going to happen. We weren't as high spirited as usual. Normally when we drank, we'd get silly and goofy, but that night Diana seemed quiet as she and Cameron shared the Jack Daniel's. Cameron seemed to be watching her. I shared my vodka with Riley. Somehow we started telling ghost stories.

There's no end of ghost stories in Vermont. We're known for them. Mrs Acosta just did a unit on them in English. We did 'The Signal-Man' by Charles Dickens, and *The Turn of the Screw* by Henry James. We had a spirited discussion that night in the graveyard about whether it was ghosts that were torturing little Miles and Flora or whether the nanny was nuts.

'Personally, I think the nanny was imagining it all,' I said. That was the explanation I liked best. I didn't believe in ghosts. I believed in psychology, and people, and motivations. I found the story fascinating.

'Why are you so sure?' Diana countered.

'Do you believe in ghosts?' Cameron asked her, as if he were teasing her.

'I just mean,' she said to Cameron, 'that maybe the writer intended it to be a ghost, in the story. Of course I don't believe in ghosts.' She gave him a playful shove.

I caught a glance between Riley and Diana that I

didn't understand. Maybe it was the vodka, but I was annoyed with Cameron. 'You aren't even in that class.'

He said, 'So what? I'm still entitled to an opinion.'

'But how do you explain it,' Diana mused, 'all the stories about ghosts? I don't mean the literary ones, I mean the local ones, the things people say.'

'Tell us a story, Diana,' Riley urged. 'You're the best one at telling ghost stories.' And she reached out to me for another swig from my vodka-filled water bottle.

Diana told us the story of Emily and the bridge. We'd all heard it before, but we always enjoyed listening to Diana's stories, and her little embellishments.

'You all know this one, it's famous,' Diana said. 'There was a girl, a long time ago, called Emily.' She paused. 'She was very beautiful.'

'How do you know that?' Cameron interjected.

'Just shut up and listen,' Diana said. 'She was very beautiful, and she was in love with a handsome young man. They were supposed to run off and be married. Perhaps their parents didn't approve of them getting married, I don't know. Maybe they thought she was too young. This was in Stowe. They arranged to meet one night at the covered bridge and run away together.'

'I've never heard that before, that they were going to meet at the bridge and run away together,' Riley interjected. 'You're making that up. I thought he jilted her and that she just killed herself at that bridge.'

'Just work with me here,' Diana said. 'He didn't show up. And she thought he'd jilted her, and she killed herself. We don't even know how she killed herself, but she did. Maybe she jumped.'

'Have you been to that bridge?' Cameron said. 'I have. It's not very high. I don't think a jump from that would kill you. It might hurt her bad, though.'

'Wait a minute,' I said. 'It's a covered bridge. How do you jump off a covered bridge?'

'It doesn't matter,' Diana said. 'Maybe she poisoned herself. Maybe she stabbed herself with a dagger or shot herself. The point is, she died at that bridge and she haunts it to this day. People who cross it hear all sorts of unexplained noises – thumping and banging and wailing and so on. And their cars get scratched if they drive over it.'

'Emily sounds pretty angry,' Cameron observed. 'And I've been to that bridge,' he said again, 'and I didn't hear anything.'

'Yeah, me neither,' Diana conceded. Then she paused, took another drink, and said, 'But seriously, there's something I've never told you guys before.' We all looked at her expectantly. 'A friend of my mother's – Mrs Whalen – swears she heard screaming there. This was a few years ago. She and her husband were driving across the bridge. There was this horrible sound of a woman screaming and shrieking and sobbing. She said it completely terrified them. When they got through to the other side of the bridge, her husband pulled the car over and got out to look around, thinking someone was there. She did too. It wasn't quite dark yet, and they couldn't see anyone. And before you say it was just the wind, my mom already suggested that and Mrs Whalen said it definitely wasn't, and her husband agreed with her.'

'They imagined it,' Cameron said.

'But you know Mrs Whalen,' Diana protested. 'She's not very imaginative. And her husband said the same thing, and he's as sober as a judge.' She paused thoughtfully and added, 'My mom was really affected by it.'

When she said that, the moon slipped behind a cloud, and I felt the slightest shiver up my spine. She and Riley shared another private, meaningful glance I couldn't quite decipher, and then Diana looked across at me and grinned.

I have to stop writing for a minute, I'm so sick at heart. We'll all be going to that church for her funeral. Diana will be buried there, in our graveyard. It makes me feel sick to think of it.

My cell phone pings, and I pick it up to look at it. I've got a text from Riley.

Are you there?

Yes.

We should talk.

Chapter Seventeen

AFTER SUPPER AND dishes, Paula Acosta pours herself a glass of wine, another one for her husband, and takes them both into the TV room. Taylor has gone upstairs to her bedroom, seemingly unperturbed. But Paula isn't so sure. She never knows what her daughter is thinking these days.

'Thanks,' her husband, Martin, says as she hands him the glass. He's relaxing after a tough week. It's Friday night, and it's their habit to have some wine and watch something bingeable on television.

She sits down beside him. 'I'm worried about Taylor,' she says.

'You're always worried,' he says absently.

'Someone around here has to do the emotional work,' she answers a little sharply.

He looks up then, alert. 'What's wrong?'

'Nothing. Everything.' She sighs. It's hard to put into words, it's just a feeling, a feeling that everything is slipping away from her, at risk somehow. 'Taylor is so quiet. She spends all her time in her room these days. She used to see her friends more.' She pauses, takes a sip of her wine. 'I don't think she has any friends any more. I saw her this morning, sitting all by herself in the cafeteria before classes started. And then—' She thinks of everything else that happened that day. 'And then the horrible news about Diana. It's such a tragedy, so awful what happened to her. She was such a bright girl. She had so much going for her.'

'I hope they figure out who did it,' her husband says.

'Me too.' She sips her wine. She knows she's not supposed to say anything, but if she tells Martin, he's not going to tell anyone. It won't go any further. 'If I tell you something, you must promise not to breathe a word of it to anyone,' she says to him.

He looks surprised. 'Of course. What is it?'

'There's something the police don't know yet.' He puts his wineglass down on the coffee table and gives her his full attention. She tells him. 'The gym teacher, Brad Turner. Diana had complained about him.'

'What do you mean?'

'I don't know, exactly. Kelly told me a while ago that she came to him and said Turner had been inappropriate with her. Kelly told me it was all just a misunderstanding. It was kept quiet. He only told me because he needed to talk to someone, and I'm the only one he confides in. Apparently that was the end of it. It was all kind of swept under the rug. I don't even know if he put a record of it in his file.'

'What did he do?'

103

'That's just it. I don't know the extent of it – Kelly didn't say – but he seems to think it was nothing. It's just – I'm not sure he's the best judge. It all got settled without anything official being done, so it couldn't have been that bad, surely?' She looks at her husband anxiously.

'So – do you – are you afraid that the gym teacher might have killed Diana?' He seems shocked.

'I don't know.' She shakes her head. 'I spoke to Kelly about it this afternoon. I asked him if he was going to mention Diana's complaint to the police investigating her murder. Kelly wasn't planning on telling them, but I convinced him he should.'

'And?'

'And he said he would tell the detectives. But he also implied that I was being terribly naïve, and that if it got out it would ruin Brad's life for nothing – because he never did anything wrong and there's no way he killed Diana.' She looks at him now, worried. 'Have I done the wrong thing? Should I have stayed out of it? I mean, just because he *may* have been inappropriate with Diana – and apparently there's no proof that he was – it doesn't mean he's a murderer.'

Martin looks back at her, considering. 'I don't know.'

She doesn't know either.

'I guess it would depend on what he actually did, if anything – how serious it was.'

She doesn't answer for a moment. She takes another gulp of wine. Then she says, 'That's just it – there's never any real proof with this kind of thing – it all comes down to who's telling the truth. To who you believe.'

Edward Farrell stands in the basement watching his wife's back as she retreats up the stairs. She's dropped this bombshell on him, and now she wants to just ignore it all, and not talk to their son about it? Cameron has *lied* to the police. He hesitates for a long moment, and then he charges up the stairs. He finds her in the kitchen. She doesn't want to meet his eyes.

'Shelby,' he says, coming up close to her, his voice low and urgent, 'Cameron didn't do anything to Diana. We both know that.' She looks up at him then, nodding. He pulls her into his arms and holds her, his heart pounding. He's trying to think. His first instinct is to go upstairs and ask Cameron to explain. But that's not what Shelby wants to do.

He's suddenly afraid. Can they ignore this? Should they? There might be a perfectly reasonable explanation. Maybe Cameron did lie about the time because of his curfew. He's just a kid, and kids do stupid things, make bad decisions. Or maybe he lost track of time, and he thought it was much earlier, but Edward finds that hard to believe – he's always got his phone in his hand; he always knows what time it is. As he holds his wife, he realizes with a sinking heart that while she might be able to live with not knowing, he can't. He has to talk to their son. He releases her from his arms and speaks quietly.

'Shelby, we have to talk to him about this.'

'No! It's better if we don't know. I'm a terrible liar. You know that. What if the police bring me in and question me—'

He stares back at her, aghast. *What the hell does she think their son did?* He's almost angry at her. 'They won't bring you in. He's not a suspect.'

'What makes you think that? They're treating him like a suspect.'

'They have to ask him questions! He was Diana's boy-friend. He was the last one to see her. He'd just had sex with her. But I think that will be the end of it. They can't honestly think it was him.' Edward looks at his frightened wife. But if she can have doubts, what will the police think?

She starts to cry and collapses against his chest. He folds his arms around her again and makes a decision. 'It's okay,' he whispers. 'We won't ask him. We'll leave it alone. Every-thing is going to be all right. Cameron didn't harm Diana, so it doesn't matter if he lied about the time. They'll find out who did it.'

But as he holds her, he decides uneasily that he will ask Cameron himself, when Shelby isn't around. He will leave his wife out of it; he'll tell Cameron that he heard him come in after one in the morning and get an explanation. And if he has to keep the answer to himself, to protect his wife, to protect his son, then he will.

Chapter Eighteen

RILEY HAD TEXTED Evan and asked him to come over. Now she takes him into the TV room. Her mother has left them alone. Riley closes the door and drops onto the couch and sinks down beside him, exhausted. Then she looks at him and says, 'I went over to Cameron's house to talk to him tonight.'

He raises his eyebrows at her. 'His parents didn't let you see him, did they?'

'I wouldn't take no for an answer. I just barged in.'

'Wow,' Evan says. 'I went over there this afternoon. They wouldn't let me in, and I just left.' He looks at her expectantly. 'What did he say?'

She bites her lip nervously. She says, 'I think he might have been lying.'

Now Evan seems wary, anxious. She can see the dismay in his face. 'Why? What did he say?'

'He said that everything was fine between him and Diana,

and that when he left her at home, around eleven, everything was good.'

'And you don't believe him?'

She shakes her head, looking directly at Evan. 'I don't know. He wouldn't look at me. And he *knew* she didn't want to go to the same college as him next year. But I know she hadn't told him that yet, so she must have told him last night, or how would he know?' She adds, 'I just can't see him taking it well, can you?'

'No,' Evan agrees. 'Maybe they argued, and he doesn't want to admit it. It doesn't mean he killed her.'

'No, I know,' Riley agrees. She can tell Evan doesn't want to believe that Cameron might be a murderer. But she no longer feels sure of anything. When she'd looked at Cameron, sitting on his bed in his childhood room, she couldn't help imagining him in a rage, his hands around Diana's neck. She couldn't get out of there fast enough.

She has to tell Evan what she did. 'I went to the police, this afternoon. I spoke to the detectives.'

He looks back at her. He's gone completely still. 'What? Why?'

'I told them that Diana was going to break up with him.'

He stares at her for a long moment. Finally, he sighs deeply. 'I guess you did what you had to do.'

When his wife retreats to the bathroom for a hot bath, Edward has the opportunity to talk to his son without her knowing. She'll be in there for a while, he knows. She often has a long bath at night to relax before bed, and she will

108

need it tonight. But now that he has the chance, he's almost afraid to take it.

Cameron is still in his bedroom, his door closed. He'd come out for supper, but he hadn't eaten much. No one had. Edward wonders what he and Riley said to each other. Now, as he climbs the stairs, he finds himself almost hoping that Cameron has fallen asleep, in which case he won't disturb him. But there's light coming from beneath the bedroom door into the dimness of the hall. He stands tentatively outside the bedroom door.

'Cameron?' he says softly.

'Yeah,' comes from within.

Edward pushes the door open. Cameron is sitting on the bed, his arms around his drawn-up knees. He lifts his tear-stained face. Edward falters. But then he closes the door carefully behind him and comes over and sits down on the end of the bed and faces his son. 'Are you okay?'

'No.'

Edward swallows. 'I know you loved her. I can't imagine how hard this is.' Cameron won't even look at him, but stares down at the quilt on the bed. 'Cameron, I have to ask you something.' His son does look up at him then, wary. 'I heard you come in last night, just after one o'clock.' His son's wariness has turned instantly to fear. Edward waits, his heart pounding. He wishes he was anywhere else; he wishes he hadn't started this. He feels like he's on the edge of a precipice; the fall will be catastrophic.

'Does Mom know?' Cameron asks in a whisper.

'No,' Edward lies. 'This is just between us.' Cameron

109

appears to be paralysed. He doesn't move. He doesn't even blink. Edward must ask. 'Cameron, why did you lie to the police about it?'

Cameron's face is a combination of confusion and terror. 'I didn't know what to do.'

'Okay. You can tell me the truth, though. It will be okay,' Edward says, lying again. But he's terrified too. What if his son – if he did kill Diana – then it can never be okay. Nothing can ever be okay ever again.

'I did come home around eleven, like I said.' He pauses. 'But then I went out again.'

Edward is puzzled. 'Why? Where did you go?'

Cameron answers. 'I went back to Diana's.'

God help him. 'Why?'

His son starts to cry, tears running down his face. 'We'd argued. We had a big fight. When I left her at home, we were both mad at each other. So I came home, but then I went back, to try to work things out with her.'

'Okay.' Edward's stomach plunges.

'I parked in front of her house and sat in the truck in the dark for a while. I didn't know what to do.' He stops.

Edward doesn't want to ask, but he does. His mouth is so dry. 'And then what?'

'That's it. I just sat there for a long time, thinking. And then I left and drove around for a while and came home again.'

'Okay,' Edward repeats, exhaling. This is bad, but it isn't terrible. His son didn't hurt Diana. He must be telling the truth. But it won't be good if the detectives find out – that

110

they argued, that he was there. That he lied to them. *Jesus.*
'What did you argue about?'

'She didn't want to go to the same college next year . . .
and . . . she broke up with me.'

Edward swallows. This is bad.

'And now she's dead!' Cameron says wildly.

'It's not your fault,' Edward says, trying to calm him. He
tries to think, but his brain doesn't seem to be working
properly. It takes him a moment to ask, 'You didn't see anything? Hear anything?'

Cameron shakes his head, then looks up anxiously. 'What
if someone saw me there in the truck?'

Edward swallows again. 'Then you tell the police the
truth.'

'Should I tell them anyway?'

Edward considers this carefully. 'I don't think so. Let's
just keep this between us, okay?'

Cameron watches his father leave his bedroom and close
the door behind him softly. He was afraid his dad already
knew about the time he came home. He'd suspected as
much in the truck on the way home from the police station.
Now he knows for sure. He and his dad share a secret, and
his father agrees that it should stay that way. At least now
he doesn't feel quite so alone.

He's still very worried that he might have been seen.

Everything is so fucked up.

Cameron had spent the day lying in bed, curled in the
fetal position, sending his parents away when they tried to

come in to comfort him. He doesn't want them, and he doesn't want to talk. He wants to stop existing.

Cameron had heard Evan come to the door, had heard his father send him away. It might have been a mistake to talk to Riley. He's worried about what Riley thinks. He hadn't liked the way she looked at him.

At least his father believes him. His father would believe him no matter what lies he told.

Chapter Nineteen

BRAD TURNER LIGHTS a rare cigarette, blowing the smoke out the open window. It's not allowed in here, inside the apartment, but no one's going to know. And he needs a cigarette desperately right now. He's got a small, one-bedroom apartment in a low-rise building on one of the small side streets in town, Ivy Street. It's quiet after five o'clock, when the shops close. He looks down on the street now. It's quite late, long after dark, and no one is stirring. There's no one to see him smoking at the window.

The apartment is mostly out of sight of the teenagers he teaches. They walk up and down the main street carousing in groups; they don't come down here. He doesn't want them to see him coming in and out of his apartment building. He doesn't want them to know where he lives. Kids like to know things about their teachers. They're nosy. They're going to *love* this, he thinks, and angrily flicks the spent cigarette out the window.

He thinks about Diana, feels a pang of something sharp. He tries to identify it. What is it? Anger? Fear? Regret? He thinks it's all of them. He's sorry that Diana is dead. Of course he is. He genuinely liked her, in spite of everything. He's angry, though – at her, and at Principal Kelly. He's scared now too. The police are investigating Diana's murder, and they'll want to talk to him if they find out what she said to Kelly about him.

His cell phone rings, making him jump. He picks it up and recognizes the name: Graham Kelly, the principal. Shit, shit, shit. Today at school, in all the turmoil, he had barely seen Kelly. He hadn't had a chance to talk to him alone; there was always someone around.

Kelly was on his side. Kelly had believed him. The whole thing had made Kelly very uncomfortable, and he'd obviously just wanted it all to go away. But what if he tells the police?

He answers the call. 'Yes?'

'Hi Brad, it's Kelly.'

There's an awkward pause, and then Kelly speaks. 'I'm sorry, Brad. I wasn't going to mention what happened with you and Diana to the police, but I feel I really have no choice. I wanted to give you the heads-up – I'm going to tell them in the morning.'

Fuck. Brad takes a breath. He says, 'I understand; you're in a difficult spot. I'm sorry. I'm sorry it ever happened.' He's still hoping to change Kelly's mind. But even if he does, who else might know? Diana said that she didn't want anyone to know, that she hadn't told her mother, or anyone else. But what if she had? Kelly must realize he can't keep it quiet, or he would.

'I'm sorry too,' Kelly says.

Brad realizes that Kelly isn't going to change his mind. 'You know this will ruin me,' he can't help saying. 'And you know she was lying.'

Kelly doesn't respond to that. He says, 'It's just that – what's happened to her changes everything. And it's unfortunate that this will now have to come out.'

Unfortunate, Brad thinks bitterly, close to panic. 'And what will come out, exactly?' he asks.

'You know – what's in the file.'

Brad closes his eyes for a moment in relief. He's read the file. He opens them again. 'Am I going to lose my job?' he asks.

'I will try to protect you, but honestly, I don't know. It depends.'

'What do you mean?'

'If it becomes known – you know how powerful parents are these days.' There's a short silence at this. Then he adds, 'Look, the police will probably question you, realize you had nothing to do with her death, and leave it be—'

'Of course I had nothing to do with it!'

'Of course not.' Kelly pauses. 'So with any luck, none of this might ever become known publicly.'

At least he knows where he stands. 'Thanks for letting me know,' Brad says. Just before he disconnects, he says, 'Keep me in the loop about this.'

'Of course.'

Brad lights another cigarette, brooding out the window, more anxious than before. His cell phone rings again, and he glances at it. It's Ellen. He doesn't want to talk to her. He doesn't know what to tell her, so he doesn't answer. She doesn't know anything about this.

Not yet, anyway.

Ellen looks at her phone in dismay. It's not like Brad to ignore her calls. Maybe he's in the shower. Maybe he'll call her back and ask her to come over tonight after all. It feels odd to be at home on a Friday night, when she's engaged to be married in a matter of weeks. But she can put the time to good use. There's so much to do when planning a wedding, although she feels a bit guilty to be preparing for such a happy event when one of her fiancé's students has been murdered.

She thinks again about the body of that young girl left in their field. She can't stop thinking about it. It's sickening. And frightening.

Her thoughts turn once again to Brad. She can understand that he feels he needs some time alone, but she thinks it would be better if he could share his feelings more openly with her.

Ellen feels a twinge of unease. She loves Brad – head over heels – but there always seems to be something unknowable about him, as if he's keeping part of himself locked away from her. Maybe that's part of the attraction. She ascribes this to his upbringing, to his being the youngest child in an unhappy, dysfunctional family. He's not used to feeling safe, to sharing his feelings, and having those feelings validated. He's had to protect himself in order to survive as a healthy human being.

She thinks about their future, how different it will be when they start a family of their own. They've bought a modest little bungalow on the outskirts of town, with the help of her parents. The sale will close on December first. It will be a home filled with love and acceptance, honesty and kindness.

Ellen wanders into the dining room. The large, formal table is littered with wedding paraphernalia. They always eat in the kitchen, so she's turned the dining-room table into her workspace. She starts working on the place cards for her wedding supper; she still has a lot of them to do.

Brenda Brewer finally climbs the stairs to bed. She's told her ex-husband to make himself up a bed in the spare room. She's suggested he might as well leave in the morning, and he agreed. 'I have to get back to Jill and the boys,' he said unnecessarily, and she walked out of the room.

Now she crawls beneath the covers and turns off the lamp beside her bed. The room is plunged into darkness. She longs for the oblivion of sleep, but even though she's taken a sleeping pill, for a long while it eludes her. Because sometime last night, someone murdered her daughter. The horror of it.

As she finally begins to drift off to sleep, she thinks she senses her daughter's presence near her, close and comforting. She knows it's just her mind, on the edge of sleep, playing tricks on her, but she clings to it nonetheless.

Chapter Twenty

GRAHAM KELLY SITS in his living room alone in the dark, tense, sipping a whiskey. He's been a mess all day. He's been swinging like a pendulum between his shock and grief about what's happened to Diana and his anxiety about the position he's in – his uncertainty about what he should do.

His wife has gone to bed, and his three kids have scattered to their various bedrooms to spend far too much time on social media and computer games that are doing them no good at all. He no longer enquires. He has lost control over them, and now all he can do, it seems, is hang on for the ride and hope it all turns out okay in the end. Parenting has been something of a nightmare for him and his wife. They have not been easy kids, but he loves them fiercely anyway. They have caused him personal heartbreak and professional embarrassment as a principal. It has certainly made him more empathetic to parents going through difficulties with their kids. He's done his best. He's come to believe that children are born with certain traits and temperaments and the most well-intentioned parenting in the world can't fundamentally change that. You do what you can. He doesn't judge.

But this.

He must go to the police station tomorrow morning and talk to them. Because Paula is right. And he's a little afraid that if he doesn't tell the police, Paula will.

They're going to want to question Brad. But it will probably be all right, he tells himself, gripping his whiskey glass tightly. Brad didn't kill her. Brad will have an alibi – he'll have been with his fiancée, no doubt – they're such lovebirds. Brad won't have to worry about any serious questioning on that point, at least. But Kelly, like the coward he is, hadn't wanted to bring up the matter of an alibi on the phone.

He knows he has always been someone who avoids bad news, skirts conflict. He's never been one to face things head-on – not in his work, or in his personal life either. It was a bit of a surprise, even to him, how he ever made it to the level of principal. But then he realized that it's all about working within the system. No one at the board level wants a maverick for a school principal. It's all about not rocking the boat, really.

He hopes this matter of Diana's complaint doesn't come out publicly, because he doesn't want to be under scrutiny for the way he handled it. He should have reported it, even if he found it unbelievable. It's not always easy to do the right thing, or to know what that is.

*

It's late when Joe Prior hears the familiar knock on his apartment door. He wonders what took him so long. Joe gets up from his chair where he's been watching the news on TV and opens it.

It's Roddy, whom he met on the job at the construction site earlier in the year. Roddy is a bit of a drifter too. He's half Canadian and spent part of his early life in New Brunswick. He's lean, as if he's underfed, but Joe knows how strong he is – he's seen him lift things at work. He's usually pretty amiable but can sometimes be a mean drunk. He lives by himself in a small trailer on the outskirts of town. Joe never goes there because he can't stand trailers. Too many miserable memories of growing up. He'll never set foot in another trailer again if he can help it.

'Hey, Roddy, come in,' Joe says. He mutes the TV.

Roddy enters the room and slumps down on the tattered black-leather couch and puts his feet up on the worn coffee table. Joe goes automatically into the tiny kitchen and comes back out with a cold can of beer, which he tosses to Roddy, who catches it expertly. Joe reaches into the fridge again and pulls out another cold one for himself. Roddy is glancing around the shoddy apartment, taking in the dirty clothes in the laundry basket by the front door, the books on the shelves.

'So, did the police call you?' Joe asks.

'They came to visit me. At my trailer.'

'Yeah?' Joe sits down in his recliner.

Roddy takes a long swig of beer. Then he lowers the can

and looks back at him curiously. 'Pretty fucking intense when all you did was flirt with her.'

'Yeah, no shit. Imagine how *I* feel. My picture all over the fucking place and all I did was talk to her. I should probably sue them.' He raises his can and drinks.

'Yeah, maybe you should.' Roddy belches and says, 'Anyways, they'll leave you alone now.'

'They'd fucking better.'

Friday, Oct. 21, 2022, 11:45 p.m.

I can't sleep. It feels like I might never sleep again. So I'm back on my laptop.

Writing is how I process things. Mrs Acosta, our creative writing teacher, has been encouraging me. She knows I want to be a writer someday. That's why I started writing this journal, just for myself, because you've got to start somewhere. 'Writers write,' Mrs Acosta says. She also says I have to find my voice. And I don't know, maybe writing about what happened to Diana will help me deal with all this.

Of the four of us, Diana was the one with the most energy, the ideas, the enthusiasm. She was the only one who understood my ambition to be a writer someday, except for Mrs Acosta. Cameron and I used to be closer, but when he became Diana's boyfriend at the end of the summer, he spent more time with her, and we've drifted apart. He's a walking cliché – tall, strong,

121

ruggedly good-looking, captain of the football team. Who else would date Diana, who looked like she should be a cheerleader? But she was too busy for that. She was beautiful and kind and a star runner, and so smart and funny too. And now my tears are falling onto the keyboard again.

Riley and Diana were always close, 'besties' as the girls like to say. I like Riley. She's smart, too, and ambitious and very competitive, especially with me. We compete for top marks in every class we're in together, which is most of them. Now our little group will fall apart. Diana was the heart and centre of it; she's what held it together. And now Riley suspects Cameron might have killed her.

I'm miserable at home. Mom is great, but my dad is an asshole. He's narrow-minded and has no interest in anything outside his own puny life. It's just hunting or watching TV and hitting the booze. He watches a lot of sports on TV and drinks beer after beer – come to think of it, he's a walking cliché too. Mom reads books to get away from him. They wanted more kids, but it didn't happen. I guess that makes me all the more disappointing, so I wish they'd had more kids too. They're obviously disappointed in each other. I don't know why they stay together – it can't be for me. Dad obviously had hoped his only child, his only *son*, would be a star athlete, like he was in his youth. He peaked in high school. But I'm hopeless at team sports and have no interest in them. I don't think my dad has ever gotten over that.

Instead, I'm applying to NYU for English and creative writing. *What the hell you going to do with that?* Dad said. Mom just looked sceptical. I think she blames herself. She always encouraged me to read. She's always read a lot herself, and our house is full of books. For as long as I can remember I've seen her sitting somewhere with her nose in a book. I tend to read the classics – *In Cold Blood*, by Truman Capote, is my favourite. I've read it three times. I think Mom maybe now wishes she hadn't encouraged my reading so much, taking me to the library all the time.

Being a big reader is a bit unusual in my peer group. Except for Diana. She read good books, and we talked about them all the time. God, I'll miss her.

Chapter Twenty-One

THE NEXT MORNING is Saturday, and Cameron lies in bed, staring up at the ceiling. He can hear his mother downstairs moving around in the kitchen. It sounds the same as every Saturday morning, but he knows that now everything is different. He realizes that he's hungry. He hasn't eaten much at all since yesterday morning, when the police interrupted his breakfast. He gets up and pulls on jeans and a sweatshirt. He doesn't bother with a shower. He doesn't care. He goes downstairs and enters the kitchen.

His mother turns at the sound of him, as if she's surprised to see him. She smiles. 'Cameron, honey,' she says, 'what can I get you for breakfast?'

'I'll get it,' he says, and grabs a bowl and cereal, takes the milk out of the fridge. He can't stand her false cheerfulness; it sets him on edge. She hovers, and he feels as if she's smothering him. He can feel her eyes on him, watching him, worrying about him, and he doesn't like it. He glances at the clock on the stove: 10:14. He slept in. 'Where's Dad?'

'Upstairs.'

The landline in the kitchen rings and his mother jumps. Cameron feels a jolt of fear surge through him. His mother stares at the phone, not moving, while it rings again. She's closest to it. 'Aren't you going to get that?' he asks, his voice tense.

She answers the phone and listens. She turns to look at him, and he knows.

'Yes, he's here.' She goes still. 'Yes. We'll be there soon.' She hangs up the phone and addresses him. 'They want to talk to you again. We have to go to the police station.'

Oh God, someone saw me. They must know he was at Diana's the night before last, after eleven, and he told them he wasn't. He tries to rise out of his chair, but his strength has left him.

'I'll get your father.'

A half-hour later, Cameron and his parents arrive at the Fairhill Police Station. His mother had insisted he finish his cereal before they left, but he could hardly get it down. His father walks beside him with his hand on his shoulder, as if silently saying, *I'm here for you.* Cameron is grateful, but it isn't going to be much help. His father can't save him. They'd had a hurried, whispered conversation that his mother doesn't know about before they left the house.

What if someone saw me?

125

Then just tell them the truth, and you'll be fine, his dad said.

'In here,' Detective Stone says, opening the door to the interview room. It's the same room they were in yesterday. 'Just to remind you,' Stone says, 'you're here voluntarily. You can leave at any time.'

Cameron nods nervously. It's the same as before – Detectives Stone and Godfrey on one side of the table, and Cameron flanked by his anxious parents on the other. He wishes his mother wasn't here, but he's afraid to ask her to leave. They start the tape.

'So, Cameron, you told us yesterday that you dropped Diana off at her house and she went inside at about eleven p.m., correct?' Cameron nods. 'Can you speak up for the tape?' Stone asks.

'Yes.'

Stone nods along. 'And then you went home.'

'Yes.'

Stone looks him in the eyes and waits. Cameron's fear escalates. They know. The way the detective is looking at him – they must know. He feels himself begin to tremble. His dad is watching him, concerned.

'Just relax, son,' Stone says. 'We just want to clarify a couple of things.' The detective is being friendly, even kind.

Cameron swallows. 'Okay.'

'Were there any problems in your relationship with Diana? Any arguments? If so, best to tell us now.'

'No,' Cameron says. It's a knee-jerk reaction. He remembers, as soon as he says it, that Diana told Riley things, that Riley knew about the college thing. She must have spoken to the detectives, and that's why he's here. Riley has always been a gossip; she should stay out of other people's business, he thinks bitterly.

Edward Farrell watches his son tremble as he sits in the chair across from the detectives. Cameron's nervousness dismays him. He glances at Shelby, and she looks wary, even alarmed. What's going on here? The vibe is different than it was yesterday, even though the demeanour of the detectives has not changed. It's his son who's changed.

'Are you sure, Cameron?' the detective says now, and waits. Cameron says nothing. The detective says, 'Because we've heard otherwise.'

'What?' Cameron says.

'We've heard that you and Diana were having problems.'

Shelby butts in anxiously, leaning forward in her chair. 'That's not true, is it, Cameron?'

The detective gives her a quelling glance, and she sits back again.

Cameron doesn't answer. Edward is worried. His son couldn't have had anything to do with Diana's death. But he knows he hasn't been telling them the whole truth, either. They just have to get past this.

'I loved her,' Cameron says at last, stubbornly. 'She loved me. We were perfect together.'

'But you must have had disagreements,' the detective presses. 'Everyone does.' When Cameron doesn't respond,

Stone asks, 'Did you argue with Diana about what colleges to go to?'

Cameron shakes his head and says, 'No. It wasn't a big deal. I thought we should only apply to the same colleges, but she wanted to apply to some others too. Because they had better vet programmes.'

'And how did you feel about that?'

'I was okay with it,' Cameron says.

But Edward knows they had a furious argument about it that night – Cameron told him. Diana had broken up with him.

'Her friend Riley told us she was thinking of breaking up with you,' Stone says.

'That's not true!' Cameron protests. And then, impulsively, 'Riley doesn't like me.'

'I thought you were friends?' Detective Stone says.

'We used to be. We all hung out together. But she didn't like it when Diana and I got together because Diana didn't have as much time for her. She was always trying to get between us.'

Detective Stone tilts his head. 'She said you were possessive.'

'She would. That's what I mean,' he says defensively. 'She was trying to split us up. But Diana knew I loved her. That's what mattered.'

'Okay. So you didn't argue last night?'

'No. Like I said, we drove around for a while, then parked and had sex in the truck and then I took her home around eleven. Everything was fine. She went inside and I left.'

Edward watches his son nervously. He knows that what he's just said isn't true. He knows they argued. But he's the one who told Cameron to stick to his story.

Stone sits back in his chair and says, 'The woman who lives across the street from the Brewers came home from visiting a friend in the hospice on Thursday night. She visits with her every night until about midnight, so she's very clear on the time. And when she got home on Thursday night, a little after midnight, she saw someone sitting in a truck outside of the Brewers' house. The truck exactly matches the description of your truck.'

Edward's stomach drops.

Cameron feels lightheaded, as if he's taken a hard hit on the football field. The detective is waiting for him to say something, but Cameron can't speak. He can feel that his face is flushed. He must look guilty as hell. He swallows, glances at his dad, who nods at him almost imperceptibly. He can't look at his mother.

'Okay, yes, I was there,' he says to the detective, stumbling a little over the words. He pauses, wondering how much he should say. He thinks of what his father told him. He swallows again. 'We did argue a bit. About the college thing. And after I dropped her at home at eleven, I did go home.' He pauses. 'But then after a while I went back. To apologize to her, to make up. I parked outside her house and sat in the truck. But I never got up the nerve to go in and talk to her. I thought she might still be mad at me.' He hangs his head. 'I stayed there, in the truck, for a while, till

129

after midnight, then I left and drove around a bit more till around one in the morning, then I went home again.'

'Why didn't you tell us this before?' Stone asks.

'Because – I thought if you knew we'd argued, and that I was there, you might think—' He can't finish the sentence.

'You should always tell us the truth,' Stone says firmly.

'I'm telling the truth now,' Cameron says, feeling desperate.

Stone looks back at him, cocks his head to one side. 'I don't think you are, Cameron.'

Cameron begins to tremble almost violently.

'Look, detective,' his dad begins. But he doesn't get any further than that.

Stone interrupts him. 'We know you got out of the truck, Cameron. What did you do when you got out of the truck?'

Edward watches his son and the detective in alarm. Oh God, what is going on here? This can't be happening. If Cameron says he didn't get out of the truck, then he didn't get out of the truck. He must believe that. Is the detective lying? Trying to trap him? But Edward knows his son has been lying all along. He must put a stop to this – now. 'Hold on,' he says aggressively. 'Are you accusing my son?'

'We just want to establish the facts, Mr Farrell,' Stone says.

'No,' Edward says firmly. 'This is over. If you want to question my son any further, it will be with an attorney present.' He should have done this sooner, he thinks.

He sees a brief flicker of annoyance in the detective's eyes, followed by resignation. 'I was just about to read him his rights anyway,' he says. 'Godfrey, please proceed.'

Edward and his wife and son listen in utter dismay as Detective Godfrey reads Cameron his rights.

'Is he under arrest?' Edward asks in disbelief. He feels like he can't breathe, like something very heavy is pressing on his chest.

'No. But we want to question him further, and it's not voluntary any longer. Call your lawyer. We'll wait till they get here.'

Stone turns off the tape, and the two detectives exit the room. Edward catches his wife's shocked, drawn face and then turns to his son. 'Cameron, don't say anything more. I'm going to get you the best criminal lawyer I can find.'

His fingers work busily on his cell phone, googling criminal lawyers in Vermont with the best reputations. He starts making calls while his wife and son sit there, frozen in fear. Neither of them utters a word.

Chapter Twenty-Two

No one knows I'm here, invisible, in this interview room. I watch from somewhere up around the ceiling. It's kind of neat, being a fly on the wall, seeing and hearing everything, but I can't enjoy it because it's all so upsetting. They think I'm dead, but I'm right here.

I still want to think this is temporary, some kind of extended, recurring dream that I'll snap out of, but I'm beginning to be afraid that it isn't a dream at all. I've been feeling cocooned somehow, not as distressed as I should be, as if I've been drugged by something that takes the edge off and makes me experience everything at a distance. But now the cocoon is unravelling, and I'm more alert, less fragmented, more aware of what's going on. Like I've been given a shot of adrenaline.

Is this boy who says he loved me responsible for my being here now, in this reduced form, drifting from place to place?

He sat outside my house in the dark for all that time.

Why would he do that? If he wanted to apologize, why didn't he text me and tell me he was outside? I would have come down. I would have let him into the house.

And then it strikes me. Maybe he did. And maybe I did let him in.

What did he do when he got out of the truck? The detective wants to know, and so do I. What did you do? I scream at Cameron. I get right up in his face and scream it over and over. He doesn't even flinch. I'm so angry. I can't participate. I can't communicate. I can only scream and scream and be ignored.

He's been lying all along. And now he's been caught out in his lies, and I want to know the truth. If he did this to me, I want him to suffer for it. I'm not an angel. Everyone thinks I'm an open book, but I'm more complicated than I seem, just like everyone else. I'm not a saint. I'm not perfect. I keep some things to myself. But that's what everyone does. Everyone has secrets – just look at Cameron. The lying bastard.

After the detectives leave the room I stare at my former boyfriend, slumped in his chair like a zombie, with his parents beside him. He's been crying a lot, anyone can see that. But maybe he's not crying about me. Maybe he's crying about what's going to happen to him.

As I watch him, I try to remember. I think about getting into his truck when he picked me up. I remember tossing my hair over my shoulder and smiling at him as I did up the seat belt, like always. And now, suddenly, staring at him, consumed with rage, I do remember. Driving along the

133

rural roads in the pitch dark, our headlights slicing into the blackness. Stopping at one of our favourite spots, in the corner of a field on the edge of somebody's farm. Now that I think of it, it's not that far from where they found my body.

Cameron was on me as soon as he turned off the ignition. I wanted to make out, too, but not as much as he did. He always wanted sex – I think that's just the way it is with teenage boys. Afterward, he complained that we always had to do it in the truck. I tried to make light of it and reminded him that in the summer we spread a blanket on the ground and did it under the stars. But since the weather got colder it had been in the truck. We couldn't go to his place because his parents always seemed to be home.

'You know, we could try your bedroom, next time,' he suggested as we pulled our clothes back on.

That got my back up right away. We'd had this conversation before, and I didn't feel like having it again.

'I mean, your mother isn't home, and it's going to get fucking cold soon. We can't come out here in the winter.'

I didn't like his complaining, and I didn't like his tone. 'Well, maybe you'll just have to do without,' I said, surprising myself. We never argued, so what happened next surprised both of us.

'What the hell does that mean?' he said.

For a moment I said nothing, because I didn't know what to say. I wasn't going to entertain him in my childhood bedroom. And I was already annoyed at him in general, for his clinginess. He had his own football schedule, but when time allowed, he crowded me. But I had things to do. I had to keep my grades up, and I had a part-time job. Cameron didn't have a part-time job. His parents felt he had enough on his plate with school and sports. But I was being raised by a single mom and I was saving for college. And suddenly his sense of entitlement – to me, to everything – pissed me off. I spoke before I thought. 'You know, Cameron, there's something I've been wanting to talk to you about.'

He looked at me like he didn't like the sound of that. His shoulders went up and his eyes narrowed, like he was bracing himself.

'I've been thinking, about college.' There was a long silence then, as if he knew what was coming.

'And?' he said.

'There are some really good veterinarian colleges I'd like to apply to – ones we haven't discussed.'

'Yeah, okay. I can apply wherever you want. I already told you that.'

He wasn't taking the hint, but I knew he wouldn't. I knew I'd have to spell it out for him. 'It's just that . . . I'm thinking it might be better if we don't go to the same college after all.' There, I'd said it.

'What? Are you breaking up with me?'

It was his disbelief that sealed it for me. He simply couldn't believe that I would want to do anything without him. That he wasn't the most important thing in my life. He looked angry then, although I don't remember feeling afraid.

'No, not right away,' I said, automatically trying to

smooth things over and hating myself for it. Sitting there in the cab of his truck, I suddenly wanted my old life back, seeing my friends, spending more time with Riley, spending time with myself. But I couldn't bear to hurt Cameron, to cut him off so suddenly, so completely.

'No,' he said.

I was a bit stunned by that. 'What do you mean, no?'

'We're not breaking up. You don't know what you're saying. You're just mad about me wanting to have sex in your room.'

Then I was *angry*. Livid. He was telling me that I didn't know my own mind, that I didn't know what I wanted. How dare he? *And how did he think that he could unilaterally decide that we were not breaking up? Fuck that. It didn't work that way. Relationships end when one person wants out.* 'You know what? We are breaking up,' I said, sure of myself then. 'Take me home. We're done.'

'You can't be serious,' he protested.

'Take me home. Now. I don't want to see you any more.'

He started the truck and peeled out of the field. He drove alarmingly fast down the dirt roads in the immense darkness. People have no business driving when they're angry. It's dangerous. Especially at night in the country where there are no lights. 'Slow down,' I said angrily, my hand out against the dash. 'You could hit something.'

'Like what?'

'Like an animal,' I said, furious.

When we got to my place he stopped in front, and I got out and slammed the truck door. I charged up to the house

136

without looking back. When I got inside, I slammed that door too. I heard him speed away, tyres squealing.

Once I got inside, I couldn't believe what had just happened, how quickly things had changed. I hadn't planned on bringing any of that up. But I thought maybe it was for the best. I thought about texting Riley, but I didn't feel like it and decided to tell her about it in the morning.

I can't remember anything after that. But now I know Cameron came back that night.

I want to remember. Or do I? Do I want to relive the terror of being murdered? Maybe there's a good reason I can't remember. Maybe I never will.

I want to crawl back inside the cocoon. I don't want to feel alive, and not be alive. But I don't think I have a choice. I'm starting to realize that none of this is a dream.

Chapter Twenty-Three

BRAD TURNER IS drinking coffee and chain-smoking at his small kitchen table in his apartment on Saturday morning. It's almost noon. He slept poorly. He's disabled the smoke detector, given up smoking by the window. He's got the lid of a jam jar on the table, and he's using it as an ashtray. He knows Kelly was planning to go to the police this morning to tell them what Diana said about him. They will want to talk to him soon.

Ellen calls him from the bakery, and it's all he can do to sound normal. The call is stressful for him. It's hard to pay attention to what she's saying, because of all that's running through his mind. They will probably ask him where he was on Thursday night. He toys with the idea of asking Ellen to say that she'd spent the night at his place, even though she hadn't. But he doesn't want to ask her. And her parents would know she was lying.

Ellen will find out about this. Should he tell her now,

he wonders, before she hears it from somewhere else? Explain to her that it was all teenage-girl histrionics? His mind is going a mile a minute, helped along by coffee and nicotine.

'Are you even listening to me?' Ellen asks. She sounds worried about him. He hasn't been following anything she's said.

'Sorry,' he says. 'I'm a bit distracted this morning.'

'Of course,' she answers, her voice sympathetic. 'What are you up to today?'

'I've got school stuff to do,' he tells her. He isn't doing it, though. He's chain-smoking, waiting for word from Kelly.

'I missed you last night,' she says, her voice softening. When he doesn't answer, she says more briskly, 'I got the place cards finished, though. Do you want me to come over after work?'

'I'm not sure. I've a lot to get done. I'll call you later, okay? I love you,' he adds suddenly, sincerely, and they end the call. He does love her. He can't lose her. She's all he has.

This will hurt her, of course. She might not want to marry him if she thinks that he'd behaved improperly toward a teenage girl. He must make sure she believes him. After all, Diana's gone, and she can't contradict him.

Brenda's ex-husband couldn't leave fast enough. He made himself some coffee, told her he was sorry he was not able to be more help, hugged her, and left. Brenda doesn't know what she ever saw in him.

She wanders around the house aimlessly, consumed with

grief. She remembers the strange sensation she had the night before as she was drifting off to sleep – the feeling that her daughter was near, comforting her. But she doesn't feel it now. Now she feels totally alone, abandoned. As she moves pointlessly from room to room, it slowly occurs to her that something is different, but she can't quite figure out what. She has the feeling that something is missing, she's almost certain of it, but she can't put her finger on what it is.

When the doorbell rings, she thinks it's the detectives back again, so she opens the door; she doesn't care that she's in her pyjamas and robe. She's surprised to see Riley and Evan, instead. She has always liked both of them very much. Evan is holding a bunch of flowers in his arms – white lilies and pink roses – wrapped in cellophane. Her tears well up again at the sight of them, at the thought that they aren't here to see Diana. But suddenly she wants to talk to someone who loved Diana, who was involved in her life – someone who's not a negligent father or a police detective. She opens the door wider and invites them inside.

She leads the way into the kitchen, lays the flowers on the table, and sits down wearily. Riley and Evan sit at the kitchen table too. It seems as if the flowers on the table are there in Diana's stead, taking her place.

'I'm so sorry, Mrs Brewer,' Riley says, her voice catching.

'I'm sorry too,' Evan says awkwardly.

She looks at them both and sees the grief and strain in their young faces. 'Thank you,' she says, her voice quivering.

Riley says, 'We're here, if you need us. Just to talk to, or to help you out with errands, if you'd rather not go out.'

'That's so kind of you,' Brenda says. She's touched by their thoughtfulness, their concern. Riley is a great girl, has spent countless sleepovers in this house. She's smart and kind, like Diana was. And she's always liked Evan. He's very bookish, like her daughter, who also loved to read. A nice change from all the jocks at the high school, like Cameron. Cameron hasn't been in touch. But maybe there's a reason for that. 'Diana's father has already left, so I might take you up on that.' She adds tearfully, 'I'm all on my own now.'

'We'll give you our cell numbers,' Evan says, and seeing a pad of paper and a pen on the table, he reaches for it and writes down his name and number, and passes the pen and paper over to Riley.

'Call us whenever you like,' Riley says, 'if you need something, or someone to talk to.'

'I could use some help,' Brenda says, feeling suddenly overwhelmed. She doesn't feel like she can do anything at all. She can't eat, or shower, or dress herself. She certainly can't plan her own child's funeral.

'We'll help you,' Riley offers. 'Whatever you need.'

It's a relief, to not have to do this all alone. Brenda struggles to her feet and begins to make them all tea. As she fumbles with the kettle and the cups, she finds herself telling them about Mrs Payne, across the street. 'She saw a truck parked outside the house around midnight, with a man sitting in it the night Diana was murdered.' She adds bleakly, 'Maybe if she'd called the police—' She breaks off. Maybe if Helen Payne had called the police her daughter would still be alive. If she'd been Helen, would she have called the police? She doesn't know.

'Was she able to describe the truck?' Riley asks.

She shakes her head. 'Just that it was a pickup. But everybody around here drives a truck like that. Cameron has one. And that man from the Home Depot, Joe Prior.' She adds, 'The detectives told me Prior has an alibi, but not a very good one.' She says suddenly, her voice breaking, 'It's all my fault, for not being home.'

'No,' Riley is quick to say. 'It's not your fault. You must never think that.'

'But it is,' she insists, 'because I wasn't home. If I hadn't switched to nights Diana might not be dead.' She begins to cry.

'But how could you know?' Evan says. 'You mustn't blame yourself.' He gets up and hands her the box of tissues that was on the kitchen table.

But she does blame herself.

Chapter Twenty-Four

WHEN THE CALL comes, Brad almost jumps out of his skin. He takes a moment to get his breathing under control before he answers. He knows from the call display that it's not Kelly. Kelly hasn't had the decency to let him know how it went at the police station. No, it's a detective, and they want to talk to him. Brad tries to sound calm. They have to know he's expecting this.

When he arrives at the station, there are reporters hanging around outside. Some snap his picture, and he doesn't like it. They want to know who he is. He decides to tell them – calmly – that he was Diana's teacher and coach and that they will no doubt be interviewing all her teachers. That makes them lose interest quickly. They go back to loafing around the steps as he makes his way inside.

Once he is sitting in the interview room and is facing the two detectives, he finds it harder to seem relaxed. He shouldn't have smoked all those cigarettes, drunk so much coffee. His mouth is suddenly dry and sour tasting, and he would like some water, but he is afraid his hand will shake as he drinks it, so he doesn't ask, and they don't offer.

'We've heard some allegations about you from Principal Kelly this morning,' Stone begins.

'What did he say?' Brad asks, keeping his voice neutral.

But the detective ignores his question. 'How long have you been teaching at Fairhill High School?'

'A little over a year. I started last September. I teach physical education, and I coach sports teams.'

'You coached Diana, we understand.'

'Yes, she was in one of my gym classes last year and again this year. She was a talented athlete, especially good at running cross-country. She was the best runner on the team.' He's feeling a bit better now that he's talking. 'It's such a tragic loss. She had so much potential.'

'But she complained about you.'

Brad eyes the detective, who is waiting for him to say something. 'She did,' he admits at last. 'She blew some things out of proportion. I put it down to teenage-girl dramatics.' He thinks he manages to sound not too defensive, perhaps even disappointed in one of his students. 'I was surprised at how she interpreted some things, but even so, I apologized. That was the end of it.'

'What did you apologize for, exactly?' the detective asks.

Now he feels uncomfortable. 'I said I was sorry if she misinterpreted my actions.'

'And what were your actions?'

He remembers the anger he felt at Diana. He must not let

144

it show. He says mildly, 'She didn't like it that I patted her on the back if she ran a good race. Sometimes I rested a hand on her shoulder and leaned in closer when I was giving her a pep talk. Things like that.' He shifts in his chair. 'I had no idea it bothered her until she complained to Principal Kelly.' Detective Stone regards him steadily, as if waiting for more. Brad asks, 'Did you ever play any sports?' Neither detective responds. 'I grew up playing sports. We were always slapping each other on the back to say well done. I just wasn't thinking. It was an honest mistake. But after that – no more camaraderie. I keep my distance. I've learned my lesson.'

'You never touched her in any sexual way?' Stone asks.

'Absolutely not.'

'She also said you looked at her in a way that made her uncomfortable.'

He allows himself to express some indignation. 'That was entirely in her imagination. I was her teacher, her coach. I have to make sure they do things properly or they could injure themselves. I didn't look at her any more than any of my other students.'

'Did you ever see Diana outside of class or the coaching environment?' Detective Stone asks.

'No.'

'Do you have any idea if anyone was bothering her?'

He shakes his head. 'No. I didn't know about anything like that.'

'One more thing,' the detective says. 'Can you tell us where you were on Thursday night, from eleven o'clock on?'

'I was at home, in bed.'

'Alone?'

'Yes.'

'Okay, thank you. That will be all, for now.' Detective Stone rises and hands him a card. 'If you think of anything useful, please get in touch.'

Brad takes the card. 'I will.'

As he leaves the police station, his relief is immense.

Joe Prior parks his truck in the parking lot of the 7-Eleven. He's driven a little over an hour to get here. He knows Josie will be here today – she always works Saturdays. Joe has been watching her for a while. He likes to spread them out. Josie here in Littleton, which is over the state line in New Hampshire. Kayla in Magog, in the Eastern Townships of Quebec. He does a lot of driving. But that's okay, he likes driving his truck, uses the time to think, to go over his fantasies in his mind.

He gets out of the truck and walks casually into the store. He knows where the cameras are and stays out of view as best he can. He must be extra careful now. He's got a baseball cap pulled low, and the collar of his jacket pulled up. He lingers in the back corner looking at snack foods as someone finishes a purchase up at the front. He watches Josie furtively, enjoying the curve of her cheek, the fall of her light brown hair, the shape of her breasts beneath her T-shirt.

The customer passes him on her way out the door and the bell tinkles as she leaves. Joe continues to survey items as he slowly walks down the aisle. He's not going to buy anything; he's just looking.

The bell on the door tinkles again. A man has come in with his little boy. The shrill chatter of the child carries across the store. Joe hates children.

It ruins it for him, and he walks out, the child's irritating patter following Joe until the door closes behind him.

Chapter Twenty-Five

RILEY IS SITTING listlessly with Evan at a picnic table in the little park in the centre of town after their visit to Mrs Brewer. It's Saturday afternoon, cold but sunny. It was awful seeing Diana's mother that way. Her daughter's death has broken her, and Riley could hardly bear to look at her. She'd spent a lot of time at the Brewers' house over the years – at playdates when they were children, and for sleepovers all through high school – and now she thinks of how empty that house will be. Her heart breaks for Mrs Brewer. She has nothing left.

Riley feels tears building again and looks away from Evan, at the swings. She thinks anxiously about what Diana's mother told them – what her neighbour saw the night Diana was killed. Eventually she turns to Evan and asks, 'Do you think it was Cameron sitting outside the house in his truck that night?' She felt he'd been lying to her.

'But Mrs Brewer said Joe Prior has a truck too,' Evan says. 'And the police think his alibi is weak. It could have been him.'

'So it could have been either one of them,' she says. 'Or anybody else.' After a minute she adds bitterly, 'You know what makes me mad? That the neighbour didn't call the police. Maybe if she had, Diana would still be alive. I'm with Mrs Brewer on that one.'

They fall silent again, sitting dismally at the picnic table. Then Evan says, 'I've been thinking. I'd like to put up a memorial, maybe a simple white wooden cross, at the side of the field where she was found. My dad should have supplies at home.'

Riley nods. 'That's a nice idea. I'll help you.'

Riley accompanies Evan back to his house, and he takes her into his dad's unused work shed in the backyard. There's all kinds of tools and scraps of wood in there. Evan soon finds a couple of pieces that will work. He grabs a hammer and some nails and constructs a simple cross, about five feet high, two across.

'I think we've got some white paint left over around here somewhere,' Evan says, studying his handiwork. 'Maybe we should put it up first and paint it when it's standing in the ground, it'll be easier. And then we won't have to wait for it to dry before we put it up. I'll just ask my mom if I can use her car, 'kay?'

He leaves her there in the shed while he goes inside. It's cold, but she's not offended that he didn't invite her into the house. It's Saturday afternoon and she knows Evan's dad is probably far into the booze by now. He doesn't talk about it much, but she knows how much it bothers Evan. She looks down at the cross lying on the floor. She can't believe that on Thursday evening Diana was alive, and not even two days later, Riley is here in Evan's shed, staring at this cross. For a moment she feels dizzy, as if the world has spun too fast, and she can't keep up.

Evan returns, with permission to use the car, and they load the cross, angling it between the front seats. Evan puts an old can of white paint, a paintbrush, and a screwdriver and hammer to open the paint can with into the spacious trunk of his mother's car. He throws in a plastic bag to put the dirty brush and paint can in when they're done, and a spade.

Riley climbs into the car with a heavy heart. As Evan drives them through the little town, she makes him stop at the florist. It's the same florist they went to earlier that day for Mrs Brewer's flowers. It's the only one in town. 'We should get some flowers for her,' she says. She leaves him in the car and runs into the shop. She chooses two small bouquets – one of white lilies and another of pink gerbera daisies. She returns to the car. 'I got one from each of us.'

Riley feels an increasing sense of disquiet as Evan takes the rural roads that will lead them to the field. She hasn't seen it yet, except in photographs, but everyone knows where Diana was found. They know where the Resslers' farm is.

As Evan drives down the gravel road toward the farm, they spot traces of yellow police tape flapping in the breeze along the fence line. He stops the car at the side of the road, and they slowly get out. They stand together, side by side at the entrance to the field, staring out at it. Riley recognizes the open green gate from the photos she saw in the news, but the white tent that stood over Diana's dead body is now gone, so they don't know exactly where she was found. Riley feels an involuntary shudder, something animal and instinctual. She imagines it, some murderer – probably the man sitting outside Diana's house in his truck – carrying her friend across this field in the dark, probably already dead. She can see it all too clearly, everything except the killer's face. She forces herself to stop.

She watches Evan put up the cross between the edge of the road and the wooden fence, next to the entrance to the field. They can't put it up in the field because it's private property, and it's farmed. When the cross is sturdily in place, Riley silently takes the paintbrush from Evan. She paints the cross reverently, tenderly, in long strokes, almost as if she's touching Diana, brushing out her long hair. When she is finished, Riley lays the two bouquets of flowers gently at the base of it. She whispers, 'I miss you so much, Diana,' wiping away tears.

Evan takes her hand in his and adds, 'They'll find out who did this to you, Diana. I promise.'

I watch them, Riley and Evan, putting up the cross, painting it a fresh white. It stands out so sharply against the natural background. Riley and Evan – I would trust them with my life.

I'm afraid, though, that I was wrong to trust Cameron. Cameron might have put me here, floating on the fringes, in this sort of half life, watching people who love me grieve. I'm grieving too, for all I've lost.

So much is missing ... whole chunks of my memory gone. I hope they find out who did this to me, because I'm not sure I'll ever remember on my own.

Edward is notified by text when Cameron's attorney finally arrives at the police station on Saturday afternoon.

'He's here,' he says to his wife and son, who have been sitting in this interview room for what feels like a lifetime, while they waited for the attorney. 'I'll go talk to him,' Edward says, standing up.

'I'll come too,' Shelby says.

'What about me?' Cameron asks.

'You stay here, we'll talk to him first,' Edward says.

Edward and Shelby leave the room and seek out the lawyer in the waiting area. He's a man in his late forties named Steven Hanlan, and he has a confident, all-business air about him. He's one of the top criminal attorneys in Burlington, and as soon as he lays eyes on him, Edward feels a little better. They no longer have to manage this on their own.

'Let's find someplace private to talk,' the attorney says, hefting his briefcase and leading them to a quieter area with some empty chairs, where they won't be overheard. He speaks in a low voice. 'What's the situation?'

Edward brings him up to speed. 'I know it looks bad,'

Edward concedes, when he's finished. 'But there's no way he did this. He's a good kid. And he loved her.' But he knows that women are often killed by men who love them. He glances at Shelby, who doesn't seem to have recovered from the shock of the police interview and is very quiet.

'I'm not going to ask if he did it or not,' the attorney says. 'My job is to defend him, and I will do that to the best of my ability.' He stands up and says, 'Let me talk to him alone.' Edward tells him where to find Cameron, and he sets off down the hall.

Once he's gone, Shelby begins to cry. He takes her in his arms. She whispers, 'Edward, I'm scared. What was he doing over there?'

Edward pulls back and looks at her. They have to get through this, somehow. 'I don't know.'

They sit in miserable silence until they are asked by Detective Stone to join them again in the interview room.

They all settle in to continue the interview, this time with the attorney present, and Stone makes the introductions for the tape. Then he takes up where they left off. 'Cameron, what did you do when you got out of the truck?'

Edward watches in fear, his heart in his throat. He's never been so frightened in his life. Not even when Cameron was born, the umbilical cord wound twice around his neck, an Apgar score of zero.

'I lied, before.'

Edward's heart jumps.

Cameron seems to prepare himself. He begins to speak in a monotone. 'When I was sitting in the truck, I texted Diana several times that I wanted to talk, but she didn't answer.' He glances at the attorney, who nods at him. Cameron pulls his phone out of his pocket. 'Here, I can show you.'

Edward wishes he could see those texts. Perhaps he should have asked his son to let him see his phone earlier, but it hadn't occurred to him.

Stone and Godfrey silently study the texts on the phone and then Stone puts the phone back down on the table, close to him. 'Okay, then what?' he presses.

'I didn't know what to do. I thought she was still mad and ignoring me, or that maybe she'd turned off her notifications. The light was still on in the living room.' Then he stares down at the table and speaks in a rush. 'I didn't want to leave things the way they were, so I – I got out of the truck and knocked on her front door. I knocked a few times, but she didn't answer.'

'And then?' Stone asks.

Edward is desperate to hear Cameron say, *I got back in the truck and went home.* The attorney looks concerned and puts a hand on Cameron's forearm, shaking his head at him.

But Cameron ignores him and continues, 'I went around to the back of the house.' He swallows nervously. 'Her bedroom's in the back. The light was on in her room. I called her name a few times. I even threw some dirt at her window, thinking that would get her attention. But she didn't answer. I figured she was still mad and ignoring me. Then I went back to the truck and drove around for a while and went home.'

154

'Is that right?' Detective Stone says flatly.

Edward can tell the detective doesn't believe him. He can't bring himself to look at his wife.

'I know it looks bad,' Cameron says in a rush, 'but I didn't kill her! I should have told you everything right from the beginning, I know that. But now I'm wondering – what if she was already dead? What if somebody killed her after I dropped her off at eleven? Before I came back? And that's why she didn't answer? Because I think she would have answered me if she could. Even if she'd turned her phone off, she would have heard me knocking at the door, or calling at her window.'

Stone looks unconvinced. He says, 'We think the killer accessed the house from the backyard. We found impressions in the grass there.'

Edward sees Cameron shaking his head, agitated. Cameron finally glances at his attorney, who doesn't look happy at all. Edward feels queasy.

Cameron says, 'I didn't go in the house, I swear!'

Chapter Twenty-Six

IT'S EARLY SATURDAY evening and Brenda is sitting with the detectives again in her living room. They tell her Cameron has retained an attorney. She finds that disturbing. It makes her feel nauseated, that she let that boy into her house. That she allowed him to take her daughter out in his truck all over the countryside at night when she was away in another town at work.

Detective Stone asks now, 'Did Diana ever talk to you about her gym teacher?'

Brenda furrows her brow in confusion. 'Her running coach? Mr Turner?' Stone nods. 'No, not really.'

'Apparently Diana complained to the principal about him.'

This takes her completely by surprise. 'About what?'

'Inappropriate behaviour.'

She's astonished. Diana had never said anything to her. It troubles her that her daughter never mentioned this. Why didn't she? Why did her daughter tell her so little? She'd always thought they were close, but now she's not sure. It adds another layer to her grief – that her daughter didn't confide in her, and now it's too late.

'She never told me about that.' She asks, 'Do you think *he* might have done this?'

'We don't know. We interviewed him. It seems unlikely, but we're keeping an open mind.' He adds, 'They've finished with the body, so you can start making funeral arrangements.' After a pause he says, 'Cause of death was strangulation, with some kind of ligature. There was no obvious sign that she was sexually assaulted. They weren't able to recover any evidence from her body for DNA analysis, and as you know, her clothes are missing. And we haven't recovered any evidence from the field where the body was found, or from the house. We will continue to search for her missing clothes, and her cell phone.'

Brenda finds herself staring at the door to the living room. Her daughter's jump rope usually hangs from that doorknob, and it's not there. That's what's different, she realizes now. She says, 'Diana's jump rope – she always leaves it hanging on the back of that doorknob,' she points, 'and it's not there. She used it to skip in front of the TV.'

'When was the last time you remember seeing it?' Stone asks.

She tries to think. 'I don't know for sure. But it's always there. And now it isn't.' The realization of what it means dawns on her, sickening her. She watches the two detectives share a glance.

*

157

When Roy sees the white cross on the edge of his field that evening, in the failing light, the flowers laid beneath it, he stops the tractor and sits in silence. He doesn't know who's put it there, but he thinks it's a nice gesture. It reminds him of those crosses you see at the side of the highway sometimes, where people have been killed in accidents, with flowers or teddy bears scattered beneath them. All of a sudden, his heart wells up with a heavy sense of life's misery. How tragic and unfair that this young girl died, and that she died so horribly, so senselessly. He finds it hard to shrug off, perhaps because it feels so strange for this to happen in their small rural town, or perhaps because she was left in his field. He can't get the image of her dead body and the scavenging birds out of his mind. He wonders if he will ever be able to work this field, or even drive by it, without thinking of it. Tomorrow he will buy some flowers.

As he sits on his tractor, looking at the cross and the flowers, silently paying his respects, he feels a lingering sense of unease, that something else is wrong in his world. He's not sure what it is, but it has to do with his daughter. Maybe everyone around here is worried about their daughters right now, he thinks, after what happened to the Brewer girl. There could be a killer here somewhere, and nobody knows who it is.

But it's more than that. Ellen has seemed quiet and strained the last couple of days, and she's admitted to him that she's worried about her fiancé. He knows they haven't seen each other yet this weekend. Roy hopes he isn't getting cold feet. The wedding is only weeks away.

WHAT HAVE YOU DONE?

Riley and I went back over to Mrs Brewer's tonight after supper to tell her about the cross we put up. We showed her pictures of it on our phones. She seemed very moved by it and thanked us. I walked Riley home again because she's not allowed out alone after dark these days.

Mrs Brewer told us something she probably shouldn't have – that the detectives have learned that Diana complained to Principal Kelly about Mr Turner, the gym teacher, for 'inappropriate behaviour' and that they'd interviewed him, but they don't think he killed her. I have to admit I was shocked. Diana never said a word to me or Riley about it. I could tell Riley was shocked too. Apparently Diana hadn't told her mother either, and I could sense that Mrs Brewer was hurt by that. I guess Diana was more secretive than we realized. It makes me wonder what else Diana didn't share with us, or at least with Riley. I was also surprised because Turner always seemed like an okay guy to me.

And now they think they know what the murder weapon was. Mrs Brewer told us that Diana's jump rope is missing from the living room. I can't stop thinking about it, how it might have happened. If she was strangled with her own jump rope, wouldn't it mean Diana was probably murdered in the house, and then taken to the field after? That seems to be what they're thinking, according to Mrs Brewer, but they're not releasing much information to the public.

159

It would have been risky to carry her to a vehicle in front of her house to get rid of her body. But her street ends in a dead end, and there's an empty field next to her house. There's an abandoned road on the other side of that field. You can't see it from the street – no one uses it. I'm wondering now if the killer could have carried her from the back of the house through the field in the dark to a truck on that road. I wonder if the police have thought of that.

Cameron and I used to ride our bikes on that road when we were kids. But anyone could have known about it, even Joe Prior, if he was watching her, if he was planning it.

I feel a dull stirring of something, cutting through all this numbing grief. If it wasn't so upsetting, I could almost imagine myself writing about it some other way. Not as a diary, but as a novel maybe. It would be a way to honour Diana. But I'd give anything just to have her back.

Life is so strange, so unpredictable – I always thought I'd write about all of us one day, Diana included. But not like this.

Paula Acosta watches the late-night news, sitting up in bed with her husband. There is no new information about Diana's murder. They show the same old footage of the tent in the field, the crime-scene figures moving about. There are no new leads, not that they're divulging, anyway. There is nothing about Brad Turner. She wonders if Kelly spoke to the police at all.

She frets about the people who were closest to Diana. Her mother. Her boyfriend, Cameron; her friends Riley and Evan; the girls on the track team. Her heart breaks for all of them. It's so dreadful that murder has come to their small town. She'd thought they were safe here.

Brenda lies in bed, late at night, all alone in the draughty house. She waits for it to come over her, the feeling she had the night before, that her daughter was close by. She yearns for her. She whispers tentatively, 'Diana, are you there?'

But there's nothing. When she finally falls asleep, she dreams of the jump rope, tight around her daughter's neck.

Chapter Twenty-Seven

THE NEXT MORNING, Sunday, Riley waits for Evan to show up in his mother's car. She'd texted him this morning about her crazy idea. She wants to go to Joe Prior's place and see if they can get a look at his truck. She wants to have a car so they can be discreet and can make a quick getaway if necessary. She's not sure about this, or what they will even do if they see his truck, but what has she got to lose? She doesn't have anything else to do today.

When Evan arrives, she climbs into the passenger seat beside him. Before he even backs out of her driveway, he turns to her and says, 'How did you find out Prior's address?'

She smiles. 'I don't know his exact address, but he lives in the building on the corner of Division and Goucher. I called one of the local reporters, pretended I was a reporter, too, and asked if she knew where he lived. She told me.' Evan looks back at her for a moment with raised eyebrows, then backs out of the driveway and heads in the direction of

Prior's apartment. It's not far. She's quiet for a moment and then says, 'There's been nothing in the news about Turner.'

'I know,' Evan says.

'I mean, shouldn't he be a suspect? If she complained about him?'

'Maybe he is, and they're just not saying anything. There's not much in the news about Cameron either, or Prior, just that they've been questioned and released.'

'I guess.' She asks him something that's been bothering her. 'Why do you think Diana didn't tell any of us about Mr Turner?'

Evan says, 'I don't know. It's not like her.'

'No, it isn't. Why the big secret?' Riley says. 'I wonder what was going on.' She's been thinking about this all night. 'If she complained about him to Principal Kelly, *he* must know. He must have done something about it. He would have to. There must be a record of it somewhere.'

'Yeah, but he's not going to tell us.'

'The police must know what happened, but they're not going to say anything,' Riley says. Then she says, 'Pull over for a minute.'

Evan turns into a side street and parks. 'What?'

She faces him. 'What if we told the press and *they* went to Principal Kelly? He couldn't deny it, could he, if the police already know?' Evan stares back at her. She adds, 'I hate to think of Mr Turner doing something slimy to Diana and getting away with it. I mean, even if he didn't kill her, he's clearly done something bad. Maybe he shouldn't even be teaching. Why shouldn't people know?'

163

'Yeah.'

It's been troubling her: why didn't Diana confide in her? She can understand why she didn't tell Evan. And she can understand why she didn't tell her mother. It's embarrassing, and they didn't have that kind of relationship – her mother was a bit old-fashioned, uncomfortable with topics like sex. Maybe that's why she simply described it as 'inappropriate behaviour' and didn't go into detail last night. But she's surprised that Diana didn't tell *her*. Riley certainly would have told Diana if something like that had happened to her, but then, she would have told her mother too. It doesn't make sense. It makes her wonder, now, whether it was just too awful to talk about. 'Maybe I should call KCVS.'

'Seriously?' Evan says. 'What would you say?'

Riley considers. 'I'll tell them Diana told me she complained to Mr Kelly about Mr Turner, but I won't give them my name.' Before she can lose her nerve, she starts to look up the number on her phone. She places the call, suddenly nervous.

A woman's voice answers. 'KCVS News.'

'I have some information,' Riley says breathlessly. 'Information that might be relevant to the Diana Brewer murder,' she says, as Evan watches.

'Go ahead.'

Riley swallows. 'Diana made a complaint about a teacher at school. Her gym teacher, Mr Turner. He was her coach. He was being inappropriate with her.'

'Where did you hear this information?'

164

'I'm a friend of hers. She told me,' Riley lies. 'I suggest you ask Principal Kelly at Fairhill High about it.' She disconnects before the woman on the line can ask her name. She turns to Evan; she can hardly believe what she's just done.

'You've got nerve, I'll give you that,' he says. He starts the engine, and they continue on their way.

Sunday morning, Shelby is on her third cup of coffee. She has barely slept, and neither has her husband. It's a terrible thing to have your teenage son suspected of murder. She can't look at Cameron the same way any more. When she looks at him, she doesn't see what she used to see. She's terrified that the police are going to come to the house any minute and arrest him. She's still surprised they released him after questioning him the day before. The way they hounded him!

She has always doted on Cameron. He is their only child. She has loved him fiercely, encouraged him, protected him, been proud of him. He's been a good, but not brilliant, student. He's made up for that by being an excellent athlete. He was a cute toddler, a good-looking boy, and is now a handsome young man. She can't pretend that didn't matter to her. She tells herself that it matters to all mothers what their children look like, even if they won't admit it. The ones with good-looking children feel superior, lucky, blessed. The mothers of the pretty girls feel special, you can tell. It confers a special status on the mother when her child is attractive and popular. And Shelby got caught up in that, so pleased that her handsome boy was dating one of the most attractive, most popular girls at school. She admits that to herself now, and it makes her feel ashamed. Because now she doesn't know what lies behind her son's handsome face.

He's a liar, certainly. He lied about when he came home. He lied about where he was that night, about getting out of the truck. The way that detective looked at him! It sent fear ripping through her guts, because she knew from his eyes that the detective thought Cameron had killed Diana. He was in her backyard that night, he had been angry, and he had lied to all of them about it. How can she ever believe anything he says ever again?

Did he kill her? She thinks about it, holding her breath. Did he get inside her house somehow and creep up to her room and *strangle* her? Or argue violently with her and lose control? And then put her in their truck and dump her body in a field? If he did, she doesn't know how he can live with himself. How he could possibly have thought he'd get away with it. That he'd even try. Is that who her son is?

She sits alone at the kitchen window, growing colder and colder. It's as if her heart has stopped, and there's no longer any blood circulating in her veins. She doesn't want to believe it's possible, but she forces herself to think long and hard about how Cameron adored Diana. How he wouldn't let her out of his sight. It was an attentiveness bordering on obsession. And she and Edward had thought it was sweet. *First love is like that*, they told each other. They were too caught up in how good the two of them looked together, what a great girlfriend Diana was, how proud Cameron made them.

But if she's honest with herself, his behaviour with Diana sometimes made her a little uncomfortable. The love that bordered on the urge to control. And yet she pretended not to see it and said nothing. She told herself she was looking for problems. They were obviously happy together. But couples can look perfectly happy, can fool everyone – until the worst happens.

She's loved Cameron, protected him – and made excuses for him. She knows he has a temper. She's seen it on occasion. There was that time that he got into a fight at school and was almost suspended. And there was his recent tendency toward jealousy, where Diana was concerned.

It was a shock to learn that Diana had wanted to go to a different college, without Cameron. It shouldn't have been if Shelby had been thinking clearly; she should have seen it coming. But she *wanted* them to stay together. She thought Diana was good for Cameron, a girlfriend who encouraged him to study, to get better grades, instead of partying all the time.

Now she wishes Cameron had never started dating Diana at all. Now she wishes her son had been a little less handsome, a little less athletic, a little less popular, just – ordinary.

Chapter Twenty-Eight

GRAHAM KELLY HEARS the knock at his front door on Sunday morning and freezes. He calls to his wife, 'Can you get that?' He's reading the paper in the kitchen – there is nothing about Turner, thank God – and he's certainly capable of answering the door, but his legs suddenly feel like jelly.

He keeps perfectly still and listens intently as his wife answers the door. 'Yes?' she says.

He hears a voice, 'Is your husband home?'

It's Brad Turner. *Fuck*.

'Yes, he's in the kitchen,' his wife says. Kelly hears their steps coming toward him and prepares himself. He hasn't spoken to Brad since he phoned him Friday night to warn him he was going to go to the police the next morning. He's ignored his calls. His wife doesn't know anything about any of this.

'Look who's here,' his wife, Sandra, says brightly. 'Can I get you some coffee?' she asks Brad.

'Yeah, sure, thanks,' he says, and she turns to the carafe and grabs a mug from the cupboard and pours him a coffee.

'I'll leave you to it,' Sandra says and exits the kitchen, glancing at them curiously.

Kelly doesn't want to risk her overhearing anything. 'Let's go to my study,' he says, getting up. They take their coffees upstairs to his office at the end of the hall. He lets Turner enter first and closes the door firmly behind them. Sandra is downstairs and has begun vacuuming the carpets.

'The detectives interviewed me yesterday,' Brad says, before they even sit down. And then he becomes petulant. 'Why haven't you answered my calls?'

This gets Kelly's back up. He hadn't answered because he hadn't wanted to talk to him. 'I already told you what I was going to say,' he answers hotly. They both take a breath. Kelly sits down heavily in one of the armchairs, and Brad sinks into the other. They lean toward each other, keeping their voices low. Kelly asks, 'So, how did it go? They can't think you had anything to do with what happened to Diana.'

'I wouldn't be so sure,' Brad says, looking tense.

'What?' Kelly asks in surprise. 'Surely you must have an alibi, though?' he asks anxiously. 'Wasn't your fiancée with you?'

'She was at home at her parents' that night.'

'I thought she lived with you.'

'No, she lives with her parents.'

It stuns him for a moment. Brad doesn't have an alibi. He hadn't anticipated this. So Brad won't be quickly discounted as a suspect, as he'd expected. They will look more closely into him, and into Diana's complaint, and how Kelly handled it. Now Kelly is deeply worried. He's required to report suspected child abuse. If it becomes known that he did nothing about these allegations of Diana's, his career will be finished. He has a mortgage, three kids. He swallows. 'Do you think the police will pursue this further?' he asks.

'I don't know.'

He gives Brad a cold, angry look. 'I've tried to protect you the best I could. It was her word against yours, and I believed you. I don't know what really happened, and I did what I thought was best. Innocent until proven guilty. I didn't believe her and I didn't want to ruin your career. But I don't want anything more to do with this.'

He experiences a plunging sensation inside him as he tells Turner this, while the younger man sits hunched in front of him, visibly nervous and smelling strongly of cigarettes. Kelly has a sudden, horrible feeling that things might be much worse than he thought, that it might actually be possible that the twitchy young man in front of him killed that young girl. He remembers what she said he'd done. He'd thought she was lying because she'd refused to go to the police. And because he thought she was a dishonest girl. She'd been caught cheating on a science assignment the previous spring. At first she'd denied it emphatically, but had finally admitted it, in tears, in front of him and her science teacher. But what if she hadn't been lying about Brad Turner? He recoils from the man across from him.

Where does that leave him now? He could have blood on his hands. He should tell the police the truth, not the milder version he gave them yesterday, the version that's written down in the file that he'd never meant anyone to see. Let *them* figure out who was lying.

But there's his mortgage, and his wife and three kids.

Still, he decides, observing the man in front of him with deep dismay, if Turner can't account for where he was that night, he must now do the right thing. Perhaps Turner senses his change of mind because he suddenly leans in closer, and his eyes sharpen.

'I'd stick to your original story if I were you,' he says.

'I must do what I think is right.'

'But, Kelly, I know about that fling you had. With Ms Desjardins. And I wouldn't hesitate to tell your wife.'

Kelly feels his face go pale. *How the hell does he know about that?*

'I saw you, one night, last spring, after dark,' Turner says, pressing close. 'I was in the park, after a run, catching my breath. I saw you knock on her door across the street and slip into her house. Saw the way you kissed her, before she closed the door. I was curious, so I stayed. You were there long enough.'

Brad Turner leaves Graham Kelly's house more unsettled than he was when he arrived. He feels like everything is closing in on him. He doesn't trust Kelly any more. He hadn't liked the way he'd looked at him in his study. His barely concealed revulsion – as if he thinks he might have

171

murdered Diana. And he couldn't have Kelly thinking that, because then what might he do? He might tell the detectives what Diana had *really* said. He'd had to threaten to reveal what he knew about him, that he'd seen him and the attractive young teacher together, quite by chance. Lucky for him that he did.

Still, he doesn't know what will happen. Kelly had been terrified. He doesn't think he's going to say anything, but he can't be sure. What if he thinks his wife will forgive him? What then?

Brad doesn't walk directly home. He walks around the perimeter of town, head down. He doesn't want to talk to anyone.

He thought it had gone relatively well with the detectives the day before. He'd handled it well. Still, they'd asked him for an alibi, and he hadn't been able to provide one. Will that be the end of it? That really depends on Kelly, he thinks now.

He's been such an idiot. He didn't seem to be able to help himself. The glances, the casual touches – he got pleasure out of it. He didn't think anyone noticed. And once he started, he didn't know when to stop.

He's always enjoyed looking at girls. At their young, developing bodies. It's one of the reasons he became a gym teacher. He likes their long, coltish legs and their swinging ponytails. He likes to watch them in shorts and skimpy tees bending and twisting and stretching. He likes to imagine them in the locker room – especially that. He likes watching the way they develop over the course of a year. When he coaches them, he likes to lean in close and smell their skin, the musky sweat on them, like perfume. To pat them on the back when they've done something well. And then he stepped over the line with Diana. What a mistake that was.

Diana, especially, was a temptation, something to be resisted. He'd been fresh out of teachers' college, and he noticed her right off, last year in September, when she was in eleventh grade. She was a natural athlete, and that appealed to him. She was beautiful, with her large eyes and lightly freckled skin, her long honey-coloured hair. She used to bend over and let her hair hang down as she gathered it up and put it into a ponytail before she started running. He'd stand behind her and stare at her in her running tights, watch the graceful movement as she flipped her head up again, ponytail swishing. God, she was something.

She caught him looking.

What is he going to do about Ellen? She knows something's wrong. All his attempts to brush off her questions on the phone seem only to have made her more certain that something's not right. She knows he's upset about Diana's death, but she doesn't know the half of it. She might soon find out, and then where will he be? Will she stand by him?

She has to.

Riley and Evan arrive at Joe Prior's building on the outskirts of Fairhill. They stare at the ugly low-rise in front of them.

Evan drives around behind the building. There are several parking spots in the lot, and some are empty. At the moment, there's only one pickup truck in the parking lot.

173

Evan parks the car on the street and they get out. Riley looks around nervously before approaching the truck. There's no one around. They both study the truck, looking in the windows, casting glances over their shoulders. They don't even know if it's the right truck, but Riley nervously takes some pictures of it with her cell phone, while Evan keeps watch. She doesn't know what she expected to find – it's not like he would have left any evidence on the back seat. But she had to look. What if the detectives couldn't because they didn't have enough to get a warrant? But there's nothing remarkable here – a dusty hardhat, a high-visibility vest, and a newspaper on the passenger seat, a dirty coffee cup in the cup holder. This truck is similar to Cameron's, which is also a black pickup. The hardhat makes it seem likely that the truck belongs to Prior, but they won't know for certain unless he comes out of the building and gets into it.

'Is something wrong?' his wife asks when Graham Kelly comes back downstairs a few minutes after Brad Turner leaves. 'Why was that teacher here?'

It's on the tip of Graham's tongue to deflect, to say that it was nothing, to make up some reason, but before he can marshal his thoughts there's another knock on the front door.

'Who the hell can that be?' Sandra says, moving toward the door.

This is it, Kelly thinks. *The police are here. What is he going to tell them?*

174

But it's not the police. It's a reporter from KCVS News. He hears her introducing herself to Sandra at the door – *I'm Jennifer Wiley, KCVS News* – and he feels trapped. Reluctantly, he joins his wife. He'd already said all he was going to say to the press at the school on Friday. They've been leaving him alone since. He can't avoid them for ever, but he's annoyed that they've come to his home.

He recognizes her; she was at the school on Friday, after Diana's body was discovered. As the principal of the high school, he'd made a statement and spoken to reporters about what a great loss it was to the school and their community, about how lovely Diana was, how much potential she had, and how important it was that they find whoever it was who did this terrible thing. He has nothing more to say. But now Jennifer Wiley looks at him and says, 'Mr Kelly, I understand that Diana Brewer made allegations of inappropriate behaviour against one of your teachers, Brad Turner?'

For a moment he's speechless. He can feel the heat rushing to his cheeks. Then he says tightly, 'No comment,' and closes the door in her face. He turns around and finds his wife looking at him with an expression of astonishment.

Chapter Twenty-Nine

ELLEN IS WAITING in her fiancé's apartment. She tidies up while he's out, washing the few dishes in the sink, wiping down the counters. She has stopped by without warning because she needs to talk to him. He wasn't home, but she has her own key. She hasn't seen Brad since Friday afternoon in the school parking lot. He'd wanted to be alone Friday night, missing their family dinner at the farm, and he'd put her off again yesterday and last night. Why is he avoiding her? What's going on? She dumps out the worrying jam jar lid full of cigarette butts, puzzling over his odd behaviour. She feels uneasy, as if a storm's about to break. Is he having second thoughts? Does he not want to go through with the wedding?

She couldn't bear it if he got cold feet and called off the wedding. All the preparations are made, the invitations have gone out, the money has been spent, and her parents loaned them the down payment for the perfect little bungalow that is going to be theirs on the first of December. What do they do about that? She takes a deep breath and tries to stop her spiralling thoughts. She knows he loves her. She must soothe his nerves if that's what this is. He comes from an unhappy home. Maybe it's no wonder he might be anxious. He needs to learn to open up, to talk to her about these things. She can allay all his fears.

She hears the key in the lock and tenses. She often lets herself in, but she usually lets him know first, with a text. She didn't text him this time because she fears he's avoiding her. She's not sure what to expect. She stands in the living room, facing the door.

The look on his face when he sees her – dismay, even panic – makes her heart sink. Things must be worse than she thought.

'What are you doing here?' he says, but he's smiling now, the dismay, the panic, erased. He approaches and sweeps her into his arms so that she can't see his face. She can feel his heart pounding against hers – it's a two-storey flight of stairs up to the apartment, after all. They hold each other tight, and she nestles her face in the crook of his neck and breathes him in. Maybe everything is all right after all, and he's just nervous about the wedding. He whispers her name into her hair, stroking the back of her head.

Finally, they break apart. She studies him. Despite the smile, he looks tense and avoids her eyes. Maybe it's too soon to hope. She says, 'Something's wrong. What is it?'

He looks at her then as if he's in pain. He runs a hand nervously through his thick, dark hair. He looks like he wants to tell her something, and her blood runs cold. But he doesn't get the chance to speak because there's a knock at his apartment door. They're both startled and turn their faces toward the sound. No one rang the buzzer, but Ellen knows that people can get in the building if they follow someone in.

In a few strides Brad's at the door and opens it. Ellen immediately recognizes the woman standing there: she's a well-known reporter from KCVS News – Jennifer Wiley.

Brad takes in the sight of the reporter and wants to close his eyes. This can't be happening. There can only be one reason why she's here, and Ellen is standing right behind him. He feels his heart thudding in his chest, pounding in his ears. He feels like he can't breathe, but it's the strangest thing – when he speaks, he thinks he sounds almost normal.

'Yes?'

She smiles, all warm and friendly. 'Brad Turner?' He nods. She introduces herself and says, 'I'd like to talk to you about Diana Brewer, if that's all right?'

He wants to slam the door in her face, but Ellen steps forward and says, 'Come in,' and he wants to kill her. Before he can think his way clear, the reporter is sitting down in his small living room with his fiancée, and Ellen is saying how awful it is about Diana, and how upset he's been about it. She seems to be excited to be talking to a minor celebrity in these parts. This person who's going to destroy him. He feels the most awful rage toward the two women in his living room. He can't ask the reporter to leave now that

Ellen's invited her in – that would look suspicious. He tells himself to remain calm. What does she know? Maybe nothing. She can't know anything for certain. And Diana is dead.

'Come, sit,' Ellen commands him, and he complies with outward good grace, because he doesn't know what else to do.

'I'm sorry to bother you,' the reporter says. 'I know Diana's death must be very upsetting for you. But you understand how torn up the community around here is, so we'd like to pay Diana tribute. I'm talking to lots of people who knew her – I'm doing a feature on her.'

He begins to relax a little. 'She was a great person,' Brad lies. 'It's terrible what happened to her.'

'I understand you were her gym teacher?' the reporter asks.

Ellen puts in, 'And her coach. She was on the cross-country running team, so he knew her very well.'

'Is that right?' the reporter says.

'Diana was a natural athlete,' Brad says, wishing Ellen would shut the fuck up. 'She had a good chance to do well in the regionals that are coming up soon.' He allows himself to get a little choked up while he thinks furiously about what else he might say about her.

'She sounds like an all-round great girl, from what I'm hearing,' the reporter says. 'Which is why I have to take it seriously when I hear she made a complaint of inappropriate behaviour at school. A complaint against you.'

The silence. He can hear the beating of his own heart, the

hum of the heating system in the apartment. He registers the utter shock on Ellen's face. It's as if time has slowed down. What does he do now? How does he save himself?

'What the hell are you talking about?' Ellen asks the reporter, not friendly now but suddenly rigid. All the colour seems to have left her face. She turns to him for an explanation.

He doesn't know what to do but deny it. 'It's not true,' he says.

'What's not true?' Wiley asks pointedly. 'The complaint, or that she made the complaint?'

He focuses his swimming eyes on the reporter; he can't bear to look at Ellen. He wonders what this woman knows. She must have spoken to either Kelly or the police. But the police got the whitewashed version – so far, at least. He doesn't know for sure what Kelly might have told the reporter; he must assume he told her the same thing he told the police, or nothing at all. Diana's dead. She can't contradict him now. And Kelly doesn't really *know* anything for sure. It was her word against his. He takes a breath, lets it out.

'She spoke to Principal Kelly about me, but it was all a misunderstanding. I don't know why she made such a big deal about it.'

'What did she say?'

'Nothing, really. It was nothing. I used to pat her on the back after a run, put my hand on her shoulder when I gave her a pep talk, that sort of thing. It was never sexual – not on my part, anyway. It was a misunderstanding. She blew things out of proportion.'

180

The reporter looks troubled, but Ellen looks much more than that.

'Kelly thought there was nothing to it. That's why he didn't do anything. And she didn't want to take it any further, or to tell anyone else – because she'd clearly over-reacted. And now, if you don't mind, I'd like you to leave.'

Chapter Thirty

RILEY AND EVAN get back into the car and sit. 'What now?' Evan asks.

Riley says, 'Maybe we just wait and see if he comes out.' Evan shrugs.

She wonders if there's any point in them being here. Her mind drifts for a while. Then she sees a large, beefy man come out the back entrance of the building and walk in the direction of the truck. She nudges Evan's arm, feels him lean forward beside her. As the man gets closer, she recognizes him from his photo – the red hair and unkempt beard. She finds her heart beating faster.

'That's him.' Suddenly she's frightened. This is the man who might have murdered Diana. Who might have sat outside her house that night in that truck. It occurs to her now that they didn't tell anyone where they were going, what they were doing.

Prior is carrying a large canvas bag in his right hand. He tosses the bag into the passenger seat and climbs in.

'What if that bag has evidence he's getting rid of?' Riley says, turning to face Evan. 'We should follow him.'

Evan says uneasily, 'You sure you want to do this?'

'We owe it to Diana, don't we?' Riley answers.

Evan waits until the truck pulls out of the parking lot and then follows at a safe distance. Prior soon drives onto the on-ramp to I-91 North. 'I wonder where he's going,' Riley says.

'Please promise me that if he turns off into the country-side somewhere to dump that bag we're not going to confront him,' Evan says.

'We'll just see where he goes, that's all.'

They drive some distance behind him, keeping the truck in sight without being too obvious about it. They follow him for well over an hour, easily keeping the truck in sight, but Prior stays on the highway. They spend much of the drive in tense silence, each alone with their thoughts.

'The Canadian border – that's where he's headed,' Evan says suddenly. 'There's nothing else up here.'

'We can't follow him over the border. We didn't bring our passports. Do you think he's trying to make a run for it?'

'Maybe.'

When they've been following Prior for an hour and a half, they reach the border crossing at Derby Line. Evan pulls over to the side as they watch Joe Prior and his truck pass into Canada.

Riley is dismayed. 'What if he's getting away!' she cries. 'Evan, what if he killed her?'

'We can tell the detectives,' Evan says. 'At least they'll know when and where he went over the border.'

Riley is suddenly convinced that Joe Prior is the man who murdered her best friend. Why else would he run? She pulls out her phone. Evan turns the car around and they begin the long drive back to Fairhill.

Ellen sits frozen on the couch as Brad closes the apartment door behind the reporter. The silence between them is like a loaded gun.

'Now that she's gone,' Ellen says, looking coldly at him, her heart beating rapidly in fear, 'you can tell me the truth.'

He seems taken aback. 'I *have* told you the truth, I swear!' He sits down beside her. 'Sweetheart, I never told you about any of this because it was all bullshit, and I didn't want to upset you over nothing. Both Kelly and I knew it was all lies, that's why nothing came of it. If I'd really done anything inappropriate, do you think Kelly would have done nothing? I'd have lost my job if there was anything to it! It was all teenage theatrics. That girl was a fantasist.'

She stares at him. This is a very different picture of Diana than what she got before. She says slowly, 'Well, which was it – a misunderstanding, or lies?'

He's silent, as if realizing he's slipped up. She presses him. 'Did she misinterpret what you did, or did she make it up?' She knows she sounds strident, accusatory, but this is all such a shock.

'Some of it she misinterpreted, but she lied too. Exaggerated.'

'Why would she do that?'

'I have no idea. It all just came out of the blue. No one was more surprised than me. You have no idea how distressing it was. I wondered . . .' He hesitates to say it.

'What?'

'I did wonder if maybe she'd had a crush on me, and when I ignored her she might have wanted some kind of revenge. That's the sort of thing teenage girls do.'

'Is it?' Her voice is hard. She's not so sure. Her experience of the world is quite different. She finds it hard to believe that a girl that everyone seemed to find so smart and kind would do such a thing. She stares at him – he's in such obvious distress – and wonders if he's lying to her.

'You don't believe me,' he says, his voice chilly. He adds, in a hostile tone, 'You actually think I was inappropriate with one of my students.'

When he says that, she's suddenly unsure, afraid of losing him. She wants to believe him. 'Of course I don't!' she protests. Because she simply can't believe it. She refuses to believe it. But now she knows why he's been so upset these last couple of days, since Diana was murdered. Not just because he has lost a student in such horrible circumstances. He's been afraid that *this* would come out, and that it would ruin his reputation, even though it was all a misunderstanding or outright lies; he's afraid people will believe this of him. She thinks suddenly of her parents – what will they believe? And now it *will* come out, because this reporter

185

knows about it. It appals her, the thought of what's ahead of them. How will she face people? This is a small town, and everyone gossips.

He takes both her hands in his and says to her, his voice serious, 'We have to be strong, Ellen.'

She nods, numbly; he's afraid of the same thing, she realizes, about how people talk.

'The detectives will probably want to talk to you,' he says.

She's confused. 'Why?'

He looks back at her as if she's stupid. 'Because I have no alibi.'

The full horror of their situation settles upon her then. He's saying that he might be a suspect in Diana's murder. It hadn't even occurred to her.

'I can help you,' he says, 'with what to say to the police.'

Cameron paces his small bedroom endlessly, back and forth, back and forth, between the desk and the wall, over and over. He's either pacing like this or curled up in a ball on his bed; there's nothing in between. He keeps reliving the long day at the police station yesterday, those catastrophic interviews. They'd questioned him relentlessly, pushing and pushing until he thought he was going to just break down and tell them anything they wanted to hear. Then his father had stepped in to protect him, and got him an attorney.

He's not sure it went any better after that.

He's made a big mistake. He should not have admitted to getting out of the truck. They said it as if they already knew.

But how could they have known? *What did you do when you got out of the truck, Cameron?* And so he'd slipped up by admitting it. He shouldn't have. They could tell someone had been in the grass behind the house, and now they're sure it's him. He *told* them he was there.

When they'd spoken, before resuming the interview, his attorney had warned him that they had enough at this point that they would soon get a warrant for his phone. He'd asked him if there was anything on it they needed to worry about. So Cameron had shown him the messages to Diana, him apologizing, begging forgiveness, saying he was outside in his truck. The lawyer told him it was okay that he'd already admitted that they'd argued, that he was there, outside her house, that he wanted to talk to her. They were going to find out anyway, as soon as they took his phone. But telling them he got out of the truck? That was on him – the attorney didn't know about that. That was a mistake. His attorney hadn't been happy about it. He should have just handed over the phone and kept his mouth shut.

Now he's the prime suspect. The police think he went in through the back and killed her. He's pretty sure that's what his attorney and his parents think too.

They will arrest him soon. Oh God, what is he going to do?

Chapter Thirty-One

JOE PRIOR ENJOYS his long Sunday drives. He goes all the way to Quebec, Canada. There's a girl there he likes the look of. She works at a Couche-Tard store. His guess is she's about sixteen. A good age.

Through the week his routine is to work and go home and have supper, drink a few beers and go to bed. Sometimes Roddy comes over for a few. Construction is hard work, but the weekends are devoted to pleasure. He'd driven to Littleton, New Hampshire, yesterday, and today it's Magog, Quebec. He likes to check out his favourites and then cruise around looking for other cute girls working the cash register somewhere. When he finds ones he likes, and he's rather particular, he tries to learn more about them. He doesn't want to know what their dreams or aspirations are – he really doesn't care. What he does is follow them home after their shift sometimes, careful not to be noticed, so that he knows where they live. And once he knows where

188

one of his girls lives, he will sometimes stay there long into the night, watching her house.

He tries to figure out who lives there with her, what their routines are. He studies the location, the doors, the windows, and how he might get in, the surroundings where he might park the truck, how he might get away. He commits it all to memory. It's all part of the fun. If it seems too risky – if the girl lives with a large family, like that girl Georgia, that was a shame – he gives up. He couldn't see any way to get at her with so much going on in that house. But it's surprising how many girls live with only their mothers. So many fathers are not around these days. That certainly makes it easier. Roddy's been asking where he goes on the weekend. Nosy little shit. Joe told him he has a buddy in Quebec with a cabin and he goes to see him some weekends, to do a little hunting or fishing. When Roddy asked him where his hunting and fishing gear was, he told him he didn't have any himself, he uses his friend's. Roddy recently asked if he could go with him there one day – he likes to hunt and fish, he grew up in New Brunswick. For fuck's sake, that's not going to happen. There is no friend with a cabin.

Ellen is numb and unbending as Brad tries to get her to stay.

He offers to make a nice dinner, asks her to spend the night. He tells her he's missed her, and that now that she understands why he was avoiding her, everything is okay. Now that she knows everything, he tells her, he just wants her near him. He tells her over and over again that he loves her, that he can't wait to marry her.

189

But Ellen is afraid she doesn't know everything, and she doesn't want to stay. She can't just accept this disturbing information and have everything go back to normal. She needs time to think, and she can't think when she's around him. This is all too overwhelming.

He's been coaching her on what to say to the police. *Just tell the truth*, he says, as if she wouldn't. And anyway, she doesn't know anything. What can she tell them? *Tell them that you know me, that you know it never happened, that she was exaggerating. You know I would never do anything like that.*

But she doesn't know, not for sure.

Something is off about all this. He seems to be ... overreacting. What is he so worried about? If what he told the reporter is true, that his friendly gestures were completely misinterpreted, and if that's all it was, why is he so scared? What are these lies Diana told that he won't share with her?

It's important that you stand by me.

He's even said it was too bad she hadn't spent the night here with him on Thursday, because then none of this would be happening. As if it's her fault he doesn't have an alibi. It frightens her that he even needs an alibi.

Maybe she should talk to Kelly, she thinks. He would know.

'So, will you stay the night?' Brad coaxes.

She thinks about going home, the questioning looks from her parents. They know something's going on. What is she going to tell them? There's nowhere she can go right now and not carry this burden with her.

190

As she watches him waiting for her answer, his cell phone buzzes.

Brad glances anxiously at his cell phone on the coffee table. His nerves spike. Fuck. Not now.

'Who's that?' Ellen asks apprehensively.

'Graham Kelly.' His voice is tight. He'd rather not do this in front of Ellen.

'Aren't you going to get it?' she asks.

She's watching him, as if it's a test. He lets it ring twice more before he picks it up. 'Yes?'

Kelly says, 'Brad, there's something you should know.' He sounds tense.

'Put it on speaker,' Ellen says. Her voice is cold.

Brad can't let this all go haywire. He thinks quickly. 'Hi Graham. Ellen's here, so I'm going to put you on speaker, okay?' He's got to hope that he can trust Kelly not to say anything stupid. But he hadn't liked the way Kelly had looked at him that morning, hadn't liked using leverage. 'I've told her about Diana's allegations. She's been great. Very supportive.' He glances at Ellen; she looks more frozen than supportive.

'That's good,' Kelly says carefully. 'Hi, Ellen.'

'Hi,' Ellen says.

'It's good that you told her,' Kelly says, 'because things are about to get ugly.' His voice is tight.

'I already know,' Brad says wearily. 'A reporter was here a little while ago. I had to throw her out.'

'That one from KCVS?'

191

'Yeah.'

'She was here too,' Kelly says.

Brad wishes he knew exactly what Kelly had said to her, but he's not about to ask now, not with Ellen listening.

'There's something else you need to be worried about.'

Brad's heart almost stops. 'What?'

'Another girl has come forward today, about you. She's gone to the police.'

'What?' Brad says, his world spinning.

'I thought you should know,' Kelly says, and hangs up, as if he wants nothing more to do with it.

Ellen leaps up and runs to the bathroom. He hears her retching into the toilet.

Chapter Thirty-Two

IN THE BATHROOM, Ellen splashes water over her mouth with trembling hands. Her mind reels. *Another girl.* The phrase repeats over and over again in her mind. Brad hadn't said anything to her about any other girl. What else is Brad hiding from her? Is everything that comes out of his mouth a lie?

She has to pull herself together. She will ask Brad about this other girl. And then she'll leave. She can't stay here. If the man she's supposed to marry can behave improperly with his teenage students, she doesn't know who he is. If it was one girl, she might be making it up. But if there was more than one . . . *another girl* . . .

And – oh God – this other girl has been to the police. What has she told them? And what will Ellen say if the police want to interview her?

He's been trying to hide it, but she can tell how frightened Brad is. There must be a reason.

Now he's knocking at the bathroom door. 'Are you okay in there?' He sounds alarmed.

She opens the door and faces him. She brushes past him into the living room, picks up her jacket and her bag, and turns to him. 'What is this other girl going to say about you?' she demands.

'I don't know,' he says, his voice climbing. 'I never did anything to anyone – not Diana or anyone else! You must believe me!'

But she doesn't believe him. Not any more.

'Ellen, sweetheart, don't leave,' he begs, his eyes desperate.

'I need some time on my own right now,' she says as she walks to the door.

'And I need to know if I can count on you,' he says wildly to her back.

She doesn't answer.

Sunday, Oct. 23, 2022, 9:30 p.m.

I got shit from my mom and dad when I got back this afternoon. I told them I hadn't expected to be gone so long.

'Where the hell were you with your mother's car?' my dad demanded, with his Sunday afternoon drunk on. He was weaving a little where he stood, looking at me blearily. I've always hated Sundays. I wondered again why my mother didn't leave him.

I decided to tell them the truth. 'Riley and I were

following Joe Prior.' My mother's jaw dropped, literally. She stood there open-mouthed, unable to speak.

'Who's that?' Dad asked vacantly. Always taking an interest, my dad.

'Why don't you go back to your game,' Mom said to him. 'I'll deal with this.'

Dad faded back into the den and Mom pulled out a chair and we sat down at the kitchen table. I told her all of it, and she wasn't happy. 'He could be a murderer!' she cried. 'Evan, you have to stay away from him!'

'It was perfectly safe, Mom,' I said. 'We never got out of the car.' A small fib. 'We called the detectives to tell them that he'd crossed the border into Canada, and then we went to the police station, after we got back here.'

That was frustrating. The detectives weren't even there when we got there. We spoke to an officer in uniform. We repeated that Joe Prior had crossed the border into Canada at Derby Line at 1:20 p.m. He took the information down. He didn't seem to take us very seriously. It really pissed Riley off, and I don't blame her.

Roy glances furtively at his daughter as they all watch TV on Sunday evening. He can tell she's been crying, although she's obviously washed her face and put on a bit of makeup to try to hide it. She's been unusually quiet all evening, not her usual chatterbox self. She hardly touched her dinner. He and Susan have been sharing quiet looks since Ellen got home late this afternoon. Something has happened, and they both know it probably has something to do with her fiancé.

'Everything okay?' he asks Ellen during a commercial break. 'You seem quiet.'

'Yeah, fine. I'm just tired,' she answers.

'You can tell us if something's wrong,' he says gently. 'Everybody has bumps in the road.'

'I'm going to bed,' she says abruptly and gets up. 'Goodnight.'

'She's not fine,' Susan says quietly to him once she's left.

'No,' Roy agrees. He tries to turn his attention back to the television programme, but he can't concentrate. He's worried about his daughter. When the programme is over, the local news comes on. There is a breaking report about the Diana Brewer murder, and Roy sits up in his chair.

Jennifer Wiley, a well-known face on KCVS News, is reporting from outside the small Fairhill Police Station. 'New information has come out tonight in the investigation into the murder of local girl Diana Brewer. The seventeen-year-old was strangled, her naked body found Friday morning in the field of a local farmer. Now it has come to light that Diana had complained of inappropriate behaviour by one of her teachers at Fairhill High School.'

The penny drops for Roy.

The reporter continues. 'I attempted to speak to the principal of Fairhill High School, Graham Kelly, today about the allegations, but he was not available. Stay tuned for more news on this breaking story.'

Roy turns to his wife. She's looking at him with a stricken expression – he knows they're both thinking the same thing.

Chapter Thirty-Three

PAULA SITS UP in bed with her hand on the remote. She's been waiting for this all weekend. 'Martin, look.' She nudges her husband's attention away from the book he's reading. 'They know about Turner. Kelly must have spoken to them after all.' She listens intently. 'What a mess this is going to be,' she says when the report is over. She wonders how well Kelly will cope. 'It's better that he came forward than they find out about it some other way.' At least, she hopes that's what happened.

'They don't name him,' Martin says.

'Not yet,' she replies. 'I wonder how long they'll be able to keep that quiet?'

She's relieved that the police now know about these allegations of Diana's against the gym teacher. She wants the matter handled properly. If there's any truth to it, if he's been inappropriate with a student, he should not be allowed to teach. She hates that her daughter – that any girl – might be exposed to that. The police will get to the bottom of it.

She thinks again of Diana, how she ended up dead in that field. If Turner had anything to do with that, surely the police will figure it out.

Shelby Farrell is watching the television news. 'Edward!' she calls, and he quickly joins her in the den. When the brief segment is over, she turns to her husband and says, 'You know what "inappropriate behaviour" means. So what if it was him? What if *he* killed Diana?'

She turns suddenly when she hears a sound at the door. It's Cameron. She's surprised to see him out of his bedroom.

'What's going on?' Cameron asks.

'We were just watching the news,' she says. She tells him of Diana's complaint about the teacher and his eyes spark with interest. 'What teacher?' he asks.

'They didn't give his name, but the police must know who it is,' Shelby says. 'Do you have any idea who it might be?'

'She never said anything about it to me,' Cameron says. He looks surprised, and angry. Then he asks, 'Can I go out for a bit? Can I have the truck?'

'Why?' Shelby asks.

'I just want to go get a burger.'

'You didn't eat your supper,' Shelby observes.

'Yeah, and now I'm starving,' he says grumpily.

Shelby glances doubtfully at her husband.

Edward says, 'Do you think that's a good idea?'

'Why shouldn't I? I haven't done anything wrong. And I'm sick of my room. I feel like I'm going out of my mind. I can't go out during the day – everybody will stare at me.'

Edward glances at him and says, uneasily, 'Sure, I guess so. Do you want me to come with you?'

'No.'

Shelby asks, 'Are you going to see your friends?'

He shakes his head. 'No. I just want to be alone.'

'You're not going to do anything stupid, are you?' she asks nervously.

'I'm not going to kill myself, if that's what you're worried about.'

It is what she's worried about. That, and anything else he might do that wouldn't be in his best interests. Like talking to his friends, saying more than he should. But she suppresses her misgivings and says, 'Just don't be too long, okay?'

Brad Turner chain-smokes until the apartment is an awful fug of fumes. He's angry at Ellen for not standing by him. He thought she, at least, would believe him about Diana. If she doesn't believe him, who will? Okay, so when that other girl came forward – perhaps it was too much to expect her to stand by him then. But when it was just Diana, she should have listened to him. She should have trusted him.

After he's had time to calm down and think about it, he feels a bit more in control. He tells himself that Ellen will come around – when all this fizzles out for lack of evidence. Because there isn't any evidence, not where Diana is concerned. And no one else has any proof either. It's just Diana and this other girl's story against his.

It must be Zoe Simpson, he thinks now. There's no one else it could be.

He has to be sure of Kelly, though. He needs to talk to him again – remind him that this could destroy him too. What Brad is really afraid of is that Kelly will lose his nerve.

He makes the mistake of watching the late news and learns that the story of Diana's complaint is out there already. They will name him soon. Everyone will know.

He's suddenly desperate to get out of the smoky apartment; he feels trapped and he needs to breathe. He leaves quickly and gets into his car. He must try to talk to Ellen again. Surely she still loves him? It can't be over, just like that.

He finds himself driving down the familiar gravel roads in the direction of Ellen's family farm. He doesn't know what she might have told her parents. Then he realizes they've probably seen the news.

A white cross suddenly looms in his headlights, completely unexpected, startling him. He comes to a sharp halt in the road, staring at it. It reminds him again, plainly, horribly, that Diana is dead. He sits completely still in the car for a minute, unnerved.

He can't talk to Ellen again tonight. He'll give her time for all this to settle down. Because he knows if it's just this one girl against him, it will be her word against his. He'll deny it and keep denying it and all this will go away, and he will marry Ellen in December.

*

Riley is in her bedroom, sitting up in her bed with her back to the headboard. She's thinking about Diana, tears rolling down her cheeks. She now thinks Joe Prior probably murdered her. Why else would he flee to Canada? He'll probably never come back, he'll disappear and never have to face justice for what he did. The officer who took their information didn't even seem that concerned.

She stares at a photograph of Prior online. He looks like a killer. She can't believe she and Evan actually waited outside his apartment and followed him. What if he'd seen them? But he'd been too keen to get to Canada. And he'd had that canvas bag with him; she keeps thinking about that bag.

Her heart is full of grief, and her tears won't stop. She can't face going back to school tomorrow. She's not ready. Her mom already told her she could stay home tomorrow if she wanted. Maybe she'll never be ready.

She goes back to her texts with Diana and reads them again. There's hundreds of them, maybe thousands. She spends a long time reviewing them. Reading them, and seeing the attached photos, reminds her of everything they've done together and occasionally even makes her smile. Finally, she gets to the last text she ever received from Diana, at 9:52 the night she died.

Cameron on his way over to pick me up.

She looks at the texts she'd written to Diana since:

Morning, see u soon

201

Hey Diana, I'm in the caf

R U there?

Then:

Hey, Diana. I miss you.

I wish you were here. I wish I knew what happened to you.

She sniffs as her nose begins to run and begins tapping.

I don't know how I'm going to make it through this. The world is so empty without you. We'll find who did this to you, no matter how long it takes.

She leans back, exhausted, and closes her eyes. A moment later there's the ping of a text. Probably Evan, she thinks. She opens her eyes and looks down at her cell. But it's from Diana.

No you won't.

She shrieks and drops the phone.

Chapter Thirty-Four

RILEY HEARS HER mother's footsteps thudding down the hall. Her bedroom door is flung open and her mother appears, clearly alarmed. 'What is it?' she cries. 'What's wrong?'

Riley turns her face to her mother. 'It's the phone!' she cries.

'What?'

Riley finds herself shrinking away from the phone lying on her bed. She says, her voice shaking, 'I was texting Diana. I don't know why – it helps me feel like she's still here, somehow. But she answered, just now.'

'What?' her mother repeats, dropping onto the bed.

Riley reluctantly picks up the phone and shows her. 'Look.'

'It's not Diana,' her mother says.

'Of course not. I know that. But who is it? Wouldn't the police have her phone?'

'The police wouldn't send a text like that,' her mother says, her face pale.

Riley drops the phone again and starts to tremble. 'It's her killer, isn't it? He's got her phone, he must have. He sent that text!' She can feel herself becoming hysterical.

The man who killed Diana has just sent her a message. No you won't. She looks at the phone as if she's looking at a snake curled on her bed. Her thoughts race. What if he knows who she is? Her name would have come up on Diana's phone. What if he's watching *her*? He might know where she lives.

'What are we going to do?' Riley asks in panic.

'Where's that card Detective Stone gave you?' her mom asks quickly.

Riley gets up off the bed and starts searching through the pockets of her jeans. She finds the card and hands it to her mother, who pulls her own cell phone from the pocket of her robe and dials the number on the card. She puts it on speaker.

The phone rings four times before it's answered. 'Detective Stone.'

'It's Patricia Mead, Riley Mead's mother. My daughter has been sending texts to Diana on her phone. Someone just answered.'

There's a short silence. Riley and her mother look at each other, waiting.

Detective Stone says, 'I'll be there as soon as I can. It will probably take me an hour to get there. What's your address?'

*

They both get dressed while they wait for the detective. Her mother checks that all the doors and windows are locked, then makes them chamomile tea, but both of them are too on edge to drink it. When the detective arrives, alone, it's well after midnight. Riley's mother invites him in, and they sit in the living room.

Stone gets right to the point. 'We don't have Diana's phone. We couldn't find it.' He looks at Riley and reaches out his hand. 'Can I see yours?'

She opens it to her texts with Diana and hands it over without a word. She's still too shocked to say anything.

Stone studies the messages, scrolling through.

'That text was sent at eleven thirteen p.m.,' he says at last, putting her phone down on the coffee table between them. 'I think we have to assume that whoever killed Diana has her phone – and sent that message.'

'Why would they do that?' Riley asks, frightened. Her voice is shrill, and her mother turns to her anxiously.

'We know that some killers take trophies. It's risky, but it's worth it to them.' He pauses. Then he says, 'But answering your text, that's a whole new level of hubris.'

Riley knows what hubris is. 'Is he after me now? He knows my name. He might know where I live!'

Her mother looks at her in alarm, then turns back to the detective. 'What can you do to protect her?'

'The best thing we can do is catch this bastard,' Stone replies. He looks at both of them calmly, but Riley can sense his excitement. 'I know you're frightened,' Stone says, 'but this is his first mistake. We'll get him.' He takes a deep breath, lets it out. 'In the meantime, I'll have a patrol car keep an eye on your place. And please keep this to yourselves.'

The next morning, Graham Kelly feels unwell as he prepares to go in to work. This is much worse than the usual Monday morning malaise.

For a while, lying in bed wide awake at five a.m., he thought about not going in at all. It would be a shitstorm. The reporters would be all over him, now that KCVS broke the news that Diana had made allegations about one of her teachers. They'd want to know who it was and what he did about it. He felt himself breaking into a cold sweat.

But he's going in because it will only look worse if he hides out at home. He has to minimize this somehow. Brad Turner has him by the balls. If he tells the truth, Brad will tell his wife about his stupid, short-lived, and much-regretted affair. His wife will want a divorce. Kelly doesn't want a divorce. A divorce will ruin him, and ruin the kids. He doesn't want his career destroyed either. It's a stark choice: tell the truth about what Diana claimed Turner did, or stick to the much milder version he's already told the police – the version that's in the file. There's no good coming to him if he tells the truth now, no matter how bad it makes him feel. He must stick to what he said in the first place.

Turner had called him late last night and made that very clear. Graham hates him for it. Brad is basically blackmailing him. Kelly doesn't know for sure what happened between Brad and Diana, but he thinks now that there must be some truth to what she said. Diana is dead, and Kelly's not sure of anything any more.

The problem is, Kelly is fundamentally a good man, and he's appalled to be in this position. He wants to make a clean breast of it and tell the police what Diana really said, and explain to them that he didn't believe her, because she refused to go any further with her complaint, and she should have if she'd been telling the truth. And she'd lied before, about the cheating. So of course he thought she'd been lying.

His wife is very quiet while he gets dressed. He's going in earlier than usual, to avoid the press. Sandra is not happy with the situation either. He has given her the same white-washed story he gave the police. She knows that Brad was over here on the weekend, that they were shut up in his office. She knows how uneasy Graham is.

He gets into his car with a troubled conscience and a quaking heart.

Ever since his daughter started working at the bakery, Roy has enjoyed their early mornings together in the farmhouse kitchen, having breakfast, talking about the day ahead while the sun is barely up. Monday morning he's alone with Ellen in the kitchen, but the vibe is very different. Susan has stayed in bed, because they both think it's better if he talks to their daughter alone.

Ellen drinks her coffee and eats her toast silently, her head down. He has to say something, even though it breaks his heart to do it.

'Ellen?' he says. She looks up warily. She looks like she's barely slept. 'Your mom and I were watching the news last night.' Ellen stops chewing. Her eyes are fixed on him with fear. His heart sinks. 'They said – they said that Diana made a complaint against one of her teachers.'

She covers her face with her hands.

'Is it Brad? Is that why you've been so upset?'

She nods listlessly and uncovers her face. 'But he says he didn't do it. That she made it all up.'

He hesitates for a moment and then asks, 'Why would she do that?'

'I don't know.'

He steels himself. 'Do you believe him?'

'I thought I did.' She looks at him, her face desolate. 'Oh, Dad, what am I going to do? He says I should stand by him, and I would, but—'

'But what?'

'But – another one's come forward.' Her voice has become a whisper. 'A second girl. She went to the police yesterday.'

Roy swallows. Another one. He's filled with revulsion. His daughter's fiancé might be a child molester. He's also going to be a suspect in a murder investigation. Does she realize it?

As if reading his mind, she says, 'He told me that the police might want to talk to me.' She looks at him, clearly anxious. 'He's worried they might suspect him of – of what happened to Diana. They've already asked him for an alibi for that night.'

208

'And?'

'And he doesn't have one.'

He regards his daughter, his heart thumping. The girl's body was left in their field, Roy thinks. Why? Because he knew the road? Knew that it was deserted at night? Is his daughter's fiancé some kind of madman?

He sees the distress in his daughter's eyes and he can't bear it. The idea of her marrying a man who might be a child molester and perhaps a murderer – he can't let that happen.

Chapter Thirty-Five

SHELBY IS IN the kitchen after breakfast when the phone rings. She stares warily at the phone on the wall for a moment before she picks it up. 'Hello?'

It's Detective Stone. She hears his voice and has to fight the urge to slam the phone down again.

'Good morning,' Detective Stone says.

She doesn't answer. Her throat is dry.

'We'd like you to bring Cameron back down to the station again later today,' Stone says.

'What for?' she asks, her voice tense.

'We have a few more questions.'

'He's already answered all your questions!' Shelby says.

'Not the ones about what he was up to last night,' Stone says. 'Let's say four o'clock? And make sure his lawyer is present.' The detective hangs up.

Shelby stands in the kitchen, her hand still on the receiver, momentarily unable to move. Then she charges up the stairs and flings open Cameron's bedroom door. 'Where were you last night?' she cries. 'What did you do?'

When Edward sees the text come in from Shelby, he's in a sales meeting. The detectives want to talk to Cameron again this afternoon. About last night.

He texts her back immediately, trying not to attract notice. What about last night? What the fuck is going on? Why are they asking about last night? Cameron had been gone much longer than he should have been last night, if all he did was grab a burger. Edward gets up, nods apologetically, and exits the meeting. He can feel everyone's eyes following him. They all know his son has been questioned by the police; he doesn't know what they think. He heads straight for his own office, closes the door, and calls Shelby.

'What's going on?' he asks anxiously as soon as she picks up.

'They want us to bring him in with his lawyer again today at four o'clock. They have questions about what he was doing last night,' Shelby says, her voice low but filled with tension.

'Did you ask Cameron?'

'Of course I did! But he said he didn't do anything, that he just got a burger and then drove around. And now he won't talk to me.'

Edward's stomach is clenching. Why did Cameron leave the house last night? What did he do?

'Maybe I should talk to him,' he says finally, his heart pounding, that crushing pain back in his chest.

*

Brad Turner is at home, informed early this morning by Graham Kelly that he has been suspended from his job for the foreseeable future. He expected as much. The call was formal, unfriendly.

Shortly after that, the call comes from the detective. Brad's heart immediately begins to race. He takes a deep breath and tells himself not to panic. He expected this too. They have to interview him again, if another girl has come forward, as Kelly told him. He will reassure them that it was nothing. They seemed to believe him last time. If he can dismiss their concerns now, that will be the end of it. As long as Kelly keeps his mouth shut.

He makes his way to the police station. When he arrives, Brad is taken once again into an interview room. He wants to get this over with. He wants it to end. He must stand his ground, that's all.

'Mr Turner,' Stone begins. 'We'd like to ask you a few more questions.' Brad nods. 'You've already spoken to us about Diana. That she had made certain allegations about you.'

'Yes. But I explained all that,' he says.

'Right. But here's the thing. Another girl has come forward. She spoke to us yesterday afternoon.' He stops there and watches for a reaction.

Brad manages to seem surprised, indignant. 'What? What girl?'

'I won't say who just now.'

'What did she say?' Brad asks. His voice is flinty. He must control his anger.

'She said that you once entered the girls' changing room

WHAT HAVE YOU DONE?

when she was there, alone. She was the last one there that day, and she was still partially undressed. She tried to cover herself up with her arms. She said that you apologized, saying you thought the locker room was empty – but that you took your time leaving.'

'That never happened,' Brad says firmly.

'She's pretty adamant,' the detective responds.

'Nevertheless, it isn't true,' he says coldly. 'She's making it up.'

Stone looks back at him, sizing him up, trying to see through him.

Yes, he was in the locker room. Yes, he stood there, staring at her a beat too long. It's Zoe Simpson who's complained about him, it must be. But he didn't touch her. He didn't go near her. All perfectly harmless, in his opinion. These girls show more in their bikinis. But these detectives clearly don't see it that way. He says, 'You know if this non-sense gets out it will ruin me. And it isn't even true.'

'Have you ever entered the girls' locker room?'

'No, never.'

'You absolutely sure about that?' Detective Stone asks, obviously not believing him. 'Because we found the girl quite credible.'

Brad stands his ground. No one else was there, and he knows there are no cameras. It's just her word against his. 'I've never been in the girls' locker room. I never touched this girl, whoever she is.'

'I didn't ask you if you touched her,' Stone replies.

Brad tries not to show his anger.

'One more thing,' Stone says. 'Where were you last night between eleven and eleven thirty?'

Brad hesitates for a moment. 'I was on my way to see my fiancée.'

'Who is your fiancée, and where does she live?'

'Ellen Ressler.' He adds reluctantly, 'She lives with her parents.'

Stone's eyes sharpen. 'Her parents wouldn't be Roy and Susan Ressler, would they?' he asks.

'Yes.'

'I see,' Detective Stone says, tilting his head. 'Your fiancée lives on her parents' farm. The farm where Diana's body was found.'

Brad feels his face grow hot, but doesn't answer.

'That's very interesting,' Stone says. 'I didn't know you had a connection to the Ressler farm.'

'Everyone knows she's my fiancée,' Brad says defensively.

'And she'll confirm that you were with her last night at that time?'

He pauses. 'No. I got halfway there and changed my mind about seeing her and went home.'

'Why did you change your mind?'

'I – I thought maybe she needed some space.'

'I see. Trouble in paradise? I'm guessing she's not that happy about what you might have been doing to your students.' He leans in closer. 'What did you do to Diana, Turner?'

'Nothing. I did nothing.'

But they continue to question him, asking him the same things over and over.

214

Chapter Thirty-Six

I hover, watching Mr Turner trying to deflect the detectives. I didn't know about the locker-room incident with Zoe. So I wasn't the only one. I wish I'd known. It's nice to see him squirm – he deserves it – but I don't think he killed me. Why would he? But I know he liked to look. It pains me, not to know how I got here. My life has been taken from me. Someone needs to pay.

I remember when it happened to me, that time in the locker room, after everyone else had gone. I was humming in the shower and didn't hear him come in. When I got out, he was standing just a few feet away. I was so startled that I gave a little scream. I tried to cover myself with my hands, while looking frantically for my towel, which I'd hung on a nearby hook.

'This what you're looking for?' he said. He brought my towel out from behind his back and smiled. He held it out to me, as if beckoning me forward to take it. I froze. I was

trying to gauge whether I could get past him, wondering if he'd locked the door. But he was blocking my way. I wondered if anyone would hear me if I screamed. If anyone would believe me if I told. All of this went through my mind in a flash. I don't know how long I stood there, but even now, I recall how anxious I felt, how afraid.

He tossed the towel to me. 'Don't tell anybody about this. They'll never believe you anyway. I'll say that you invited me in for a look.' And then he left.

I didn't tell, just as he expected.

After that, I kept my distance. But sometimes I'd catch him looking at me, as if we were sharing a dirty secret.

Maybe he was more dangerous than I realized.

Edward returns home, unable to wait even until lunchtime to talk to his son. Shelby, who has stayed home from work to be with Cameron, is glad to see him, but Cameron is not. He's entered Cameron's room without his wife, thinking he'll get more out of him if she isn't there.

'What's this about?' he asks his son. He's perhaps more abrupt than he has been. His nerves are getting the better of him.

'I don't know,' Cameron says defensively.

'Where did you go last night?'

'I got something to eat and then I just drove around, that's all.'

'Drove around where? You must have done something to get on their radar, or why would they want to ask you about it?' He's almost shouting now. Cameron looks back at him in fear. But Edward can't help himself. He demands loudly, 'Are you trying to hide something?'

'No!'

'Where did you go?'

Cameron recoils from him, shrinking back against his bedroom wall. 'I went to a place I used to go to with Diana – an empty field. I just parked there and sat for a while.'

'Why?'

'Because I miss her!' He starts to sob.

Edward softens toward his son. 'Where is this field?'

'What does it matter?'

'Tell me.'

'It's where Pickering Road meets Town Line.'

Edward feels a chill come over him. 'But – that's right near the Ressler farm, where Diana was found.'

Cameron says nothing, and for the first time, Edward believes it's actually possible that his son is a murderer.

Brad Turner finally leaves the police station, waving off the reporters eager to take his picture, shouting questions. They know Diana made a complaint against one of her teachers, and here he is, served up nicely for them on a platter. That bitch from KCVS is front and centre.

'Mr Turner,' she calls, saying his name loudly, 'do you have any comment on the allegations made against you by the murdered girl?'

He meets her eyes briefly, seething with rage and trying not to show it. He's afraid of what will happen when they find out about Zoe. He turns away, without answering. He gets into his car and drives home. He takes a long, circuit-ous route, to make sure none of them are following him.

Once he's home, Brad collapses on his sofa, his head in his hands, his fingers tearing through his hair. He has to call Ellen. He considers getting an attorney. He doesn't like how that will look, but he's scared.

He lights a cigarette and calls Ellen at work. Her phone rings and rings, then goes to voice mail. She always picks up even if she's busy at the bakery. There's his answer, right there.

Shelby has been out of her mind with worry since Detective Stone called the house that morning. She hopes her hus-band can get something out of Cameron. She confronts Edward now as he slowly comes down the stairs. 'What did he say?' she whispers.

Edward shakes his head and directs her farther away, into the kitchen.

She's way past worry – into panic territory. 'What do you think happened last night?'

'I wish the hell he hadn't gone out!'

'You're the one who said it was okay. I didn't want him to go!'

'Oh, so now it's my fault?' Edward shoots back.

She takes a deep breath and says, 'Sorry, no, it's not your fault. Of course it isn't. I'm just upset.' She wrings her hands in distress. He moves closer to her and says, 'He said he went to a field he used to go to with Diana.' He pauses. 'A field near the Ressler farm.'

She feels herself swaying, as if she might faint. She clutches her husband's arm for support. 'Why?'

'Because he misses her.'

She stares back at him in fear. 'I just wish he'd be honest with us, then maybe we could help him,' she whispers.

'Help him how?' Edward asks, his voice lowered.

She regards him tentatively. 'I don't know – what if he was trying to, to, I don't know . . .'

He fills it in for her. 'Destroy evidence?'

So they understand each other. She waits for his response, afraid.

'You would do that?' he asks. 'Help him destroy evidence?'

'Wouldn't you?'

Chapter Thirty-Seven

RILEY WALKS WITH Evan to the park in the chilly October air. It's sunny and bright, but they're in low spirits. They'd both skipped school and visited Mrs Brewer again, spending a couple of hours with her helping to plan the funeral, which is to be on Wednesday.

Planning the funeral has upset Riley. Mrs Brewer had told them it would be a closed coffin. Riley was relieved to hear that, but Riley doesn't like to think of Diana in a coffin at all, being lowered into the cold, deep ground in the cemetery. The sound of the dirt hitting the coffin, with Diana inside. Her being covered by the weight of all that earth. Riley thinks that when the time comes, she might have a panic attack. 'I don't know if I can do it,' she says.

'Do what?' Evan answers, turning to her. They're at the park now, headed for the empty swings.

'The burial. I think I can do the funeral, but I don't think I can do the burial, in the cemetery.' She stops walking. She begins to tremble, and Evan regards her with concern. 'The idea of her underground, for ever . . .' She knows she must look like she's losing it. She stares intently at Evan. 'What's happened to her, do you think?'

He stares back at her as if confused by the question. 'What do you mean?'

'Do you think she's up there, watching us? Or is she gone, and there's nothing left of her at all?' She's shaking now uncontrollably. It's not fair that Diana died so soon. So young. Is that all there is? She hopes there's more, that Diana isn't gone for ever. It's bad enough, the thought of her body disintegrating in the cold, dark ground, the worms – it's terrifying.

'There's no such thing as life after death,' Evan says.

'How do you know?' she cries. 'Maybe she's still here, with us, watching us. Maybe she can't rest until they find her killer.'

'That's ridiculous,' Evan says. He seems uneasy, as if he doesn't know how to manage her and her outburst of emotion.

'I'm not so sure,' she says. She takes deep breaths, trying to calm down. 'There's something you don't know. Something we did once, that we never told anyone.'

'What the hell are you talking about?' Evan says.

Riley starts walking again, toward a nearby bench, and sits down. He sits beside her. The cold of the bench quickly seeps through her jeans.

'We didn't tell you guys, we didn't tell anybody, because we thought you'd make fun of us.' She takes another deep breath and tells him. 'We had a sleepover, a couple of months ago. At Diana's place. Sadie Kelly was there too.' She pauses, then continues. 'You know how Diana liked to tell ghost stories.' She looks at him. 'That night she was telling some wild ones, and we were all laughing, just joking around. And then she suggested we try calling some spirits.'

'Seriously?' he says dismissively.

'No, wait, listen!' she says urgently. 'Sadie said, *How? It's not like we have a Ouija board handy.*' Riley stops suddenly, remembering how strange it was, how unsettling. 'And Diana said we could make one.' She continues. 'So Diana wrote down all the letters of the alphabet, and Yes and No, and the numbers one through ten on a piece of paper, and then cut them all out in little squares. And then she put them down on her hardwood floor in a circle. We were all sitting there in our pyjamas. Nobody was taking it seriously. We were eating crisps and drinking wine Sadie had brought and laughing. Diana went downstairs and got another wineglass and a candle. Her mom had gone to bed already. Diana lit the candle and turned out all the lights. Then she flipped the wineglass upside down on the floor inside all the letters and we sat there in a circle. Diana told us to put a fingertip on top of the upturned wineglass. I thought it was a bit ridiculous, but Sadie and I went along with it. Diana told us that she'd heard about doing it this way, that it worked better than some store-made Ouija board. So the three of us sat in the dark, with the candle flickering, with Diana saying, *Is anybody there? Are there*

any spirits around tonight? Any lost souls? It was creepy.'
Riley stops and shivers involuntarily.

'So that's it?' Evan says.

'No.' Riley shakes her head, takes a deep breath. 'Then it got weird.'

Chapter Thirty-Eight

'GO ON,' EVAN prompts.

Riley says, 'The wineglass began to move. On its own, I swear. It wasn't like anyone was pushing it. We all had our fingertips on it just very lightly, and it spelled out *hello*.' She remembers it so clearly; it had made a strong impression on her. It was so scary and unexpected. 'And Diana said, *Thank you for coming. What is your name?* And it spelled out *Simon*. It was a bit slow, but very clear. And Diana asked, *How old are you?* And he went to the numbers 1 and 2. So Diana said, *You were twelve when you died?* And he went to the word *Yes*.' Riley stops and studies Evan for his reaction. He's transfixed, but she can't tell what he makes of it. 'Then Diana asked, *Where did you live?* And he spelled out *Here*. And she said, *Here? In this house?* And we all looked at one another, completely freaked out. But he said *No*. So she asked if he lived in Fairhill, and he answered *Yes*. He said his house wasn't there any more. Diana asked him what year he was born, and he said 1861. Then she asked him how he died.' She stops again, as Evan looks at her doubtfully.

'You have to believe me, Evan. There was a boy, a spirit, no question about it.' She carries on. 'It was the strangest thing I've ever experienced. He went quiet for a bit, and we thought he'd gone, but Diana asked him again how he died, and he spelled out *Sick*. And Diana was going to ask him more about it but then the wineglass just started flying around and around so fast in circles on the floor, as if he was angry and we were all terrified and took our fingers off the glass and it stopped.'

Evan's looking at her in disbelief. He says, 'Sadie was manipulating the wineglass, manipulating both of you. You know what she's like.'

'No.' She shakes her head vehemently. 'I was there, you weren't! We all swore we weren't making the glass move, and then we all put our fingertips back on and tried to push it around, but it was obvious when someone was doing it. And we couldn't get it to go round and round in circles like that. It wasn't the same. It wasn't one of *us* that was answering. It wasn't Sadie. It was a spirit. I'm sure of it.' She takes another deep, trembling breath. 'And now I wonder if Diana is here somewhere, like that boy Simon.' She adds, 'And I wonder if she's as angry as he was.'

Evan clearly doesn't believe her, Riley thinks. He thinks she'd been duped. She regrets that she told him. She gets up suddenly and starts walking briskly away.

'Wait, where are you going?' Evan calls after her. He begins to follow.

She doesn't answer. She's angry at him for not believing her, and she would prefer to be alone, but after that text last night from Diana's phone she's too afraid to be by herself, even in broad daylight. She stops and looks back over her shoulder and sees with relief that he is following her.

He catches up, but trails a few paces behind her, giving her some space. She walks to the United Church. It's almost noon, on a bright Monday, and the churchyard is deserted. She heads for the cemetery, the one they used to hang out in, but probably never will again. She wonders where Diana will be buried, and if she will bring flowers for her grave. But she can't bear to think about that.

She makes her way directly to the older section of the cemetery, the part she likes best, where the gravestones are ancient and pitted and sometimes covered in moss. Some are rather grand and beautiful, but many more are quite simple, the gravestones reflecting the wealth of the dead person's family. Others are stone plates set into the earth that have been walked on over the years and are hard to read. Some mark the deaths of multiple children at once. It's sad, but the deaths were all long ago and feel removed from real life. Not like the newer part of the cemetery, where they will soon be digging a grave for Diana.

Riley has done the math. If Simon was born in 1861 and was twelve years old, he must have died in 1873.

'I know what you're doing,' Evan says beside her.

'Then help me look,' she says.

They walk slowly up and down the rows, reading each headstone carefully. But there is no Simon, born in 1861

226

and buried in 1873. There is no Simon at all, and no one with those exact dates.

Evan stands beside her. She can sense that he wants to say *I told you so*, but he refrains and she is grateful, at least, for that.

Ellen is grimly silent as she works in the bakery, moving like an automaton through the kitchen, putting rolls in the oven, taking them out again, hardly aware of what she's doing. Her phone chimes, and she ignores it. The other girls in the kitchen aren't speaking either. They must have heard the news. They all know her fiancé has been questioned; the reporters have caught him coming out of the police station. They think he's some kind of pervert, and that the police might suspect him of killing Diana. Ellen wants to scream and tear off her apron and run away.

She vacillates constantly. Sometimes she thinks Brad is being wrongly accused, that things will all work out somehow, and she will have her old life back – with her optimism, her beautiful wedding, and the cute house waiting for them on December first. But most of the time she thinks that Brad must have done something he shouldn't have. They wouldn't make it up. Why would they? But – you do hear stories of people making false claims that destroy lives. People lie. Girls can do terrible things. She remembers a story in the news recently – a teenage girl murdered a homeless person in cold blood, for no reason at all . . . Maybe Brad is a victim. It's certainly possible. And so she goes, back and forth, driving herself mad.

If only she'd been with him the night that Diana was killed. If only they would catch the real killer, so all this would go away. Because Ellen doesn't believe for a second that Brad murdered Diana. He didn't do it, so they won't be able to find any evidence that he did. But she's afraid that he might have been inappropriate with Diana and this other girl. Maybe Brad is the liar.

Apart from everything else, it's personally humiliating. She thought he loved her, that he desired her, that she was everything to him – or at least enough for him. But maybe not. And the fact that she could make such a mistake, that she didn't detect this *perversion* in him – how can she trust her own judgement any more? The very thought of it turns her stomach. Brad possibly leering at teenage girls, wanting them, touching them. It's disgusting. She doubts everything. And her parents – how can she face her parents after all this?

But how will he ever prove that he didn't do it? He can't, that's the thing. He might be able to win in court, if it comes to that, but he will never be able to completely convince her that he didn't do something to those girls.

She knows she can't marry him if she's uncertain. If there's *any* chance that he molested these girls, it's over. And she will have to cancel the dream wedding and give up the cute house that she's been redecorating in her mind, as well as the bright future they'd been planning together.

Chapter Thirty-Nine

Monday, Oct. 24, 2022, 1:30 p.m.

Riley is mad at me, but I can't help it if I don't believe her. I'm not going to pretend I do. All this about spirits and the Ouija board. It was either Sadie up to some prank, or some kind of group hysteria.

Although I admit it would have freaked me out if we'd found a grave for that boy with the correct name and dates.

My parents have gone to work and I'm alone in the house this afternoon. I need to think, to write. But I might go back to school soon.

The killer sent a text to Riley. It made the hair rise on the back of my neck this morning when she told me, in confidence. Why would he do that? I can tell Riley is frightened. She's afraid he knows who she is, that he might be watching her. That she might be next. She had a complete freak-out in the cemetery this morning, telling me this, after we couldn't find that grave. I calmed her down eventually. She asked me to walk her home. She even asked me to wait, after she unlocked her front door, while she checked the house to make sure it was empty. I offered to come in and help her look. It was bizarre, the two of us going all over the house, checking the closets and under the beds, confirming the windows and doors were locked. I think Riley is losing it. But she has a point. There's a killer out there and nobody knows who he is. And they seem to think he killed Diana inside her house. And he had the audacity to text Riley. Why would he send that message? What's to be gained from it? Other than to scare her?

The police took her phone – they said they wanted it in case he sent another text. But I doubt he will. If he *is* watching Riley, he'll know that the detective went to her house last night, and why. It would be risky to con- tact her again.

Riley called me first thing this morning from her land- line and told me everything. Her mom had to go to work, so as soon as the stores opened I picked Riley up and we went to buy her another phone, a cheap one, because she didn't know when she'd get hers back. And then we went to Mrs Brewer's, to help her with the funeral. She doesn't seem to have anyone else. It's so sad.

I think I might go to my last class this afternoon and

hang around a bit after. See what people are saying. Especially since it hit the news about Mr Turner. Everyone knows now that Diana complained about him. Looks like Riley's call to the news station did the trick. But it seems hard to believe that he might have killed her. He seems like just a regular guy. But then so does Cameron.

Paula knocks quietly on Principal Kelly's open office door. She's on her free period, and Kelly's alone in his office, looking haunted. He glances up at the sound of her tap and seems to relax a little when he sees that it's her. He waves her in.

'Graham,' she says, closing the door behind her. She comes in and sits down in the chair opposite his desk. 'How are you holding up?'

'Well, you've seen the news, I'm sure,' he says testily. 'Everyone has.'

She nods. 'You did the right thing, going to the police. You had no choice.'

He draws a hand down his face. 'I might as well tell you,' he says. 'It's probably going to be in the news soon enough. There's another girl who's come forward. She's already gone to the police with similar accusations.'

She looks at him in dismay. No wonder he seems so upset. This is what she feared – that what Diana claimed might have been true. That she might not have been the only one. Had Graham known about this other girl? Her voice sharpens. 'Who?'

231

'I can't tell you that. The police called me and asked if I knew anything about it, but I didn't. I had no idea! She never came to me. That's God's honest truth.' He adds abruptly, looking at her with his troubled eyes, 'Brad doesn't have an alibi for the murder.'

She swallows, her throat suddenly dry. Because Graham looks as if he thinks Brad might have killed Diana. That wasn't his feeling when she spoke to him on Friday.

He clears his throat nervously. 'Paula, you know me, you know I'm a good person, right?'

She nods, but she can't bring herself to speak.

'I try to do the right thing.' He leans closer toward her, lowers his voice. 'When Diana came to me and made those allegations against Brad – the three of us were here in this room. He strenuously denied them. It was her story against his.' He hesitates and adds, 'I haven't told you this, but she'd lied before.'

'What?' Paula starts in surprise.

He nods. 'She was caught cheating on a science assignment. She denied it, over and over. But then she admitted it. So I wasn't inclined to believe her.'

Paula is completely taken aback; she would not have believed it of Diana.

'And there was another thing,' Graham continues. 'She didn't want it to go any further – in fact she insisted that we tell no one, that it stay very quiet. I suggested she go to the police, but she wouldn't. Because of that, too, I didn't believe her. I thought she was lying.' His eyes shift away from hers.

'But I didn't exactly follow protocol. I didn't report it. I kept it unofficial – just a note in my own file. The only ones who knew about it were me, Brad, and Diana. And you.' He looks at her then.

Paula, shaken, says, 'You're required to report it, whether you believe it or not.'

He nods, clearly distraught. 'I should have, and I didn't. I should have believed her. And now she's dead.'

Paula leaves, distressed, to get to her next class. It's Graham's fault that he's in this mess. He's obviously mishandled things. She's shocked that Diana was caught cheating, and that she lied about it. She's troubled, too, by what Graham said. He'd suggested Diana go to the police, but she refused. So it must have been something fairly serious, not something minor, like he told her before.

She wonders again what exactly these allegations were, and why Graham now seems to think he has Diana's blood on his hands.

Chapter Forty

CAMERON IS IN his room when he hears voices from outside. He peers out his bedroom window. The police are here. There's a police van parked on the street in front of their house. Cameron is already anxious about having to go back to see the detectives at four o'clock, and now this.

He cocks his head and listens from behind his closed bedroom door. He can hear people talking downstairs, his mother's voice rising in fear. He opens his bedroom door, walks a few steps, and stops abruptly, looking down the stairs into the living room. There are people everywhere, and they're obviously looking for something. His dad is still here, standing at the foot of the stairs with his mom; he hadn't gone back to work after he came home earlier that day. His parents look as if they've had another shock.

'What's going on?' Cameron asks, coming to stand beside them.

'They have a search warrant,' his dad says. His mother seems incapable of speech. She can hardly meet his eyes.

'Why? What are they looking for?' Cameron says stupidly, as he watches them head up to his bedroom.

Neither of his parents answers.

'We need to go back down to the station now,' his dad says. 'It's almost four o'clock.'

'No,' Cameron protests. He says it automatically. He can't face it. He doesn't want any of this to have happened. He just wants to hide.

'Come,' his father says firmly, his hand on his shoulder. 'Let's get this over with.' He tells him the lawyer will meet them there.

His mother doesn't come with them, for the first time. Cameron wonders if she's staying behind to see if they find anything. They have to take the car, because the truck is being searched. His mind goes blank on the short drive to the station.

His father tries to nudge him out of his stupor. 'Cameron?'

He turns reluctantly to his father. *What now?*

'Is there anything I should know?' his dad asks, his voice serious.

But Cameron can't speak.

'What are you going to tell them about last night?' Edward asks, staring grimly at the road ahead. 'Maybe we should talk about it.'

Edward is quietly panicking as they resume their places in the room and the taped interview begins. Cameron is still

235

not under arrest, but Edward is terrified that it's only a matter of time. It's getting harder and harder to know what to do. Everything has become so blurred in Edward's mind. He doesn't know truth from lies, or right from wrong. Edward remembers his whispered conversation with his wife earlier that day. They want to help their son if they can, no matter what he might have done. Diana is dead, and nothing can change that now. What is to be served by their son spending the rest of his life in jail? If Cameron *is* to blame, he must have lost control. Surely he would never do something like that intentionally?

But how can they be certain that he would never do it again? How would they ever live with themselves if he did?

And how best to help him now? He's been caught out in too many lies already. Edward had no idea until now what a liar his son was. They'd discussed, on the way to the station, what he should say. Should he admit he was out last night? Edward had clenched his hands around the steering wheel and tried to think. Someone might have seen him go out in the truck, so he should tell the truth. That's what they decided. But Edward suggested – God help him – that he not mention the field that he and Diana used to go to, so close to where her body was found. He told him to say he went somewhere else – anywhere but there.

The voice of Detective Stone pulls Edward out of his thoughts.

'Cameron, we have a simple question. Where were you last night, between eleven and eleven thirty?'

Cameron looks at the detective. 'I went out, in the truck.'

'Where did you go?'

'I went to get a burger. And then I just drove around.'

'Why?'

'Because I'd been stuck in the house for three days, and I was going out of my mind.' He says this with a raised voice, his desperation showing.

The attorney interjects. 'Why does it matter? Why are you asking him this?'

Stone says, 'Diana's cell phone is missing. Do you have it, Cameron?'

Cameron shakes his head. 'No.'

'Well, someone has Diana's phone, and sent a text message from that phone to Riley Mead at eleven thirteen last night.' He adds, 'We think that whoever killed her kept her phone. We're looking for it right now at your house, Cameron, but we're not going to find it there, are we? Because you've hidden it somewhere else, haven't you? And you were looking at it when that text came in from Riley, weren't you?'

Cameron shakes his head, insistent. 'No.'

Edward feels the blood rush from his head. Cameron doesn't seem very worried that the police are going to find Diana's missing cell phone in the house. Is that because he doesn't have it, or because he knows it isn't in the house? God help him, he and his son alone know where Cameron was last night. What if he *did* kill her, and hid the phone somewhere in that field? What did the text say?

Stone leans forward, slightly aggressive. 'Tell us exactly where you went last night.'

Cameron hesitates and then says, sullenly, 'I went to the graveyard, at the United Church.'

'Why?' Stone asks.

'It's a place we used to go, Diana and I.' He adds, 'I just wanted to be alone.'

Now Edward is very much afraid that the phone is somewhere in that field. They can't have the police finding it, possibly with Cameron's fingerprints all over it. Maybe, he thinks, if he could get Cameron to tell him where it is, he could go get it and get rid of it. Destroy it.

'You don't need a truck to go to the church from your place,' Stone observes.

'I told you – I drove around for a while first,' Cameron says.

'Right,' Stone says, obviously not buying it. 'We know you were in Diana's backyard that night. We think that whoever killed her moved her body out through the back of the house and across the empty field to an abandoned road, where he had a vehicle waiting. You must know about that road, Cameron. You grew up here.'

'No, I didn't know about it.'

'Stop lying to me, Cameron. It's like a reflex with you.'

Brad is in a state. Ellen doesn't want to see him. She hasn't answered his calls or texts. He doesn't want to leave the apartment, now that all this shit has hit the news. He's lost his fiancée, and he's clearly going to lose his job and probably his teaching certification too. He thinks it's time to get himself an attorney. He's searched online and chosen a couple to call. He needs Kelly to keep his damn mouth shut.

The detectives arrive with a search warrant and a team early Monday evening. He looks at the warrant carefully before he lets them begin. But there's nothing he can do to stop them.

It doesn't take them long to search the small apartment, but it's one of the worst experiences of Brad's life, worse even than the interviews he's been subjected to at the police station. They tear everything apart as he watches, helpless. He's worried that they might try to plant evidence – something of Diana's. He doesn't trust the police. He tries to keep an eye on each of them, but they're everywhere all at once. He watches them, while Detective Stone watches him. 'What are you looking for?' Brad asks.

But the detective doesn't answer. Detective Stone doesn't search much himself; he just wanders around rather aggressively, glancing here and there, letting the others ransack his apartment with abandon. But they find nothing. Brad feels the most tremendous relief.

After they leave, he reaches for his phone with trembling hands and calls an attorney.

Chapter Forty-One

Monday, Oct. 24, 2022, 7 p.m.

Everything is so different now. The world feels as if it just stopped when Diana died and then started spinning in the opposite direction. Nothing is the way it used to be. I don't know what to think about anybody any more.

I think about Cameron a lot, stuck in his house, not talking to anyone except the police. We used to be close friends, but he changed when he started going out with Diana. We could all see it. It took Diana the longest, but she got there in the end.

Cameron's always been a bit full of himself because he's so good-looking and athletic – a sports star. That's what matters around here. It all seems to come so easily to him. But I never thought he was particularly bright. I'm thinking about that text and whether Cameron could have sent it. Riley says the detectives thought it was a sign of hubris, and yes, I can see that. Would Cameron be that arrogant? Possibly. It's a fact that people tend to think good-looking people are smarter than they are – I read that somewhere. But I haven't seen him since Diana died. I don't know how he's handling all this. Riley saw him, and she said he seemed devastated and lost, but I suppose he could have been putting on an act. I just don't know.

I'm worried about Riley. It's funny – I never thought I'd worry about her. She's never seemed to be someone anybody would have to worry about. She's very cap-able and self-reliant. Strong. But Diana's death has really thrown her. And this thing about the text has really fright-ened her. She seems to be falling apart more and more by the day. She doesn't think she can manage the burial, on Wednesday, but I have told her she has to try. I told her that I will be there to support her.

All that competitive stuff between us has disap-peared. Who cares about school and marks and academic prizes when Diana is dead? Riley is very different from Diana. Not as buoyant and carefree. But she is beautiful, too, in her own way.

That stuff about the Ouija board, though – it's all very weird. It seems to have upset Riley even more. I wish she wouldn't think about that stuff. I think she should see one of the counsellors at school. It might help. I suggested it to her today, but she said she didn't feel like going back to school. I told her she had to go back sometime, and she just shrugged. I told her I was going to start going back to classes regularly tomorrow, and that she could just text me if she needed me and I'd be there.

I was at school for a bit this afternoon and all people were talking about was Mr Turner. And now – it was in the news tonight – another girl has come forward with complaints about him. They're not saying who she is because she's a minor. Just how much of a creep is he? Could he be a murderer?

I hope they get to the bottom of all this and identify Diana's killer. She deserves justice. But even if they find out who did this, she'll never get her life back. And we'll never get her back in our lives either.

Edward Farrell decides to tell his wife everything. He can't carry this heavy load alone.

The police had found nothing in their search of their home and truck that afternoon. Edward wasn't surprised by this because Cameron hadn't seemed particularly worried about the search. But that evening, sitting at the kitchen table, while Cameron is closeted in his room, Edward tells Shelby what happened at the police station – about the missing phone, and the text.

Shelby looks back at him in fear.

'He told them he went to the graveyard, to be alone,' he says. She stares back at him, her eyes large, her face drained of colour.

'What?' she whispers. 'But he told you he was at the field that they used to go to, near the Ressler farm.'

He swallows. 'I told him not to tell them where he really was. It looks . . . bad.'

'But he doesn't have her phone,' Shelby says. 'They didn't find it.'

He can't believe he has to spell this out for her. Her mind can't be working properly – it's the fear. 'No, not here.' He watches as it dawns on her, and she becomes even more frightened.

'You think he hid it somewhere else.'

'He says he doesn't have it,' Edward says tersely. 'But what if he does? What if he sent that text? But why the fuck would he? I'm pretty sure that's what the detectives think.'

'What did the text say?'

'I don't know.'

'We have to find it first,' Shelby says. 'You have to make him tell you where it is!' Her eyes are wild and her voice unnatural. 'You have to get rid of it!'

Edward is tortured. 'But is it the right thing to do?' he whispers. 'If he killed her—' He can't go on.

'We don't have a choice!' she whispers back fiercely. 'This is our son! We can't let him go to prison for the rest of his life!'

'He won't tell me.' Edward shakes his head in defeat. 'I tried. In the car on the way home. You know how stubborn he can be. He denies everything. But he's told so many lies.'

'What are we going to do?' she asks plaintively.

'Maybe he hid the phone somewhere in that field where he went last night. I know where the field is; he told me. Maybe I'll go out there and look around.'

'How are you going to find a cell phone in a field?' she whispers desperately.

'I don't know! Do you have any better ideas?'

But she didn't.

Edward waits until dark, then gets in the truck, which they've searched but not taken away, leaving his shattered wife at home with their son, who is holed up again in his bedroom. He doesn't tell Cameron where he's going, or even that he's leaving the house. Edward brings a strong flashlight with him. He drives out of town, and down the country roads to where Pickering Road intersects with Town Line, about ten minutes from Fairhill. He is relieved no one is around. It's completely dark, except for his own headlights.

He drives slowly until he finds the field he's looking for, right where Cameron had said it was. He sees the open gate, bumps into the field, and turns immediately to the right, pulling into the corner, which is sheltered on two sides by thick trees along the fence lines. He turns off the ignition and sits in the utter darkness, listening to the ticking of the engine. Nobody can see him here. Nobody would have been able to see his son and Diana in this truck either.

Slowly, with a feeling of dread, Edward gets out of the truck and begins to search. Perhaps the police have searched here already, if it's not far from the field where the body was found; he doesn't know. If they did, they didn't find anything. If Cameron hid the phone, it's probably somewhere along the fence line, not in the open field. He starts from the corner and goes first in one direction, then the other. He looks for hollow logs, large stones that seem to have been disturbed, anything. He looks for cavities in trees, hidden nooks in branches. He spends two hours searching, until he is frozen to the bone, but he finds nothing.

Finally, he gets back into the truck, defeated.

As Edward pulls left out of the field onto the gravel road, he spots the headlights of another vehicle far behind him, turning onto the same road. *Shit, shit, shit.* Where did they come from? It was deserted a second ago. Edward tries to remain calm. Maybe the other driver didn't see him come out of the field at all. But he panics – he hits the gas and floors it. He wants to get the hell out of here. He doesn't want anyone to know he's been anywhere near where Diana was found.

Chapter Forty-Two

ROY RESSLER IS on his way to town to pick up some ice cream to go with the apple pie Susan has made. He likes to have something sweet with the late-night news before bed. He's hoping the drive will take his mind off his troubles.

At the end of his long driveway, as he's turning left onto the rural road, he sees what looks like the lights of a vehicle coming out of one of his fields. It startles him. Nobody has any reason to be in his fields – they're private property. He immediately thinks of Diana, so brutally murdered and left in another one of his fields along this same road. He sees the red taillights of the vehicle ahead of him and tries to catch up to it, but it's too far in front of him and puts on an impressive burst of speed and disappears. By the time Roy gets to the crossroads in his old truck, there are three possible directions the other vehicle could have taken, and he has no idea which way it went.

Roy never makes it to the store. When he arrives at the

police station, he's got himself all worked up. He worries that there might be another girl, dumped in one of his fields, and he feels a terrible sense of urgency.

The detectives aren't there, but officers from the state police are available to talk to him. He tells them what he saw, but he can't give them a description of the vehicle at all. 'There's no good reason for anyone to be in one of my fields at night,' he says anxiously.

'Do you remember exactly which field it was?' one of the officers asks him.

Roy nods emphatically. 'Yes.' He knows his fields like the back of his hand. He's known them all his life.

'Let's go take a look,' the officer says.

Roy gets into his truck and two officers follow him in a police cruiser. When they reach the field, they park on the side of the road and get out of their vehicles. 'How far is it,' the officer asks Roy, 'from here to the field where you found her?'

'Under half a mile,' Roy says, 'down this same road.'

The officer studies the entrance to the field with a strong flashlight. 'Tyre tracks,' he says.

'I told you,' Roy says, feeling vindicated. But mostly he's afraid. If someone has dropped another dead girl on his property, he's not sure he can survive it.

'I'm calling Stone,' the officer says to his partner. 'He's going to want a thorough search.'

Paula is quiet and thoughtful all evening. She's worried about her daughter, Taylor. She saw her sitting alone again today at lunchtime, on a bench in the hall outside the cafeteria. She had her lunch beside her, and she was reading a book. Students passed her, going in and out of the cafeteria, without talking to her, without even seeing her. It broke Paula's heart.

She hesitated. She considered going to her daughter and asking her what was wrong, but she thought it might be better if she asked her at home. It might have embarrassed her at school.

It pains her deeply. Why doesn't Taylor seem to have any friends? Where have they all gone? Why has she become so quiet? She had lots of friends at middle school. Is something going on online? She needs to get into her daughter's phone somehow and see if she's being bullied. But how? Her daughter's not going to let her see her phone. If Taylor won't talk to her, how will she help her? She's becoming more and more withdrawn.

She had spoken to her about Turner, specifically, when the news came out about him and Diana. She'd asked her daughter if he'd ever been inappropriate with her, or if she'd ever seen him behave improperly with anyone else, but Taylor had again turned away in embarrassment and said no. She'd had to ask. At least, with Turner gone, she won't have to worry about Taylor and the other kids at school any more.

Paula suspects Taylor might be struggling socially because her mother is a grade nine English teacher. Paula reminds herself that other kids survive going to school where their parents teach, but she can't help feeling guilty. Maybe she

should try to find a job further away. Would that help? Or
has the die already been cast for Taylor at Fairhill High?

She has a serious talk about it with Martin. He's also
worried about how Taylor's managing but doesn't think
that Paula being a teacher at the same school is as big a
problem as she does. He agrees they should talk to her.

They go to Taylor's bedroom after supper. Paula knocks
on her closed door and says, 'Can we come in?' She hears a
grunted assent and enters the room.

Taylor looks startled and seems wary. Paula studies her
for a moment – she's such a pretty girl, with her fine fea-
tures and sleek brown hair. But she's not open and smiling
like she used to be; she doesn't look happy. Paula can tell
she doesn't want to talk to them. Paula is getting used to
this, to being shut out. Are all teenagers like this? Taylor is
her only child; she doesn't know. She knows how the kids
she teaches act at school, but not how they are with their
parents.

'Is everything all right, honey?' Paula asks gently, sitting
down on the end of the bed. Her husband remains standing
awkwardly by the door.

'Yeah, fine. Why?'

'I just – I've noticed you're so quiet lately. Always stuck
up here in your room.'

'So?'

Paula hesitates and then says, 'I saw you at lunch today,
sitting by yourself.'

Taylor flushes.

'Why weren't you with the other girls – your old

friends – Kiley and Petra? What happened to them?' She tries to keep her voice light, but her heart is breaking in two.

'They're around. I just don't hang out with them so much any more.'

'Why not?'

'I don't know.' She turns her head away.

'Taylor, is it causing a problem for you, that I teach English to a lot of your classmates?'

'No.'

'Are you being bullied?'

'No.'

'Can I see your phone?'

'No.' Taylor has her hand on her phone and pulls it closer to her.

Paula looks up at her husband helplessly. He's looking back at her as if she should have all the answers. She finds herself getting angry at him for not being more helpful. She doesn't know what to do next. Does she take her daughter's phone? She doesn't know the password. She decides to retreat in defeat, for now.

'Okay. But you know you can always talk to me – to us – about anything, right?'

Taylor nods but doesn't answer; she clearly just wants them to leave.

Paula, upset, leaves her daughter's bedroom and goes to the den. Martin follows and pours them both a drink. 'That went well,' she says sarcastically.

'We'll get to the bottom of it,' Martin says, but he looks more concerned than he did before.

'What should we do about her phone?'

He shakes his head helplessly. 'I don't know. What do other parents do?'

She will find out what other parents do. Maybe they should take her phone away unless she agrees to show them what's on it. She's only thirteen. How much privacy is she entitled to? There shouldn't be anything on there that her parents can't see, should there?

She sips her drink, worrying about Taylor. On top of that, she keeps remembering her meeting with Principal Kelly earlier that day. It's so distressing, all of it. That Diana is dead. That Turner was bothering her – and another girl, it turns out. That he doesn't have an alibi for Diana's murder. And there's the fact that the body was found on his fiancée's family farm. *Could he have killed her?* It's making her sick to her stomach, thinking about it all.

She and her husband watch the news together. It's out in the open now, about this other girl, it's on the news. A shit-storm is about to come down on Graham Kelly's head. She thinks that he probably deserves it. He hadn't handled it properly, and it looks like he will have to pay the price. He will probably lose his job over this. He may never be able to work in education again. She suspects a female principal might have handled it differently.

Chapter Forty-Three

ON TUESDAY MORNING, Joe Prior is on the job site when his foreman approaches him and tells him that two detectives want to speak to him. Joe doesn't like the look on his foreman's face, as if he's wondering what the hell he's done now. Joe's already told him that all he'd done is chat that girl up at the cash register at the Home Depot. Now his foreman is obviously wondering why the detectives are here. Well, that makes two of them.

Joe looks past his foreman at the two people standing near the foreman's trailer. He recognizes them. It's the same two detectives who interviewed him before about Diana Brewer.

He approaches them, and the foreman heads back inside the trailer, eyeing them suspiciously. Joe faces the detectives.

'What can I do for you?' he asks pleasantly. He thinks the detectives look a bit ridiculous in their suits in the middle of a construction site. Be a shame if a beam hit them, and them not even wearing hardhats, he thinks to himself. But no chance of that, really.

'Just a couple of questions,' Stone says.

'Okay.'

'You crossed the border into Canada on Sunday afternoon,' Stone says.

Shit. How do they know that? Are they watching him? Following him? They can't do that. They don't have sufficient reason to follow him. He thinks fast, considering his options. He can't deny it, they know he crossed the border. It's a worrying development, if they start to look at where he's been, what his habits are. 'Yeah, so what?'

'What were you doing in Quebec?'

Joe shrugs. 'Just went for the day, shopping.' It's a stupid thing to say. He doesn't make a habit of shopping. But he's been caught off guard.

'What did you buy?'

'I can't remember.'

'Do you have receipts?'

'What the hell is this?' he says, looking warily at them.

'We'll take that as a no,' the detective says. 'One more thing – where were you on Sunday night, between eleven and eleven thirty?'

'I was at home, why?' Joe answers. He wonders if they're just trying to shake him up, let him know they've still got their eye on him.

Stone glances at his partner.

'Thanks, we'll be in touch.' Then the detectives turn and head toward the foreman's trailer. Joe turns around to go back to his worksite, but glances over his shoulder to see Stone knock on the trailer door. Joe stops to watch, apprehensive. The foreman appears, closes the door behind him, and walks with the two detectives over to the area where Roddy Donnelly is working. Joe can see the detectives talking to Roddy. Now he's worried. He wishes he could hear what they're saying. But he's afraid he knows. If Roddy was just confirming what he told them before it would be a short conversation, but this goes on for too long. Stone is questioning Roddy hard, getting into his physical space. Joe can tell, even from here, from Roddy's body language – he can tell the moment that Roddy capitulates. He's not looking at the detectives any more – he's looking at the ground, shaking his head. The detectives are nodding as Roddy keeps talking. Stone claps him on the shoulder.

Fuck.

Brenda's lost track of what day it is. With each night that passes she becomes more convinced Diana is here with her; she can sense her in the house. She talks to her daughter as if Diana can hear her, as if they're having a conversation. Perhaps all this is making her lose her mind.

She hasn't been eating much. She feels rather faint, dizzy when she stands up or climbs the stairs. She must take Riley and Evan up on their offer to run some errands for her. She's out of bread.

It was on the news, about the other girl. Brenda wants to know what the gym teacher did to her, what he did to Diana. She may never know.

She texts Riley and Evan and asks if one of them could come over after school. A minute later Evan answers, saying he'll get Riley and they'll be there in fifteen minutes.

When they arrive, she's surprised at how glad she is to see them. They're the only ones whose company she seems to want these days.

'You shouldn't be missing school,' she says.

'I haven't gone back to school yet,' Riley tells her.

Evan volunteers, 'It's no problem. I'm on lunch now, and I've got a free period after that.'

'I was hoping you could pick up a few things for me.'

'Of course,' Riley answers.

She hands her a list, some money, and some cloth bags. 'You're such a help, you two,' she tells them gratefully, sitting down heavily at the kitchen table. She's quiet for a moment, fighting tears. At last she asks plaintively, 'Do you think we'll ever know who killed her?'

They both look back at her gravely. Finally, Evan nods. 'I think we will, Mrs Brewer. You've got to have faith.' And then they leave to get her groceries.

She wanders around the house, talking out loud to Diana. Asking her, if she's there, to give her a sign.

I'm back at the police station. The detectives have brought in that horrible Joe Prior. I watch him sit down in the interview room. He's just like I remember him, big, unkempt, with shaggy red hair and a scruffy beard. His jeans and shirt are dirty, and his jacket has seen better days. He's got small eyes. He smells of days-old sweat, as if he doesn't bathe enough or wash his clothes. I recognize that stench, from when he would bother me at the cash register at Home Depot. I could always smell him coming. I associate that odour with a feeling of dread. Even after he left, the stale smell would linger.

Now, I watch him sitting in the interview room and try to remember if I ever noticed that awful smell of him anywhere else. I read somewhere once that smell triggers memories. I breathe it in reluctantly and hope it triggers something now. But it doesn't. All I feel is disgust. Revulsion.

Detective Stone tilts his head at him. 'So,' he begins, 'your alibi didn't pan out.'

Prior looks annoyed.

'With friends like that, who needs enemies, huh?' Stone says.

'Well, I shouldn't have asked him to lie for me,' Prior says. 'It was a stupid thing to do, especially since I don't have anything to hide anyways.'

'Right. You have nothing to hide, so you asked someone to lie for you,' Stone says.

'Look. Try to see it from my point of view.' Joe makes his voice sound reasonable. 'My photo had been all over the news in connection with this dead girl. It looked like I was a suspect, for Chrissake. That's why I came in voluntarily to talk to you as soon as I could, as I'm sure you remember.' Stone regards him steadily. 'I had nothing to do with it and just wanted to get you guys off my back. I didn't have an alibi because I was home alone that night. But I thought if I could get someone to vouch for me that would be the end

of it.' He leans back in his seat. 'You have no idea what it's like, having your picture on the news for something like this. People look at you funny. My foreman was asking me about it. People at work were talking about me. I just wanted it all to go away. I had nothing to do with this dead girl.'

'You harassed her at her job. You showed interest in her, and it wasn't reciprocated.'

He shrugs.

And then I remember something I'd forgotten, about that smell.

Stone says, 'We've been looking into you. You're a loner. You move around. We're in the process of tracking your previous addresses, your movements.'

'Knock yourselves out,' Joe says.

I gaze down at Prior. I remember where else I found his particular, offensive odour. It was one night after work, when Aaron, my manager, walked me to my car. I never bothered locking it. There was nothing in the car worth stealing, and it was an old beater anyway, not worth stealing either. I got in the car and there was this stink. I thought maybe some homeless person had been inside my car, and I rolled down the windows to let the air in. After that I always kept it locked. But now I think it was him – Joe Prior. He was in my car. What was he doing there? And then I realize. I kept the ownership and registration in the glove box. He could have found my address.

I want to scream this at the detectives. And I do, but they can't hear me. They don't even flinch. It enrages me that I *can't reach them. But now I'm remembering something else, something frightening.*

I'm standing at my bedroom window, late at night, looking out at the backyard, and someone is there. I see the dark shape of a man, looking up at me. I don't know who it is, and I'm terrified.

Now, looking at Joe Prior, I feel the same terror that I did then.

Chapter Forty-Four

JOE PRIOR HAS had a shit day.

He hadn't enjoyed being grilled by the detectives, but they'd let him go, and he'd returned to work.

Now, as work finishes at four o'clock, he waits for Roddy at Roddy's truck. When the bastard sees him, he stops in his tracks and looks like he's about to shit his pants.

'So,' Joe says, his tone both pleasant and menacing. He's furious at the betrayal. Furious, too, that he can't even beat the crap out of Roddy because if he does the police will find out. Roddy will tell them and then it will look like this alibi is really important to him. And he doesn't want to be charged with assault. So he can't touch the fucking bastard. But Roddy's too stupid to figure that out, so at least he can scare him a bit.

'I'm sorry, man,' Roddy says. 'I didn't want to rat you out. I didn't have a choice.' He sounds terrified.

'There's always a choice, Roddy,' Joe says, 'and you made

the wrong one.' It takes all of his self-control, but Joe knows he has to let this go. He has to minimize it. He's already admitted to the detectives that he got Roddy to lie for him just to get the police off his back after his photo went out on the news. He gives Roddy one last contemptuous look and walks away, to his own truck, and doesn't look back.

As he drives home, he thinks things over. He's worried about this fucked-up alibi business. He never should have said anything to Roddy. He thought if he provided an alibi, they'd move on and forget about him. He thinks maybe he should get an attorney. He doesn't care how it looks. He needs to stay out of jail. He can't survive in jail. Just the thought of it brings on the sweats.

He tries not to think about all the shitty places he lived in when he was a kid. The cheap apartments where his dad would lock him in a closet and pretend to forget about him for days. He finds it hard to catch his breath for a minute, as his breathing becomes shallower and shallower. Those times when he was curled up on the closet floor in the dark, nothing to eat. Nothing to drink. Crying and soiling himself. Unable to get out. But the trailer was the worst.

When he gets home, he finds the police waiting for him, with a search warrant.

After school, Paula does something she's been thinking about for a couple of days. It's Tuesday, and it's time she paid a visit to Diana's mother and offered her condolences. She's heard that the funeral will be held on Wednesday, at the United Church. She imagines nearly everyone in town will go, and probably people from further away too. The school will close early so that staff and students can attend. She's dreading it. She realizes that her own worries about Taylor pale in comparison to what Mrs Brewer has to deal with.

She knocks on the front door, noting how forlorn the house seems. She knows that Mrs Brewer is a single mother, and that she has no other children. How can she be bearing it?

The door finally opens, and she's appalled at the visible change in the bereaved woman. The last time Paula saw her, in the spring, was at a parent–teacher conference. Brenda Brewer always attended the meetings, while many other parents didn't bother. She was so supportive of her daughter, so proud of her. She is a mere shadow of that woman now. Her face is colourless and slack, her hair limp and untidy. She looks older. Paula remembers her as being much more robust, cheerful and energetic. Paula finds that she wants to cry at the sight of her.

'Mrs Brewer,' she says, 'I'm Diana's English teacher, Paula Acosta. May I come in for a minute?'

The other woman nods and says, 'I remember you.'

'I just wanted to tell you how truly sorry I am about Diana,' Paula says.

She nods again and invites Paula into the living room, where they sit down. There's an awkward pause, as Mrs Brewer doesn't seem inclined to speak. 'We all miss her so much,' Paula says. And then she feels incredibly stupid, because of course her mother misses her more than anyone.

She reaches into the bag at her feet. 'You know I thought Diana very bright and talented. It's still early in the school year, but I thought you might like to have some of the work she did – some essays and creative pieces.' She hands her a folder of the assignments Diana had submitted since the beginning of the semester. Mrs Brewer takes it, slowly opens it.

'She did a very good essay for our unit on the ghost story.' Brenda looks up at her then. Paula flushes, realizing it was a tactless thing to say. She says, 'I understand she wanted to be a vet, but she was also an exceptional English student.'

Brenda nods absently and says, 'She loved to read.' Her eyes travel around the living room and then come back to rest on her. 'She's here, you know.'

'Pardon?' Paula says.

'Diana. She's here, with me in the house. Her spirit. I can feel it. I know it.'

Paula stares at Brenda Brewer, startled.

'She's here right now, watching us,' she says. 'Say hi to Mrs Acosta, Diana. Isn't it nice that she's dropped by?'

Paula is worried for the other woman's sanity. She's delusional. She needs help.

'It's such a comfort to have her with me,' Mrs Brewer confides. 'But I do worry.'

Paula stares back at her, confused, alarmed.

'I'm afraid it's selfish. I like to have her here with me, but I worry that she can't find rest. Because she was murdered, you see? I think if someone dies young, so tragically, so unfairly, they can't move on. And that's a horrible weight for a mother to bear. On top of everything.'

All Paula can do is nod.

'She's going to be buried tomorrow,' Brenda says. 'Do you think, after the funeral, and the minister's blessing, she will find peace? Or maybe when they find her killer? If they ever do. But then I'll be all alone again.'

Paula doesn't know what to do. She reaches out and touches the other woman's arm. 'I'm sure she will find peace. We must all pray for her.'

She stays a little longer, and then she takes her leave, wondering who she can call to help Mrs Brewer, who seems to have lost her mind.

Chapter Forty-Five

I watch all this in dismay. I don't know how my mother can sense my presence, but it seems she can. Nobody else does. Unless she thinks I'm always here, even when I'm not. I can tell that what she's saying is making Mrs Acosta uneasy. She thinks Mom has lost it. If I were Mrs Acosta, that would be my reaction too.

Mom has always worried about me, and I guess she always will. That's what parents do. Now she's worried for my eternal soul, that I will never find rest. I haven't even thought about that. I never think about the future any more. I live in the present and think about the past. Is that what limbo is?

I worry about everything my mother has to bear. And I can't help her, I don't know how.

At least I can think about the past, and that's what I do, when I'm not spying on the living. I'm watching everyone trying to make sense of what happened to me. It's so frustrating, the way things come back to me only in snatches, in fragments. I guess that's what happens with trauma. I try to remember what happened that night but it's like someone has pulled a dark screen down over it. I try to remember more about the man in my backyard, but every time I do I feel overwhelming terror. It's just a blank. It makes me think of that poem we studied in school, Tell all the truth but tell it slant, *by Emily Dickinson. Mrs Acosta explained that one interpretation of the poem was that it meant that the truth can be too much to take in all at once, that sometimes you must approach it in a roundabout way. It makes me wonder what Emily Dickinson knew about trauma. Maybe more than we realize.*

I find myself thinking about Mr Turner, and what happened when I finally told Principal Kelly about what he did. I remember that well enough.

I hadn't enjoyed gym class or running practice since he'd walked in on me in the locker room, and I didn't want to be on the running team any more, but I stuck with it because I didn't want Cameron or anyone else asking why I'd quit. Everyone knew I was the best runner on the team. So it took me a couple of weeks before I did anything about it. The longer I went without saying anything, the harder it got to come forward. I thought Principal Kelly wouldn't believe me – I didn't have any proof, and it was my word against Mr Turner's. Mr Kelly had caught me in a lie before. I also didn't want anyone else to know what had happened, mostly because I was worried about what Cameron might do if he knew. I didn't even tell Riley. But finally, I got so

265

tired of Turner's dirty little glances that I went to Principal Kelly to get it to stop. I thought I could keep it among just the three of us. I asked for a meeting, Mr Kelly, Mr Turner, and me. I told Mr Kelly what was happening and that he had to set Mr Turner straight. That it couldn't happen any more.

He denied everything, like I knew he would. I could tell he was surprised and angry that I'd finally come forward – he thought he'd gotten away with it. He was all bluster and hurt feelings, saying it was just a misunderstanding, that the looks, the touches were just him doing his job, being a supportive coach. As far as what happened in the locker room – he blamed me, like he said he would. He said that I'd invited him into the locker room and dropped my towel, that I was lying. That maybe I had a crush on him. I was so outraged I could hardly speak. Kelly looked back and forth between us; he looked like he felt cornered.

Kelly sided with Turner. They're friends. They're men. I told him that I didn't want to make a formal complaint, that I didn't want anyone to know. I told them that I just wanted him to stop. That I didn't want it to go any further. We left it at that.

And now he's trying to weasel out of what he did. I should have handled it differently, but I refuse to see any of it as my fault. It infuriates me that Mr Turner blamed me for his appalling behaviour. But isn't that what they do? She shouldn't have been wearing that. She was into me. *And all the rest of it. I wish now that I'd told someone else about what happened, not just Mr Kelly. I should have told Riley. Or my mother. I should have told them everything. Because now I can't speak, and he gets to tell it his way.*

Joe Prior watches them search his apartment. It's a little embarrassing, because the place is a mess. He glances around the apartment and sees what they see. Walls that need fresh paint. Floors that need cleaning. The obviously secondhand furniture. There's wet towels on the floor in the bathroom and dirty dishes and beer cans on the coffee table. But he knows there's nothing here for them to find. He even says to the female officer looking through his things, as if he's a retail worker in a store, 'Can I help you find something?' She doesn't smile.

He tenses slightly when they look at his bookcase. He has a collection of true crime paperbacks, lots of serial killer stuff. They go through it carefully. One of them, the humourless woman, looks back at him, holding up his copy of *I'll Be Gone in the Dark*. That's not ideal, but lots of people read true crime; it doesn't make them murderers. They can't hold that against him.

But he wishes he'd never asked Roddy to lie for him.

Ellen stares at the series of messages on her phone early Tuesday evening. She promised herself she wouldn't look at them, but she hasn't been able to hold herself to it. Since the news hit about the other girl, she's been living in an unimaginable hell. Her parents are shocked, and being here

267

at the farm with them she feels smothered by their sympathy and concern, although they don't say much. They don't have to.

Her dad had been in a panic the night before, afraid that they'd find another dead girl in one of his fields. He'd been up long into the night – they all had, while that macabre search went on – but they'd found nothing. And there was that unspoken subtext the whole time – *What if it was Brad?* She'd felt like she was inside a fun house, where everything was distorted, or a Hitchcock film. How relieved she'd been when they found nothing. Completely wrung out.

She wants to forget all about Brad Turner, forget he ever existed. And yet –

There are the messages.

Ellen, I love you.

I did not do what they're saying. It's all lies. You know me. I couldn't do something like that.

How could I do something like that when I have you?

You're everything I've ever wanted. Please don't leave me.

I have an attorney. We had a good meeting and he told me that I have nothing to worry about. There is no evidence against me, for anything. He says this will all blow over. It's just that girl's word against mine, and no one will believe her.

Please talk to me.

A text pings on Brad's phone, startling him.

What did the attorney say, exactly?

He'd given up on hearing from Ellen, but now his heart leaps. He types the answering text quickly. Can you come over and we'll talk?

No. Just tell me.

Fine, he texts back. It's better than nothing, Brad thinks. At least she's talking to him.

He said it was good I called him. He said I had nothing to worry about. The stuff in the file at school is, in his opinion, minor. He was able to see Kelly and he showed him what was in it. The actual file is with the police, but he took a copy, and like I told you, it was nothing. It's not enough to cause me any real harm. As far as the attorney's aware (he has contacts in the police) they don't have any actual evidence against anyone in Diana's murder. The media is just trying to make more of this than it is, because of the murder. He sees it all the time.

He might be making things sound a bit better than the attorney did, but he thinks the gist of it is right. Kelly's file makes no mention of the incident in the locker room with Diana or of the ugliness that happened after. Kelly was trying to cover his own ass, because he was required by law to report it whether he believed it or not, even if Diana didn't want him to.

But Brad is still worried. Even afraid. He doesn't completely trust Kelly to keep quiet. But Brad tells himself it's too late for Kelly to tell the truth now. He'd be in deep trouble. He's made his decision, and he's going to have to live with it. Zoe coming forward now is a little worrying, but it's her word against his and she never went to the school about it at the time, which makes her look like an attention seeker. He's practically in the clear.

I would like to see that file, Ellen texts.

And then he sees his way clear to everything. If he could show Ellen that file then she would be reassured. She has no reason to think Kelly would lie for him. He's never told her about Kelly's affair with the young teacher; she doesn't know that he has this to hold over him. She will forgive him and come back to him. It won't look good if she doesn't. They will get married in December and all this will go away and be forgotten.

I'll talk to Kelly. If I can get a copy, will you come over here and look at it?

Yes.

Ellen stares at their text conversation. Is she doing the right thing? If Brad really did nothing wrong, if Diana was making it up, exaggerating and lying like he said, then he's

270

the victim here, and she should be supporting him 100 per cent. She allows herself a little hope. If the attorney is so sure, and if the account in the file is as mild as Brad says it is, then this nightmare might soon be over. Maybe the other girl only came forward after the murder for her little moment of fame. Maybe she's lying too.

Chapter Forty-Six

GRAHAM KELLY IS having a drink at the end of the day. It's been hell – the way everybody starts panicking when a teacher has been accused of sexual impropriety. It's something every principal, and every administrator, fears. And now it's happened on his watch. He rues the day he ever hired Brad Turner.

He finishes his scotch in one gulp and pours himself another. Sandra walks into the living room and catches him.

'What's going on?' she asks him uneasily.

'You know what's going on,' he snaps. He's told her what's in that file that he gave to the police, and she said it didn't seem so bad to her. She told him that as far as she can tell, he's done everything right. He documented the complaint, and after Diana died, he went to the police.

She eyes him carefully. 'I'm just wondering if there's something more you aren't telling me.'

He wonders what she would think if he told her the truth.

Should he? Would it be easier to bear? 'I might have made a mistake,' he says.

She steps closer. 'What mistake?'

He looks at her, uncertain. 'I should have reported it. And I didn't actually put the complaint in his official file. I kept it off the record, so to speak, in my own file.' He adds, 'And now the higher-ups know, and they aren't happy with me.' It's just a fraction of the truth, a mere crumb.

'Why the hell would you do that?'

She's upset. If this has upset her, then he certainly can't tell her the rest of it. 'Because Diana didn't want me to report it, she didn't want it to be official,' he says testily. 'She was adamant that it remain among just the three of us. She didn't want it to go any further. It's why I didn't believe her.'

She regards him suspiciously. 'Why didn't Diana want it to be official? Why complain at all then? That doesn't make sense.'

'No, it doesn't – unless she was lying. And that's what I thought, so I just kept a record for myself, and as far as I know, she was satisfied, and that was the end of it.'

She appears to think for a minute. Then she says, 'But you should have reported it, and documented it officially, whether she liked it or not. You should think of yourself. You can't afford to lose your job! That isn't going to happen, is it?'

'No,' he says, annoyed at her. 'They're pissed at me, but they don't want it to look any worse than it is.' At least, he hopes that's true. But he fears it isn't.

'Good,' she says.

273

She walks briskly out of the room, leaving him alone with his thoughts. He sits alone with his drink.

He has so many regrets. He wishes he were a different kind of man. A man of action, or at least a man who confronts things head-on and tries to put them right. He hasn't confronted the problems in his marriage. He and his wife have drifted apart. They don't sleep in separate rooms, but they might as well for all the distance between them. They had been in love once; it seems like a long time ago. He can still remember it, but they are different people now. Instead of facing this and trying to make things better – by going to marriage counselling, for instance – he'd avoided his problems at home by having a stupid fling with Cally Desjardins, twenty years his junior. She was a young, attractive new teacher who, it turns out, was only interested in him for what he might do for her career. It had all come crashing down around his ears. He'd felt like a fool, ashamed of himself. He wasn't afraid of Cally saying anything; it would not have reflected well on her either. He'd never realized that anyone knew. That Brad knew. Brad had seen them together. And now he's blackmailing him.

Graham Kelly sits alone in the living room, nursing his guilt and fear.

Paula is getting dinner ready, but her mind is somewhere else. She's thinking about Brenda Brewer and how alarming her behaviour had seemed this afternoon. She feels that she ought to do something. She needs to get her some help, but where?

Taylor wanders into the kitchen and asks, 'How long till supper?'

'About half an hour.'

She wanders out again.

That's another thing. Paula had spoken to a friend of hers, who has a daughter roughly the same age as Taylor. It hadn't been much use. Because Karen, apparently, had set up firm boundaries from the very start when she got her daughter her own phone. She knew her daughter's passwords for both her phone and computer and could go on them whenever she wished. Even as she'd listened to this, Paula asked herself if her friend was deluding herself. Or lying to her. Parenting can be so competitive. Maybe she had the passwords but was too afraid to look. Maybe her daughter had changed her passwords ages ago and Karen didn't know, and was living in wilful ignorance, as Paula suspects many parents these days are. Then Karen had admitted that, to be honest, she hadn't checked for months because her daughter gave her absolutely no cause for concern. It wasn't very reassuring.

Once she's got supper in the oven, Paula decides to seek out Taylor. She finds her in the den, looking at her phone. She sits down beside her on the old leather couch in front of the TV. She clears her throat and says, 'Taylor, honey, can we talk for a minute?' Her daughter looks up at her warily, like last time. *What's happened to her?* Paula thinks. *We used to be so close. Is this normal?* 'You don't seem so happy these days.'

'What is there to be happy about?'

Put that way, Paula's not certain how to reply. There's so much wrong with the world now – wars, climate change. *What a burden we have saddled our children with*, she thinks.

'Well,' she tries, 'we're very fortunate. We have a family, a home, our health, our freedom. You can pursue whatever dreams you want.' She knows as soon as she says it that this isn't the way to reach a thirteen-year-old. Taylor rolls her eyes.

'I'm thinking of changing schools,' Paula says.

'What? Why?'

'Because I don't think you having to go to high school where I teach is good for you, socially, I mean.'

'What? No.'

'I know what they say about me. Students will always complain about their teachers, I know that. It must make things awkward for you.'

Taylor shakes her head. 'No, mostly they think you're great. I mean, they think you're strict, but they respect you. Not like some of the other teachers.'

This is a pleasant surprise; maybe she's got it all wrong. But then what is bothering her daughter? She sees tears forming in Taylor's eyes, and then the dam breaks.

Chapter Forty-Seven

ELLEN LEAVES THE farm without telling her parents where she's going. She doesn't want them to know in case they try to stop her, but they'll figure it out anyway. Where else would she go?

She drives her little car down their long driveway and turns onto the gravel road at the end of it. It feels creepy, now, when she drives down this road. As she passes the fields, and approaches the one where the body was found, she sees the white cross again, at the side of the road. At the sight of it, she feels a stab of anxiety and asks herself what the hell she's doing. There's a hysteria inside her, hovering just beneath the surface of her skin. She's lost her natural optimism, her innate sense that everything is all right with the world. She has carried that within her from childhood, instilled in her by her parents, or perhaps she's just made that way. She's never had to doubt much of anything. Until now, when she's doubting everything. She needs to know the truth.

She wants to see this file. She wants to know exactly what Diana Brewer said about her fiancé. He says it's exaggeration and lies. She doesn't know whether to believe him. She'd like to speak to this attorney too. Is it true that Brad's got nothing to worry about? What about the other girl who's come forward? She wishes she could talk to her; maybe she could tell if the girl is lying.

When she arrives on Brad's street and parks, she glances up and sees him at the window, watching out for her. Her heart stumbles. Is this the last time she will ever come to this apartment? Is this the last time she will ever let herself see him? She observes his outline; he's smoking a cigarette, flicking the ash out the window. He's so effortlessly handsome, standing in the window, that it gives her a pang. He could have anyone, and he chose her. Why would he bother with teenage girls – unless there's something wrong with him, unless he's not normal? She doesn't like that he's taken up smoking again with a vengeance. It's a disgusting habit, she thinks. And that makes her worry about what other disgusting habits he might have.

She climbs the stairs with dread, and Brad opens his door before she even knocks.

'Ellen!' he says and takes her in his arms. She allows herself to be held, but she's stiff, and she doesn't hug him back. She doesn't say anything. When he releases her, she walks into the living room, takes off her coat, throwing it on the back of the sofa, and turns to face him, her arms crossed. 'I want to see this file.' It's why she's here – to see the file, not to see him.

'Yeah, sure, of course,' he says and goes into the kitchen.

She watches him pick a file up off the kitchen table and bring it to her in the living room.

'Fortunately,' he says, 'Graham photocopied it before he gave it to the police, so he made another copy for me.' He looks only slightly apprehensive as he hands it to her.

She sits down silently and opens the file. It's short, just a couple of handwritten pages. It outlines how Diana Brewer had requested a private meeting with him and Brad Turner. The meeting took place after school on the afternoon of October 11, 2022, in his office. Diana told them she felt that Turner looked at her inappropriately and suggestively, that he touched her unnecessarily and inappropriately on multiple occasions, and that it made her uncomfortable. She said she didn't want to make a formal complaint, but she wanted this behaviour to stop. Kelly notes that he did not find her convincing, that he didn't believe her account, that he was inclined to believe Turner and think that Diana had either exaggerated the situation or made the accusations up. He wasn't going to take it any further because Diana did not want him to, which further made him believe she'd invented it all. Kelly felt it hadn't happened at all, or that, at worst, it was all a misunderstanding. Turner denied most of it, but apologized to Diana in front of him for any apparent misunderstanding and said that nothing like that would happen in future.

That's all.

Ellen finishes reading and stares down at the pages, getting her thoughts together. It's just as Brad said it would be.

Kelly was there, and he clearly took his side. Kelly believed Brad, not Diana. It's just that . . . this other girl has come forward now. What is she going to say?

Finally, she nods and looks up at him. She still doesn't like it – any suggestion that her fiancé might have looked at a teenage girl the wrong way, that he might have touched her inappropriately, even if it was a 'misunderstanding'. She would prefer that he'd had better judgement. She would prefer that she could be certain that Diana had made it all up. And this other girl too. But is that what really happened?

'What about the other girl?' she asks. 'What's she going to say?' Brad flushes and looks down at the carpet. And then she realizes. 'You already know. What is she saying?' Ellen asks, her voice sharp.

'She's lying, making stuff up, just like Diana,' he says. His voice is bitter. 'The police interviewed me, yesterday morning. She's claiming I walked in on her, in the girls' locker room. It's bullshit. It never happened.'

Ellen's heart sinks again.

He narrows his eyes at her, annoyed. 'There is no record at the school of this other girl ever complaining about me, so my attorney says I shouldn't be too worried. It makes her look like an attention seeker, coming forward now.'

Ellen looks back at him uneasily, not completely re-assured. Does he really love her? Or does he just need her to stand by him?

Prior is sitting in his recliner at home, his feet up. Working construction is physically exhausting, and it's been a stressful day. The police have finally cleared out of his apartment. He's scrolling through the news on his phone as he eats the thick beef sandwich that he's made for supper, washing it down with a cold beer. He sees the news about that teacher and another girl. Good. Maybe they'll leave him alone now, he thinks. They found nothing at his apartment, and this teacher looks like he might have done it.

He continues to idly look through the news. There's a story that catches his immediate interest. MISSING GIRL FOUND DEAD. There's a photograph of her – a school photo, familiar. That photo was plastered in the media for weeks. They've found her in upstate New York, far out in the woods. He's put the sandwich down. He reads the article. Found by a hunter. It's always a hunter. Or a hiker. Somebody with a dog. The grave had been disturbed by animals, and the hunter's dog discovered it. He gets up and grabs himself another beer.

Chapter Forty-Eight

PAULA HUGS HER daughter while she cries. Then, she listens, trying not to let her face reflect her dismay at what she's hearing. It all tumbles out. Sadie Kelly has been making her daughter's life hell. Mocking her. Singling her out and making fun of her at school and online. Turning her friends against her.

'Why would she do that?' Paula asks.

'Because she can,' Taylor answers with a sniffle. 'She always has someone she's picking on, and lately it's been me. No one stands up to her.'

'Why didn't you tell me?'

'Because she said if I complained about it she would get you fired, because her dad is the principal.'

'Oh, honey, I wish you'd told me. She can't get me fired.' Paula's always known Sadie is a handful, but she didn't know she's a bully. The fact that she's been picking on her daughter and using her own job there as leverage – she's

282

almost speechless with anger. How can she do such a thing? How does she get away with it? Why do the other girls follow her lead? What's wrong with these kids?

'There's something else I didn't tell you,' Taylor says. 'About Mr Turner.'

Paula's stomach takes a turn. She'd already asked her daughter before about Turner and been reassured. She'd believed this offensive behaviour of Turner's was something confined to Diana, and then this other girl. 'What?'

'Sometimes, when no one else could see, he would stare at me, at my chest.' She flushes pink. 'I didn't like it.' She adds, more firmly, 'He knew I didn't like it, but he just smiled and did it anyway.'

'Why didn't you tell me this before, when I asked you?'

'I'm sorry I didn't tell you – but it's embarrassing.' She adds uncertainly, 'He never actually touched me, so I wasn't sure if I should say anything.'

'Oh honey! I'm so glad you've told me now.'

She should have insisted that something be done about Turner the first time Kelly told her about it. It's not her daughter's fault that she didn't have the confidence to go to the principal, or to her. She's only thirteen. She should have been protected from this sort of thing. They have all failed her. All she can do is hold her daughter, comfort her, and say, 'The police know about him now. You don't need to worry about him any more. He's been suspended from work, and I don't think he'll ever be back.' She doesn't verbalize her growing fear that he might be a murderer. She cups her daughter's tear-stained face in her hands. 'I'm so glad you told me all this, Taylor. You shouldn't have to deal with any of this on your own. Him, or Sadie either.'

'Will I have to go to the police,' Taylor asks anxiously, 'like that other girl?'

'Maybe. I think we probably should,' Paula says. 'But you don't have to decide right now.'

It's late, almost eleven p.m., and I'm hovering in the interview room at the police station. They have brought Prior back in, and I'm watching him with equal parts revulsion and curiosity.

Detective Stone says, 'Let's cut to the chase. This has happened to you before.'

'I'm sorry?' Prior says.

I prick up my ears.

'You've been questioned by police before, in connection with a missing girl. Katie Cantor.'

'Who's that?' he says, but he looks uncomfortable, as if his casualness is forced.

'You remember,' the detective says. 'You must, because it's no fun being questioned by the police, being under suspicion for something like this – you've already told us you don't like it.' Stone is leaning toward him now. 'Katie Cantor, sixteen years old, went missing in upstate New York, near Albany, approximately two years ago. A pretty girl, worked in a corner store. You used to bother her at work too. You were questioned and released. Maybe you haven't heard. They've found her body.'

I gaze down at Prior in horror.

The police keep hammering at him, but he doesn't crack. I wonder if he killed this other girl. That's what the detectives want to find out. I want to know too. Have there been more? Am I one of many? I feel for this girl, Katie Cantor. I wonder if she's around here somewhere, floating about, like me. I wonder if I can find her. Maybe we could be friends.

Now they are pushing him, hard. 'You drive around in that truck of yours a lot. Why? What are you doing? Are you looking for girls? Is that what you were doing in Quebec? A little too hot at home right now, is it?' Detective Stone stares hard at Prior. 'They have her body. And they may be able to get DNA evidence from it,' the detective says. 'I guess you thought she'd never be found.'

Prior shakes his head. 'I had nothing to do with that girl. Or with Diana Brewer. I want an attorney.'

'Sure. Call an attorney. Two girls you chatted up are dead. You had Roddy lie to give you an alibi. We're going to hold you overnight. We'll question you again tomorrow, with your attorney.'

I watch him struggle when they take him down to the cells. And then I go home, to my mother.

I find her in the house, talking out loud to me, calling out to me across the rooms, the same way she used to when I was alive. It's like she's trying to pretend that nothing has changed. It makes me sad.

I think for a long time about Prior. He'd probably been in my car and knew where I lived. He'd chatted up two girls at retail stores – me and Katie Cantor – and we both ended up dead.

Tuesday, Oct. 25, 2022, 11:15 p.m.

I like to write at night when the house is completely quiet. Dad is dead to the world – he's usually had a few by bedtime. I'm the only light sleeper in this house. The smoke detector went off once in the middle of the night, and I'm the only one that got up. Mom takes sleeping pills and often sleeps in the guest room, away from Dad. She says it's because he snores, but I know she can't stand him. I wish she'd leave him. Maybe when I go off to university she will. I'll tell her she should.

These are strange, disorienting days. I'm feeling nostalgic, anxious. I miss Diana so much. I miss our old crowd, our old life.

Mrs Brewer acted odd today when Riley and I went to see her again after school. I can't quite put my finger on it, but she seemed to be not quite all there. Riley noticed it too. She seemed very distracted, but the funeral is tomorrow, and must be weighing on her.

I'm worried about Riley, too, about how she'll cope tomorrow. She's really anxious. And she has these bizarre ideas about Diana's spirit hanging around because she was murdered. I hope she doesn't go any farther down the crazy road. I know she's grieving. I know she's scared. That text from Diana's phone really upset her. I suppose lots of girls in Fairhill are feeling scared now. Diana was murdered, and taken from her home, in our sleepy little town.

Everyone is on edge.

Chapter Forty-Nine

THE NEXT MORNING, the morning of the funeral, Riley wakes early and lies anxiously in bed, dreading what's to come. She's thinking about Diana, and where she is now. Then, from out of nowhere, she remembers the abandoned cemetery on the outskirts of town. She can picture it, on a low rise surrounded by trees, quite overgrown. She'd forgotten all about it. There's no church there; as far as she knows, there never was. It's just a small cemetery, and she hasn't looked there.

After breakfast, she tells her mother she's going out for a bit with Evan, that she won't be long. It's a lie, she's not going to bring Evan. She's nervous, going out on her own, but it's something she must do. The day is cloudy, with a chill in the air. She gets on her bike and rides out of Fairhill, turning left at the edge of town. She pedals down a gravel road for a couple of miles and then she sees it, just as she remembered. She stops and gets off her bike, breathing heavily from the exertion. There's a sign inside the fenced area: MACKLIN CEMETERY. She hesitates before she opens the gate. What if she doesn't find him? What if she does?

She walks solemnly among the gravestones. The thought of Diana's grave, waiting for her this very afternoon, is never far away. She wanders slowly from the front of the cemetery toward the back, reading the headstones, sometimes straining to make out the names and dates – and then she finds him.

Simon Foster, born 1861, died 1873.

It's a shock. She stands in front of the modest marker, frozen in place. And then she collapses, sinking to her knees on the cold ground. The discovery deeply unsettles her and makes her worry for Diana. What if it's true, about Emily at the bridge? What if she's been hanging around, angry and lost, all this time, because she'd been jilted and killed herself? What if Diana is stuck, also angry and lost, because she'd been murdered?

Riley stares at the marker with Simon's name, feels the chill seep up from the ground into her bones. She can't talk about this with Evan. He'd just tell her it was a coincidence, that coincidences happen all the time. She can't talk about this with anyone, not even her mother. They'd think she was cracking up. The only one she could share this with is Diana, and she's gone.

But then she realizes that there *is* one person who might not think she's nuts – Sadie Kelly. She was there that night too.

The day is grey and grim; very appropriate for a funeral, Edward Farrell thinks, staring out the bedroom window as he dons his black suit. The funeral is at the United Church at one p.m. The whole town has pretty much shut down, according to Shelby, who'd been out earlier. She is in the bedroom with him, putting on a black dress. Fortunately, Cameron had a decent dark suit in his closet from the recent wedding of a second cousin. Edward prays that they all get through it okay, that Cameron doesn't break down, that there are no ugly scenes. He's particularly afraid that there might be ugliness directed toward his son, and toward him and Shelby. A lot of people who will be at the funeral probably think Cameron did it. Edward is afraid of that himself. Cameron has certainly given them lots of reason to doubt.

And Edward hadn't helped the situation, by going out to that farmer's field at night. He'd seen in the news that they'd searched that field the same night. He thinks it's because he was seen. He felt like he couldn't breathe when he found out, that his actions had tipped them off. What if they'd found what he could not? But they hadn't found anything – or, at least, they haven't said so.

They had discussed whether they should even go to the funeral but had decided that more harm would be done by staying away. People would talk either way. Better to put in an appearance, to hold up their heads. And so the three of them, in their mourning clothes, get into the car together without speaking.

As they arrive at the church, Shelby watches people anxiously. She is nervous about the funeral. She just wants to get through it, can't wait for it to be over. They will attend the service, and afterward walk to the burial site behind the church to pay their respects, but that's it. They have sent flowers. But they have decided not to approach Mrs Brewer to offer condolences. It's too risky. They don't know what she might do, or say, at the sight of Cameron.

People in town have been avoiding Shelby, knowing that her son is a suspect in Diana's murder. Everyone knows that he's been questioned repeatedly, that he saw her that night, that he's retained an attorney. She feels as if they have been shunned, cast out. Because what could be worse than parents who raise a child who kills another child? All sympathy is on Brenda Brewer's side. There's a great outpouring of that. And while Shelby understands that, and even agrees with it, she can't help but feel bitter at what she has suffered, and is suffering, as Cameron's mother. And if he *didn't* do it, think of what Cameron is suffering!

The truth is, they don't *know*. They might not ever know. Sometimes, she thinks that is the best she can hope for.

Cameron, even in his misery, despair and anxiety, frets at the tight fit of the shirt collar around his neck, the unaccustomed formality of the suit. He feels so out of joint with the world. He and his parents arrived early and slipped into one of the back pews in order not to make an entrance. He avoids meeting anyone's eyes, and as he sits, he tries to keep his gaze on the floor or on the back of the wooden pew in front of him. But he can't help his eyes straying sometimes.

Now he sees Riley and Evan, entering the church together. They start up the aisle, Riley in a plain black dress Cameron has never seen before, Evan in black trousers with a sharp crease and a white shirt, no jacket. He doesn't have a suit, apparently. Riley is already crying, but Evan looks stoic, like he's desperate to hold it together. Riley's mother and Evan's parents follow after them, looking grim. Cameron forgets to look down at the floor and stares at them, his former friends. As they reach the front of the church to take their seats, Evan turns and glances around the church as if surveying who is there. He happens to catch Cameron's eye and holds it for a second. Cameron refuses to look away, wondering if Evan and Riley think he killed Diana. He's not going to let Evan – or anyone else – intimidate him. He has every right to be here – he loved her.

His eyes suddenly blur with tears. Can't they see he's hurting too?

The funeral has created a crisis of its own in Ellen's world, which was already in turmoil. The murdered girl was found in the Resslers' field. Ellen's father feels that therefore he and her mother must go. But he delicately suggested that she stay home.

Should she? She would like to hide until all of this is over. She didn't know Diana Brewer personally. She's embarrassed and humiliated at the gossip and rumours swirling around Brad, who, as far as anyone knows, is still her fiancé.

After she read the file yesterday, she felt a bit clearer in her own mind. It was as he'd said, but this other girl was worrying her. It's not the detectives she's worried about.

They can't reasonably think Brad murdered Diana. What possible motive could he have had? She'd made a fairly minor complaint, really. It was laughable – nobody would get murdered over that. She's inclined to stand by him, to ride it out, for now. But there's this niggling doubt, gnawing away at her.

Her parents are less forgiving. They are appalled at the allegations made against their future son-in-law. They are of the 'where there's smoke there's fire' school of thinking. They want her to break it off, cancel the wedding. But Ellen considers herself more open-minded. She's more apt to consider that the girls might have made it up – that it's at least a possibility. They had argued about it, the night before at the kitchen table. Backed into a corner, Ellen found herself staunchly supporting Brad, while her mother and father listened in dismay. She told them about the file, how Principal Kelly, *who was there at their meeting*, had fully supported Brad's version of events, and firmly believed that Diana had not been telling the truth. She told them that Diana hadn't wanted to go to the authorities, and that made it more likely that she *was* lying.

'But everyone said she was a good, honest girl,' her mother said doubtfully. 'Why would she do that?'

'Teenagers do stupid things,' Ellen shot back.

'So do men,' her mother said, and Ellen found herself unable to answer.

'I have to stand by him,' Ellen insisted finally, becoming tearful. 'What else can I do? The wedding's in less than two months. We're buying a house—' And then she hadn't been able to speak for crying.

Brad was going to go to the funeral. He could hardly stay away, he told her. It would just make people think he had something to be ashamed of, and he didn't. He wanted Ellen to go with him, to show the world that she believed him. He insisted that she go, that she be at his side.

But her parents wanted her to distance herself from him, to go with them, or stay home.

In the end, Ellen decided to go to the funeral with Brad. She felt that if she didn't, her wedding would be off. And she wasn't quite prepared to make that decision just yet.

So now, here she is, walking into the church on Brad's arm, a little bit late, because they wanted to slip in the back unnoticed. When they arrive, it's standing room only, so they press their way in. The service has already started.

Ellen stands, eyes front, focused on the minister.

Chapter Fifty

BRAD TURNER HOLDS Ellen's hand firmly, as if he's afraid she will turn and run. He needs her here with him. How would it look if she deserted him now? It was touch and go whether she would come to the funeral with him at all, and he's angry at her for putting him through that, although he's had to hide it. That she could even consider such a public snub, at a time like this. But she's coming around. Thank God for the skimpy notes Kelly wrote; he'd left out so much damning information.

He looks out over the packed church. The coffin is up at the front, surrounded by flowers. It's difficult to pick out who people are, from just the backs of their heads. But that's Diana's mother, right at the front, bent over and sobbing quietly. There's a man beside her – Diana's father? And also in the front row, Evan and Riley, Diana's friends. That makes him think of Cameron and wonder where he is. He glances around and doesn't see him, but it's packed in here. Many of the people he recognizes as staff and students from the school. Kelly is there, in a rare family moment, with his wife and three difficult children. He spies Paula Acosta, and her daughter, Taylor. He bites his lower lip. She might be a worry. He continues to survey the crowd and spots the two detectives that he despises so much, Stone and Godfrey. Of course they're here, he thinks bitterly. And then he sees that little bitch, Zoe, sandwiched between her parents. His heart rate spikes.

Graham Kelly doesn't like being in church. Not with Diana lying in her coffin up there in front of him, people weeping all around him. Not with the guilt he's carrying on his conscience. Maybe he contributed to her death. And here he is in church, before God, sticking to a lie that he is finding it increasingly difficult to live with. Maybe he will have to tell the truth, even though he might lose everything. Maybe he will have to go to the police after the funeral and tell them what Diana *really* said, all the ugly things he left out of his notes. He's come to realize that he's a weak man, a coward, someone who runs away from problems. He didn't want to get involved; he wanted to pretend it wasn't happening. He didn't want to face things. Diana didn't want to go to the police, but he should have. He should have gotten rid of Brad Turner. He should have protected her.

Paula is standing beside Graham Kelly, her feelings in tumult. She has always found funerals difficult – who doesn't? And Diana was so young and died so horribly. Her husband is with her, their daughter, Taylor, between them.

She glances at Brenda Brewer, in the pew on the other side of the church. Her head is down and she's weeping throughout the service, clutching a tissue to her nose and mouth. Paula remembers how she was in her house yesterday, talking aloud to Diana as if she were an ethereal presence, sitting right there with them. It had made Paula uncomfortable, and afraid for the woman's sanity.

She can feel the distress coming off Kelly beside her. She is wound up tightly herself. She has not yet had the opportunity – and this is hardly the time and place – to tell him about Taylor's problems with his daughter, Sadie, and with Brad Turner. She's angry that her daughter had to experience this, and while most of her anger is directed at Sadie and Brad, some of it is for Kelly, who should have prevented it. She knows it will be difficult, but Taylor must tell the police what happened to her. This kind of thing can't be ignored. People like Brad Turner shouldn't be allowed to teach children at all. They shouldn't be allowed anywhere near them. *And what if he's a murderer?*

Brenda Brewer is trying to say goodbye. That's what funerals are for, and it's time to say goodbye to her daughter. She had a long, painful talk this morning with the minister. She was honest with him, and told him that Diana was still here, living at home. She told him her concerns – that Diana might never find rest for her eternal soul. She confessed her selfishness and guilt for wanting her daughter to stay.

He'd seemed surprised but had recovered his composure.

He talked a lot about the Bible, and quoted Scripture. He tried to be comforting and reassuring, told her she should forgive herself for any selfish feelings at such a difficult time. But he clearly had no bloody idea how long Diana would be trapped in her shadow existence, a tortured ghost, or what it might take for her to find peace.

The service is over, and Riley realizes she hasn't listened to a word. The minister spoke, and Diana's father and Evan did a reading, and there were hymns and more readings, but it has all passed over her. She simply stared at the closed coffin the whole time, knowing that Diana was in there. At one point she felt herself sagging, when they were standing for a hymn, and Evan propped her up.

And now it is time to filter out to the graveyard. The pallbearers carry the coffin quietly and reverently out of the nave and down the aisle as the mourners watch. Now there are louder sobs and muted weeping. Riley can feel the tears streaming down her face.

She holds her mother's hand as they walk out of the church into the grey, blustery day, and follow the crowd to the gravesite. This is the part that Riley has been most dreading. She can feel her anxiety climbing; she is lightheaded.

They are gathered around the grave now. The freshly dug pit is in front of her, a deep, dark rectangle, like a gaping, monstrous mouth without teeth. Riley feels a tremor begin throughout her body. What is it about the burial that bothers her so much? The pile of earth beside the grave looms in the corner of her eye, somehow threatening. The

297

coffin is lowered slowly into the ground. Evan is standing beside her. The minister speaks a few words.

'We therefore commit this body to the ground, earth to earth, ashes to ashes, dust to dust . . .' His voice fades away.

She sees roses, soft and white, drift down onto the top of the coffin, silently and as if in slow motion. But then she hears a sharp *chunk*, as the first fistful of damp earth hits the coffin in the ground. She faints.

How many people get to observe their own funeral? Maybe more than we think. It's very difficult for me to watch. Imagine it for yourself, seeing the people who knew you, and how they react. It's upsetting seeing so much genuine distress. Of course, someone is faking it. Someone here might have killed me. Unless it was Joe Prior, who as far as I know is still in a cell at the police station.

It's my mother I feel the worst for; she is suffering the most, and she's the one who will miss me the most. She will probably never recover from this. My father – I doubt he cares that much. After my mom, it's Riley I feel the most for. This is tearing her apart. And Evan – he is clearly strug-gling too. Kelly seems tortured – I bet he's sorry now that he didn't listen to me. I'll never forgive him for believing Mr Turner over me. I dismiss him with contempt. I search through all the people who have come to see me off, look-ing for Cameron, looking for Mr Turner. I see Aaron Bolduc, my manager at the Home Depot, the one who always walked me to my car at the end of the night. I think he was sweet on me, but he was too respectful, too much of a gentleman to show it.

I find Cameron first. He's way at the back, staring at the back of the pew in front of him. There are tears in his eyes at least. Are they for me or for him? I don't linger because I find I can't bear to look at him. I turn away, and then I see him standing by the exit: Mr Turner. He has a cool, unmoved look on his face. He should at least be faking it. That must be his fiancée's hand he's holding. She looks far away, as if her mind is somewhere else. What kind of woman would be with a man like that? I look back again at Mr Turner, at that subtle smirk.

And suddenly, it happens again – the overwhelming fear – and I'm no longer in the church.

I'm back in my bedroom, the man in the dark outside my window, and I'm terrified. I move quickly away from the window and hit the light switch on the wall so the room goes dark. My heart is pounding. I sit on the bed and I'm fumbling around for my cell phone, but I've left it downstairs, in the kitchen. I freeze and listen, but I can't hear anything. I creep over to the window again and peek out. I don't see him. I don't know if he's gone, or if he's somewhere near. I haven't been down to lock up the house yet, and I know the back door is unlocked. And then I hear it opening, quietly.

I freeze. I'm quaking with fear, furious with myself for leaving my cell phone downstairs. I'm breathing so fast I think he must be able to hear me. But he already knows where I am. He saw me in my bedroom window. There's no lock on my bedroom door. I consider making my way to the bathroom and locking the door there. I don't know if it will hold if he tries to break it down. I can hear him now, his footsteps downstairs. My legs trembling, I decide to dash for the bathroom at the end of the hall. But I've waited too long. When I slowly open the bedroom door a crack to look down the hall, he's right there, standing at the top of the stairs. I try to slam my bedroom door, but suddenly he has his foot in it, and his hands are on the edge of the door. I see black leather gloves. I scream and retreat further into my bedroom; I won't be able to make it past him to the bathroom now.

And that's where the memory stops, his face in the dark, his hands on the door, the gloves, me screaming . . .

But now I know who killed me.

It was my teacher. Mr Turner.

I feel a fresh surge of grief and rage. I don't want to be here, on the other side of the veil. I want to be there, where I belong. I want to make him pay. I want to haunt that bastard Mr Turner for the rest of his miserable life – if I could just figure out how.

Chapter Fifty-One

JOE PRIOR PACES his cell nervously. He doesn't like being caged. It reminds him of when his father would lock him in the closet for days at a time, so it triggers all sorts of unpleasant things for him. The thought of a long stretch in prison makes him break out in a cold sweat. He's afraid he's done for this time.

He thought he'd gotten away with Katie Cantor. He was questioned about her, but they'd had to let him go because there was no evidence. When he buried her, so far out in the middle of nowhere, he thought she'd never be found, but even so, he moved out of state, this time to Vermont. It's just sheer shitty luck that her body was found *now*, when they're looking at him for Diana Brewer, a girl he didn't kill.

But these fucking detectives had found out that he'd been questioned about Katie because he'd flirted with her at her cash register. Fuck, fuck, fuck. And now another girl he chatted to in a store is dead, and they've probably communicated with the police in New York State, and they're going to come and arrest him and have him taken back to New York, and they'll get a fucking warrant to get his fucking DNA because they'll probably have DNA from Katie Cantor's body. Fuck. His entire body is clammy inside his clothes.

He had nothing to do with the girl at Home Depot. He chatted her up, but she was never going to be a target. He'd learned his lesson after he'd been questioned because they saw him chatting to Katie on the surveillance footage. He never talks to his targets any more, is careful never to be captured on camera. It's just his shitty luck that someone murdered the Brewer girl. And if they get his DNA they'll have him cold for Katie Cantor. He can't squirm out of this one.

He hears someone coming and stops pacing.

'You're wanted upstairs.'

'I want my lawyer.'

'He's already here.'

Upstairs, he takes his place in the interview room. It's Wednesday, early evening. The detectives took their time, but apparently they were at the girl's funeral. His lawyer barely looks at him. Joe stares back at Stone and Godfrey, hating them with his whole heart. What happened? His luck ran out, that's all. And he made that stupid mistake with Roddy. If he hadn't done that, would he be sitting here now? Maybe. Maybe not. He wouldn't have had to make that stupid mistake in the first place if someone else hadn't murdered the girl from Home Depot.

Detective Stone informs him that he's under arrest for the murder of Katie Cantor and that New York State Police are on their way to collect him and take him back to New York to answer charges. Then he says, 'I understand they do have crime-scene DNA. So they won't have much difficulty getting a warrant for yours, to see if it matches.'

Joe turns to his lawyer. 'Can they do this?'

'Yes,' the attorney says.

'Do you have anything to say?' Stone asks.

Joe says, beginning to sweat, 'No comment.'

'Is there anything you want to tell us about Diana Brewer?'

'I didn't kill her.'

'Maybe not,' Stone concedes. 'Diana wasn't bound with wire. Katie was.'

'I didn't do it,' Joe protests wildly. 'I didn't fucking kill her! I didn't kill anybody!'

Joe lunges up out of his chair but is quickly restrained.

Wednesday evening, Graham Kelly sits in front of the two detectives as if he is in front of a tribunal sitting in judgement on him. He's not a religious man, but after the funeral in the church today – that wretched hour – he couldn't live with himself any longer. And he didn't want that bastard Brad Turner to do any more harm, to possibly get away with murder. He found he wouldn't be able to live with himself after all.

First he told his wife about his stupid, short-lived affair – she didn't take it well – and then he went to the police station. He has told them everything Diana told him, unburdened his soul, he has even wept; all that remains is to see what the fallout will be. For Brad. For him. For his family. He knows he is finished as an educator. Perhaps he can sell life insurance. Or cars. He likes cars.

Now Stone says, 'I wish you had told us this earlier.'

He lowers his eyes in shame. 'I do too.'

Turner has been called down to the police station. It's rather late. They didn't say why, just told him on the phone that they had a few more questions. The news had broken earlier that evening that Joe Prior had been arrested in the two-year-old murder of a girl in New York State. Turner had been pleased when he'd heard that about Prior. An arrest for the murder of Diana Brewer will surely follow, he told himself.

But he is worried about Graham Kelly.

He'd called his attorney and asked him to meet him there. Ellen doesn't know; she'd gone back home after the funeral earlier that day.

'We know a lot more about what happened between you and Diana Brewer than we did last time we spoke,' Stone begins.

Brad feels the blood drain from his face, but he tries to brazen it out. He shrugs. 'I don't see how. Nothing happened between me and Diana, other than what I've told you already.'

'That's not true though, is it?' Stone says, becoming aggressive. 'Graham Kelly has just been in here, and he told us a very different story.'

Brad tries not to show his alarm. *Fucking Kelly. What has he said? Has he told them everything?* He shrugs again, with feigned nonchalance, but says nothing.

'We know that you entered Diana's house uninvited – through the unlocked back door – the night before she died. We know that you wore gloves. We know that you frightened her, that you made her take off her clothes and looked at her. We know you warned her not to tell, because if she did, you would say that she *invited* you over – that she'd initiated it, just like in the locker room. Oh yes, we know about the locker room. You told her no one would ever believe her. We know that she went to Graham Kelly the next morning, for a second meeting, that she told him all this in front of you. She threatened to go to the police if you ever came near her again. But, rather conveniently, she was murdered that very night.'

Brad tries to show no emotion. He can't speak. He can feel his lawyer beside him looking at him in dismay.

'You had motive for killing her – to stop her going to the police. You didn't think Kelly would tell the truth because he'd covered up for you already about the locker-room incident, and it would make him look bad, end his career. And you knew you could blackmail him with your knowledge of his extramarital affair. But you know what you didn't factor in?' Stone leans forward across the table. 'Unlike you, Kelly apparently has a conscience. And he couldn't live with it any longer. He believed you after the first meeting, but he wasn't so sure after the second. Then he learned you had no alibi, and then you tried to blackmail him.' He adds, 'He's afraid you killed her.'

'That's ridiculous,' Brad says. 'He's lying. You only have his word for it. None of that ever happened. Diana was lying! He's trying to set me up!'

'Now why would he do that when he has so much to lose? His job. His wife. His family. His standing in the community.' Stone adds, 'Oh, and by the way, guess who else has come forward. Taylor Acosta. Remember her?'

Chapter Fifty-Two

ELLEN IS BACK at the farm with her parents. They are distraught, and she is sorry for it. She is feeling sorry for herself too. They told her that there was a lot of gossip at the funeral, and afterward, about Brad, about what he's accused of. They have urged her to break off the engagement. They have reassured her that they can get out of the house deal somehow. Or maybe, they suggest, she can still get the house on her own, if she lets them help her. There are ways to fix this, they keep telling her, as long as she doesn't marry him. She wants to shut her eyes and cover her ears with her hands, but she just sits perfectly still at the kitchen table while they bombard her with advice. At the very least, they implore, she should wait.

They'd heard the news earlier about Joe Prior, that he has been arrested for the murder of another girl. Does that mean he probably murdered Diana too? Ellen doesn't know. She hardly cares. If Brad interferes with young girls, that's enough for her to end their engagement. If it's true. But she doesn't know who or what to believe.

When they sit down to watch the eleven o'clock news together in the living room, they are all depleted and on edge. What they hear is unexpected and shocking. It's that familiar reporter from KCVS who deals the blow. She stands in front of the Fairhill Police Station, her hair blowing around her face.

'Vermont State Police have arrested local man Joe Prior in Fairhill for the murder of Katie Cantor two years ago. The missing schoolgirl's body was discovered recently in an isolated wooded area in upstate New York. Prior will be taken back to New York State to face charges there. Police hope DNA evidence will confirm whether Prior is the man who raped and murdered the sixteen-year-old, who had been missing until her body was discovered just yesterday. In other breaking news, high school gym teacher Brad Turner has been arrested for the murder of popular schoolgirl Diana Brewer, whose body was found last Friday morning in a local farmer's field. More details as we get them.'

Ellen stares at the TV in shock. She feels a kind of total emptiness, which is completely disorienting. She can feel her parents watching her in horror and pity. So, now she knows. She won't be getting married after all.

Paula watches the TV news, stunned. She'd taken Taylor to the police station earlier that evening, where Taylor told her story.

'Jesus,' her husband breathes beside her.

She turns to him, her mind reeling. 'Finally,' she breathes.

'They've arrested him for murder, and he was targeting our daughter, the way he targeted Diana . . .' It makes her nauseated, to have her worst fears confirmed.

'They've got him now,' Martin says. But he seems to be in shock. 'He won't be hurting any more girls.'

She remembers earlier that day, at the school gym, where Kelly had arranged a casual wake after the funeral. The gym was packed, and they'd soon run out of sandwiches. She'd sought Kelly out to tell him that he'd done a good job with the wake, that it was thoughtful of him to do it, but there was something else she wanted to say to him. She got him alone in a corner and told him about what his daughter Sadie had been doing to Taylor. He'd looked very upset and said, 'I'm sorry. I'll deal with her.' Then she'd told him about what Brad had been doing to Taylor. He'd seemed to stand a little straighter and repeated, 'I'm so sorry,' and then he'd left her.

Now she wonders if he's the one who gave the police information that led to Turner's arrest. She wonders what he might have known all this time, remembers how he'd looked as if he felt he had blood on his hands.

They might have had a narrow escape, Paula thinks. But for the grace of God, she might be in Brenda Brewer's shoes right now. She can hardly breathe.

Wednesday, Oct. 26, 2022, 11 p.m.

Diana is dead, and they've arrested Prior for the murder of some other girl, but not, apparently, for the murder of Diana. Because they've arrested Mr Turner for that, finally. I wonder what information led to his arrest. Poor Diana. I wish she'd felt able to confide in someone. It might have made a difference.

I texted Riley repeatedly tonight after the news to talk to her about it, but she didn't answer. Maybe she's asleep. Maybe her mother gave her something to calm her down. She had a very difficult time with the funeral.

The funeral . . . It was all so tragic. It was a nice service, though. I think Mrs Brewer can at least be happy that the funeral was beautiful, and there were so many flowers. The church was absolutely packed. Everyone was there. My reading went okay, although I was really nervous. I get anxious when I have to do any public speaking, but I wanted to honour Diana. I stumbled over the last line, then somehow made it back to my seat, lightheaded with grief. I was afraid that Cameron might try to speak to Mrs Brewer, so I stayed close to her as much as I could. But he didn't come anywhere near her.

After her, my main concern was Riley. I kept a close eye on her. I know she was anxious about the funeral, and the burial especially. She seems to almost have a phobia about it. Still, I was surprised when she fainted. One minute she was standing there beside me – swaying a little, so I put my hand out to steady her – and then she just slipped through my fingers and was down on the ground on her back, her face white, her black hair tumbling on the grass. I got down on my knees beside her, calling her name, while everyone looked on. But her mother pushed me away, and a doctor in the crowd stepped forward. Riley came to pretty quickly, and her mother put her arm around her and bustled her out of the churchyard home. I turned and went back to the gravesite, but things were essentially over. I went home with Mrs Brewer and stayed with her a while and made her a cup of tea. Her ex-husband left before too long. Mrs Brewer hadn't arranged any gathering afterward; she hadn't wanted to. So Mr Kelly had organized sandwiches and coffee in the gym at school for anyone who wanted to go. But after I left Mrs Brewer, I just went home. I was too tired and depressed to do anything else.

Chapter Fifty-Three

RILEY WAKES SLOWLY, having at last fallen fitfully to sleep only around dawn. Her body and limbs are heavy, and she stares at the ceiling and feels a kind of smothering dread hanging over her. She'd gone straight to bed after the funeral yesterday, knocked out by half a Valium her worried mother had given her. She'd risen many hours later and had watched the late news with her mother. Turner had been arrested for Diana's murder. She couldn't believe it.

Immediately the texts came fast and furious from Evan, but she ignored them. She couldn't face talking about it any more that night. She just wanted to be with her mom, pretend that none of it had ever happened. But then afterward, because she'd slept after the funeral, she'd hardly slept that night.

It's over, she tells herself now. She should be feeling some sort of relief, but what she feels is an increasing anxiety, as if there's something she hasn't dealt with, as if there's something unacknowledged that she must face. She feels she must gather her strength, but for what?

And then she realizes – she must gather her strength to face a long life without Diana in it. Grief takes time, she keeps hearing, and she realizes she's hardly even begun. She feels that she is sinking under the weight of it.

She makes her way down to breakfast. Her mother has stayed home again, in case she needs her. Riley tries to think of what day it is and realizes it's Thursday, because the funeral was yesterday. Her mom asks her if she wants to go to school, but she doesn't want to, not yet. It seems like such a betrayal of Diana, to even try to go back to a normal life when she is lying there in the cold ground, all that earth pressing down on her. Riley starts to feel her anxiety rise, and with it a kind of breathlessness, as if she can feel the earth pressing down on her too. She remembers those stories about witches in New England being pressed to death – boards placed on top of them and then stone upon stone added until they finally died. They weren't all burned at the stake or tied to a chair and thrown in the river. So many awful ways for a woman to die.

Her phone pings and she glances at it. It's Evan.

She looks at his text. Riley are you okay?

I'm fine. Just needed some sleep.

Want to talk?

She needs to talk to someone, or she will break in two.
Okay. Can I come over there? I need to get out.

Yeah, sure. I can't face school today. My parents have gone to work.

K. Maybe in an hour?

K. See you then.

Riley steps into the shower. Grief makes her move in slow motion. She lets herself cry under the water for a long time. Then she puts on jeans and a shapeless sweater, thinking that maybe Evan's right, and she should see a counsellor.

She walks to Evan's house. It's not far. It's another cold, grey day, toward the end of October. Riley notices the Halloween decorations that have gone up, seemingly overnight, or maybe she just didn't notice them before. The ghosts on people's lawns, and swinging from trees, make her think of Diana, and of the dead boy who visited them in Diana's bedroom, whose grave she found yesterday. It makes her feel gloomy.

She arrives at Evan's house, and he invites her in. He offers to make coffee. As the coffee is brewing, they sit in the living room and talk.

'Turner killed her,' Evan says. 'I can't take it in.'

She nods wearily. 'They must have solid evidence, if they arrested him.'

Evan shrugs. 'I don't know.'

She considers. She tilts her head at him and says, 'What if

they don't? What if they're just under pressure to make an arrest?' Her voice rises in volume and pitch. 'What if he's not the one who did it? What if the killer is still out there?'

'He must have done it, or they wouldn't have arrested him,' Evan says, as if trying to soothe her.

It irritates her. She doesn't want soothing, she wants the truth. For Diana. For her own peace of mind. 'You know that's not true. The wrong people get arrested all the time.' He looks back at her uneasily, as if he's afraid she'll get hysterical. She's changed her mind about not telling him. 'There's something I haven't told you,' she says.

His eyebrows go up. 'What?'

'I found another cemetery.'

'What other cemetery? What are you talking about?'

'There's another cemetery, a really old one, on the outskirts of town. And I found him.'

'Found who?'

Is he being dense on purpose? He must know what she's talking about. 'Simon Foster. I found his gravestone. Born 1861, died 1873.'

He looks at her as if she's lost her mind. He doesn't need to look at her like that – it's a fact. She saw it with her own eyes. She'll take him there and make him see it for himself. 'The dead boy we spoke to in Diana's bedroom that night.'

He shakes his head at her impatiently. 'You can't seriously believe in that stuff.'

Suddenly she wants to make him understand, to accept the possibility. She leans forward and speaks urgently. 'But it's true. I was there. I saw him communicate through the

Ouija board with my own eyes. And I found his grave! I'll show it to you.' As he observes her sceptically, she says, her voice notching higher, 'What if Diana is out there too, and we can speak to her through the Ouija board, and she could tell us who her killer was? Maybe we should try!' It's a step too far.

'Riley, the police have it handled,' he says. He stands up. 'I'll get the coffee.' He leaves her and goes into the kitchen.

He's trying to give me time to calm down, Riley thinks. *I'm not going to calm down. I think it's a good idea. If he won't try it with me, I'll find someone who will.*

But she'd already asked Sadie, yesterday, after she'd found the stone marking Simon's grave, and Sadie hadn't wanted to try contacting Diana to find her killer either. The idea seemed to make her uneasy. She said she wasn't sure any more what had happened that night, because she'd had so much to drink. She thought maybe it hadn't happened the way Riley remembered. Riley hadn't had too much to drink, and she remembered it very clearly. But Sadie had refused to go back and look at the gravestone with her.

Evan brings their coffees into the living room and sets hers down in front of her.

There's an uneasy silence as each waits for the other to speak first. Finally, Riley says, 'Never mind, forget I said anything.' He looks relieved. 'I think maybe you're right, that I should see a counsellor,' Riley admits.

'I think it would help,' he agrees.

Suddenly everything seems too much, and she begins to

cry. Maybe she *is* losing it. 'I'm sorry. I didn't sleep much last night.'

He says, 'You don't have to apologize. You look worn out. Why don't you lie down for a bit. You can use my parents' room if you want.'

She hasn't got the energy to protest. She feels utterly drained, by her sleepless night, by the funeral, by everything. She hasn't got the energy right now to go home to her own bed. She lets him show her upstairs to his parents' bedroom. She's suddenly grateful at the sight of a bed. He leaves her there and she lies down, thinking she'll fall asleep immediately. But she doesn't. The smell of his father's cologne is overwhelming; she can't stand it.

She finally gets up and quietly crosses the hall to Evan's bedroom. It's impeccably neat, the bed tidily made. She slumps onto his bed and rolls over onto her side, facing the wall. But she can't get comfortable, and she turns onto her stomach, pushing her face down into the edge of the bed. She catches a glimpse of something bright red and sparkly on the floor in the corner under the bed, something familiar. She looks more closely.

Her eyes snap wide open. She's staring at the back of a phone case – one she recognizes immediately.

It's Diana's.

Chapter Fifty-Four

I watch Riley with Evan, crying her eyes out. I know she's struggling with this, we're both struggling, but we're on opposite sides of a void and we can't support each other. It seems so cruel.

I remember that night, with the Ouija board – how could I ever forget it? I remember that dead boy. Maybe I can find him, and then at least I'll have some company. But I don't want a dead little boy from a different time. I want Riley. I want my mother. I want my life back.

Evan always was close-minded about things that can't be proved scientifically. A bit strange, perhaps, for someone who wants to be a novelist. He's interested in stories, in people, in their motivations. Story is all about emotions, surely? And those aren't scientific, they can't be measured. Maybe he'll figure that out, or he won't be a very good novelist.

He shut Riley down pretty fast. I wonder if she will try

the Ouija board anyway. And if she does, would I be able to reach her? What would I say to her? I could only tell her how much I miss her, how angry I am to be here, with no idea of how to move on. It would only upset her. Would I be less lonely? I don't know.

She cries for a long time, while I observe the two of them, my two best friends, sharing their pain. I follow them upstairs and stay with Riley when Evan goes back downstairs. I watch her lie down in his parents' room. But she's like Goldilocks, something is bothering her, the bed isn't comfortable, perhaps? She gets up and quietly moves across the hall and I follow her into Evan's room and watch her lie down on his bed.

She turns over, and I'm about to leave her there, when her body goes completely rigid. She's staring at something underneath the bed. I move in and take a closer look too.

It's my phone. In the corner underneath Evan's bed. What the hell is it doing there? A wave of confusion rolls over me.

And – seeing my phone there, hidden under Evan's bed – I suddenly remember all of it, every traumatic thing that happened to me, and it's a fresh wave of horror all over again.

I remember that night in my room, what Mr Turner did to me. How he made me strip naked, how he stared at me as I trembled in fear. How he left me there, warning me not to tell.

And all at once I remember the last day of my life, how it began, and how it ended. How I got out of bed, having hardly slept that night – and went into school early to confront Mr Turner in front of Principal Kelly.

I told Mr Kelly how Turner had broken into my house

the night before and what he'd done – and watched him deny it. He was white-faced, angry, and said it was sheer fabrication, outrageous, and how could anyone believe me? He said I was making it up and no one would believe me because I hadn't even been raped, and there was no evidence. I sat there looking at him, remembering the leather gloves, and thinking he was a monster. I couldn't understand why Mr Kelly didn't believe me. Why would I make something like that up?

'What do you want me to do?' he asked helplessly.

'I want you to know,' *I said. Then I turned to my tormentor with loathing. 'If you ever come near me again, I will go to the police, and I will bring charges against you.'*

I should have gone directly to the police that morning. But there were a lot of complicated reasons why I didn't. I was afraid they wouldn't believe me, just like Mr Turner said, and he was probably counting on that. After all, there was no actual evidence. The door was unlocked – he just walked right in. He never touched me. I didn't want to go through all that and be called a liar. But mostly, it was Cameron. I was afraid of what he might do if he knew what Mr Turner had done. I thought Cameron might attack him, and be charged with assault, and ruin his own life. I didn't want that. I loved Cameron, I just didn't want to spend the rest of my life with him. And . . . I was afraid Cameron might blame me a little. I was afraid he might think I'd led Mr Turner on somehow. Cameron was so possessive, so jealous, so insecure where I was concerned. Kelly didn't believe me, and I wasn't at all sure Cameron would either.

That morning, I left Kelly's office, pulled myself together, and went through the school day pretending to be fine, but inside I was a complete mess. The rest of that day was uneventful – up until the terrible argument that night with Cameron. I hardly remember that day, even though it was my last day among the living. I should have appreciated the sun on my face more, the way food tasted. But I had no idea then that I wouldn't see another day. I just pretended that everything was normal, faking it for everybody, even Riley, while thinking the whole time about what I should do. But I didn't go to the police that day.

And that night, after Cameron dropped me off, I was so angry. Cameron and I were finished. It was a relief, really. I had no space in my head any more for him and the time he took and his controlling ways. I was tired of making decisions based on him and how he might react. A man had crept in my back door and had terrified and humiliated me and I couldn't even tell my boyfriend – or anyone else – for fear of how he'd react. That wasn't love. That wasn't right.

I locked the doors, afraid that Turner might come back. But that night, after Cameron had behaved so badly, after what I'd endured, I decided that the next day I would go to the police and tell them everything. I couldn't let myself live a life governed by fear. Cameron had to take responsibility for himself. I was no longer willing to take responsibility for him.

And then, just a few minutes after I'd got home, I heard a knock at the front door. I didn't answer it because I thought it was Cameron again. But then I got the ping of a text. It was from Evan. Are you home? Can I come in?

321

I wasn't in the mood to see anyone, but I let him in.

'What's up?' I asked, as he entered the house. I remember looking out at the empty street – there was no truck out there then. I locked the door behind him.

'I'm glad you're home. I need my Moby Dick *back, for an assignment I'm working on tonight – pulling an all-nighter.'*

'Shit, right, I'm sorry.' I'd borrowed it and forgotten to bring it back to him at school that day as promised, because I'd been so absorbed in my problems with Mr Turner. I went up to my room to grab it and came back downstairs and handed it to him.

'Not out with Cameron tonight?' Evan asked.

I figured I might as well tell him. 'We were out, but we had a fight. I broke up with him.' I shrugged. 'So I'm home early.'

Evan sat down, uninvited. 'You finally broke up with him? Why?'

I sighed. I didn't really want to get into it right then, but Evan was a friend. 'It's a bunch of things. But mostly he's more serious about us than I am. He thinks it's for ever. I want to go to a different college, and he won't hear of it. I didn't really have a choice.'

'Wow,' Evan said, looking at me. 'Good for you.'

'You mean that?'

'Of course. Cameron's being a dick. He's too controlling. A girl like you – you need your independence. You're too . . . glorious . . . to be tamed.'

That made me a little uncomfortable. Especially because he was looking at me in a way he hadn't before.

'Anyway,' I said, standing up, 'I'm really tired, and you've got that assignment to do, so . . .'

He stood too. We were standing there in the living room. I remember it all so clearly now. I understand why I blocked it out – because it's too shocking, too horrible.

'You know I love you, Diana,' he said. 'Don't you?'

I stared back at him, surprised. I felt acutely uncomfortable. It was too much. After everything that had happened to me in the last twenty-four hours, I was approaching hysteria. I didn't know what to say, so I laughed. I was trying to make light of the situation, to reduce the tension in the air for both of us. But it was a mistake.

His face transformed. In an instant, he wasn't the familiar Evan I knew, but someone cold, different. Everything changed in that moment. I had misread him. I'd misunderstood him, all these years. He was not someone to laugh at, he was someone to be afraid of.

'How dare you laugh at me,' he said quietly.

'Evan, I'm not laughing at you,' I said desperately. 'Honestly. I'm just really tired. I think you should go.' I turned away from him then, to move toward the front door, to get him to leave. I noticed that the heavy curtains in the living room were drawn, and no one could see in. And then he knocked me down.

The blow to my head was crushing. I think I blacked out for a second. I was so confused. I remember trying to crawl from the living room, but my limbs weren't working, and I just collapsed. I wanted to escape. But his voice.

'Oh no you don't. You don't get to ridicule me,' he said.

323

There was so much nastiness in his voice. I tried to lift my head and saw him pull my jump rope off the living room doorknob and I thought, in disbelief, He's going to tie me up and rape me.

But I was wrong. He pulled me back by my legs and turned me over in the middle of the living room floor. He climbed on top of me to hold me down, pinning my useless arms to the floor with his legs, and wrapped the jump rope around my neck and pulled. I was so afraid. I remember us looking into each other's eyes for a long, grotesque moment. I felt my eyes popping, the crushing pain in my throat, knowing that I was dying, as he looked down at me with rage. The last thing I heard was my phone ping with a text.

And then I woke up in that field, looking down at my naked body, assaulted once again by those ugly birds.

How many ways, I think, can a girl be assaulted? I never got to live my life. I never got to live to be old enough, to become unattractive enough, to be left alone. To finally just be.

Chapter Fifty-Five

RILEY STARES AT Diana's phone under the bed, her heart pounding.

She suddenly understands why Evan doesn't want to speak to Diana's ghost. Because Diana must know who killed her, and now Riley does too.

She quietly pushes the bed a little bit further from the wall to get a better look. It's Diana's phone, no question. Evan must have sent that text. He killed Diana, and he thinks he'll never be found out. But why? She doesn't want to touch it. She leaves it where it is.

Her hands are shaking as she calls 911 on her cell.

'What is your emergency?'

For a moment she can't think. How does she describe this situation?

'My name is Riley Mead. I'm at Seventeen Beecher Street, Fairhill. The Carr residence. I'm in the house with a murderer.' She keeps her voice as low as possible, afraid that

Evan will hear. What if he does? Will he kill her too, and get rid of the phone? She says in a rush, 'Evan Carr killed Diana Brewer. I found her phone in his room, under his bed. Send police, quickly!'

'Please don't hang up, ma'am, keep the line open.'

To her horror, she hears steps padding up the stairs. He's heard her. She hides her phone under his pillow, ending the call first so he won't hear the woman's voice on the other end. She hears him stop outside his parents' bedroom door.

'Riley?'

A few quick steps and he's standing over her. She's feigning sleep, lying on her stomach, her face buried in the pillow.

'Riley? Are you awake? I thought I heard something. What are you doing in my room?' His voice is strained.

She pretends to wake. She rolls over, blinking. 'What?'

'What are you doing in my room?'

He must sense her fear, she thinks, because he knows. His face changes, as if he's someone else, someone unrecognizable.

'*What have you done?*'

'What do you mean? I haven't done anything,' she says, trying to smile at him, but wholly unnerved by the stranger staring back at her. It's not the Evan she knows, it's someone else. 'I couldn't sleep in your parents' bed, so I came in here. I hope that's okay.'

He stares at her, indecisive. He sees her hand, under the pillow. 'What do you have under the pillow?'

'Nothing.'

He rips the pillow off the bed, sees her phone. 'Did you call someone?'

She can't hide her fear now, her voice trembling as she answers. 'No, why? What's wrong, Evan? You're acting weird. You're scaring me.'

He picks up her phone and looks at it. It's locked. 'Open it,' he says.

She unlocks the phone with dread and he sees her last call. Then he looks at her as if he wants to kill her. It's as if time has stopped. Then they both hear it at once, the police sirens coming down the street, getting louder, closer. The rage in his eyes as he realizes it's too late, that there's no way out.

Ellen knows the truth, now. Everyone knows that Evan Carr has been arrested for the murder of Diana Brewer. They have evidence; he had her cell phone in his bedroom. No one knows why he did it, but they seem pretty sure he did. Her former fiancé is not a murderer after all. And she'd almost believed he was.

Nonetheless, all of this has shattered her view of the world. Her former sunny outlook, her optimism, her belief in the inherent goodness of people – that's all gone. Maybe it will come back some day, but she doubts it. She knows now that she was naïve, perhaps even wilfully blind. If she's really honest with herself, there were times when she caught Brad noticing young girls when they were out together, standing in line at the movie theatre, or having an ice cream cone at the park. A glance here and there – which she ignored.

She hasn't been to see him. Instead, she went to Graham Kelly's house. She'd heard that it was Kelly who'd gone to the police, who'd told them something that led to Brad's short-lived arrest. She wanted to hear what it was from Kelly's own lips.

She knocked on his door, which was opened by his rigid, unsmiling wife. 'Can I talk to Mr Kelly for a minute?' she asked. She wondered what was going on behind Mrs Kelly's eyes.

Graham Kelly had come into the living room and his wife had marched out, neither acknowledging the other. He looked as bad as Ellen felt. She was angry at him too. He'd withheld the truth, and he should pay the price. Maybe his wife felt the same way, and that's why she was so angry.

Ellen sat down abruptly on the edge of an armchair, braced herself, and said, 'I want you to tell me everything. All of it.'

He nodded in defeat. 'Okay.'

He told her what Diana said had happened in the locker room. He told her the rest of it – how Diana told him that Brad Turner had crept into her unlocked house at night, how he'd made her strip off her clothes so that he could look at her. How he'd intimidated her, telling her that no one would ever believe her because there was no evidence.

Ellen felt the bile rising up her throat. It was all so ugly, so unbelievable. Yet she believed it.

Kelly was weeping then. 'She said he was a monster,' he

said, 'and I didn't believe her, not then. And then when I learned he had no alibi, I thought maybe he'd killed her. I couldn't live with that on my conscience anymore.'

'How could you live with it on your conscience at all?' she asked coldly.

'Brad was blackmailing me,' he said bluntly.

She felt a chill come over her; she hadn't thought it could get any worse, yet here they were.

'I might as well tell you,' Kelly said. 'I've already told my wife. Brad knew about an affair I'd had, and he threatened to tell my wife about it if I told anyone what Diana said he'd done to her.' He added ruefully, 'You might have noticed my wife isn't speaking to me.'

Ellen left the house, sickened by what she'd learned. An innocent man wouldn't have resorted to blackmail.

Now, she hopes Brad goes to jail for what he did, although she doesn't know how they will ever prove it. She never wants to see him, or that little bungalow, again. She decides she'll leave Fairhill and make a new life somewhere else, she doesn't care where. She can't live here any more.

I linger in a corner of the interview room, watching Evan. It's just the two of us, although he's not aware of me. He doesn't believe in ghosts.

I think about that awful moment, when Evan realized that Riley knew, and that she'd called the police. I'd watched in horror – the same chilling transformation had come over Evan when he killed me. Like he was someone else, someone completely different.

329

I remember Evan – the great pretender – at my funeral. How touched I was by his reading. The nerve of him, when he's the one who put me here.

The desire for revenge, though – the desire to haunt my killer – is fading. Evan will pay the price for my death. He will suffer for what he's done.

Chapter Fifty-Six

EVAN IS ALONE; the detectives have to wait for his attorney
to arrive. His mother and father are somewhere in the police
station, in shock.

It's the first time he's been in an interview room, and he
studies it with interest. The table is bolted to the floor.
There's no two-way mirror on the wall so that whoever is
in here can be watched unobserved. For that you probably
had to be in a big city.

He would have loved to be on the other side of a two-
way mirror, watching everyone who came into this room
over these last few days to be questioned about Diana's
death. They probably videotaped everything, and he has an
overwhelming desire to see all those tapes. He wants to
watch the interviews they'd done with Cameron, and
Turner, and Prior. All writers have a bit of the voyeur in
them, and an insatiable curiosity. It would be so helpful to
him to have that material.

They have Diana's phone. He knows he's done for. He should have gotten rid of it. But he was never a suspect. He thought he was safe. He thought if they were ever growing suspicious of him, he would know it, and would have time to get rid of the phone. But he liked having it. He liked having something of Diana's, something so personal. Something that revealed to him so much of her life.

He waits for his attorney to arrive. He remembers that night so clearly; it will always stand out vividly in his mind, more vividly than anything before or since. He'd only walked over to Diana's to get his book back. She'd forgotten to return it, which was not at all like her. He hadn't meant to harm her. He was glad when she told him that she'd dumped Cameron. But he wishes now that she hadn't told him. Because in that moment, when she told him she was free, she looked so lovely, and he was filled with such longing for her, that he confessed his love for her on the spot. And she *laughed*.

Something came over him. It was something he was aware of, but it surprised him, nonetheless. He'd never shown that side of himself to anyone before. But she asked for it. She laughed at him. And then she asked him to leave. As she turned away to go to the door, he hit her with the only thing he had in his hands – his big, heavy, hardcover copy of *Moby Dick* – and she dropped to the floor. He thought he'd knocked her out. He stood there for a moment, staring down at her, slumped on the floor. Then she stirred and tried to crawl away, but it was a feeble attempt, and it made him feel powerful. He grabbed the jump rope dangling on the doorknob. He pulled her into the centre of the living room, turned her over, and straddled her. Her arms and legs were limp; she was still barely conscious from the blow. He wrapped the jump rope around her neck and squeezed.

It took a long time for her to die. She stared at him with wide open, bulging eyes; her eyes were screaming, though she could not. He grimaced back at her with the effort of killing her. The only sounds were his rasping, laboured breath and her gurgling death rattle. Her phone pinged with a text. It startled him, but he didn't let up on the pressure of the jump rope.

Finally, she was gone.

He rolled off her and caught his breath. He made sure there was no pulse. Her phone pinged again. He picked it up off the living room floor and looked at it. It was Cameron.

I'm outside, in the truck. Can we talk?

Fuck, fuck, fuck. Evan's heart was pounding with effort, adrenaline, and now, alarm. The living room lights were on, so Cameron would know she was still up. Should he answer the text? He decided not to. She'd broken up with him. She'd ignore him. Evan stayed down on the floor, below the window, even though the curtains were drawn. He must not be seen. He lay beside Diana, trying to think of what to do next.

Cameron kept texting.

Diana, I'm sorry. Please, can we talk?

I love you.

Please answer me.

I was an idiot. I just want to apologize. I just want to talk to you.

Then, to Evan's relief, the pinging finally stopped. Evan thought he'd given up. He waited for the sound of the truck leaving. What he heard instead was a truck door slamming and then Cameron knocking on the front door. Evan froze in fear. The knocking came again. And again. Evan remained rigid on the floor. He heard Cameron trying the doorknob, but remembered with relief that Diana had locked it after him. Eventually he heard Cameron leave the front door and walk down the side of the house. Evan's heart pounded furiously. He heard Cameron calling Diana's name from the backyard. He was terrified that Cameron might come inside the house. Was the back door locked? Jesus, what was he going to do? He didn't think he could overpower Cameron.

He lay on the floor beside Diana's body, waiting, afraid. Finally, he heard the sound of footsteps at the side of the house again, the truck door opening, and Cameron driving away. He had to wait another few minutes before his heart rate went back down to anything near normal. Then he made a plan.

First, he held Diana's phone up to her face, and fortunately it recognized her, even though her face was now a more grotesque version of itself, her eyes wide and flecked

334

with blood. He changed her password to a number code, so that he'd be able to get into her phone.

He eventually got up and turned off the light in the living room. He unlocked the back door and slipped out, leaving it unlocked for his return, and crept across the field to the lane. He walked home from there carrying his book – not bloodied at all – and returned it to his bookshelf. He waited until both of his parents were fast asleep. Then he grabbed a pair of gloves, went into the garage, and put a shovel in his mother's boot. He drove back out to the unused road, parked, and entered Diana's house through the back door that he'd left unlocked. He didn't want to leave Diana in the house, because what if someone had seen him knock on her door? Better if she was found somewhere else. He took the jump rope with him and carried her out the back door, and across the field. She was heavier than he expected, and he'd had to stop a couple of times and put her down, but he knew no one could see him there. He was sweating with the effort.

He got her into the trunk of his mother's car and drove out of town. He found a quiet road, parked behind a clump of trees, and carried her out to the middle of a farmer's field. He wanted her to be found, but he didn't want to throw her in a ditch. He stripped all her clothes off her, to get rid of evidence and to make it look like a sex killing. He took a good look at her, lying naked in the moonlight.

He left her there and drove twenty minutes in another direction and used the shovel to bury her clothes and the jump rope deep in a secluded wood. But he kept her phone.

Evan hears a sound outside the room and looks up. His attorney has arrived. His parents shuffle in, unable to look at him. He ignores them. Evan tries to listen, but his mind drifts. It's turned out quite differently than he expected. He never thought he'd be caught. When Turner was arrested, that was perfect. What a great book this will make, he'd thought. But now they have her phone, found hidden in his bedroom, with his fingerprints all over it.

Someone is repeating his name, and he looks up and tries to focus on the detective. Stone is suggesting he confess. Asking if he really wants to go to trial for murder in the first degree as an adult, and face life in prison, or if he would like to plead guilty to second-degree murder and get twenty years, or quite possibly less, given the mitigating factors of a guilty plea, his young age, and his previously clean record.

Maybe he *should* plead guilty, Evan thinks. He's only seventeen. He'll have time to get a degree and to write in prison. He knows he's not allowed to profit from committing a crime, so he can't make money from anything he writes about Diana's death. But does it matter? He'll have time to perfect his craft. He'll have notoriety and fame as a confessed murderer. He'll have a name. He'll have life experience. It's not the worst way to launch a writing career these days.

His journal is basically a lie. He'd never expected to be caught, never intended to reveal himself as the murderer – either they would get the wrong person, or it would remain tantalizingly unsolved.

But now he realizes that his journal is one kind of truth; it reflects the Evan he has been most of the time – earnest, decent, good. The Evan who loved Diana, in his way. That's who he *wants* to be. The journal was a kind of pretending, of self-soothing, of lying to himself, because he doesn't really want to be this other Evan. The one who murdered Diana in an unguarded moment.

He knows this other Evan has always been there, threatening to surface. He just doesn't know whether he'll surface again. Or how much of this he will reveal in his book. It will be interesting to write.

He enjoyed writing that journal. It's fun to play with the truth.

Isn't that what writers do?

Dear Reader,

I thought you might be interested in a little bit of information behind the writing of this book . . .

I set this one in Vermont because it has a rich history of ghost stories, which was ideal for what I had in mind. I also wanted to place this novel in more of a rural setting, perhaps because not long ago my husband and I moved from the city of Toronto to an abandoned old farm in Ontario. I love it here, but it is very dark outside at night – and even a little creepy. There is no ambient light at all, the way there is in the city.

I've always enjoyed a good ghost story. I consider myself to be open-minded on the question of ghosts – I'm really not sure one way or the other if they exist. But I had one formative experience that made it into What Have You Done? *As a young teenager I lived on a farm in rural Ontario, and one night, a family friend came over and created a homemade Ouija board by cutting out letters and numbers written on a piece of paper and placing them in a circle on the coffee table. We used an upturned wine glass and placed our fingers on it. This woman conjured the spirit of a boy named Simon – I reused the name – who answered a few questions and then got angry and sped the wine glass around the table in furious circles until we removed our fingers, at which point the glass immediately became still. I was terrified. This experience has stayed with me, and I have never tried to use a Ouija board since!*

Thank you for reading What Have You Done? *I hope you've enjoyed it!*

Very best,
Shari Lapena

Acknowledgements

I HAVE SO many people to thank, not only for this, my eighth thriller, but for the previous seven thrillers we have put out together. Seven *New York Times* and UK *Sunday Times* and *Globe and Mail* bestsellers! We truly are a dream team!

In the UK, as always, I'd like to thank Larry Finlay, Bill Scott-Kerr, Sarah Adams, Tom Hill, Jen Porter, and the rest of the dream team at Transworld. A special thanks to Larry Finlay – we will miss you! In the US, as always, I'd like to thank Brian Tart, Pamela Dorman, Jeramie Orton, and the rest of the dream team at Viking Penguin. A special thanks to Ben Petrone – we will miss you too! In Canada, as always, my thanks to Kristin Cochrane, Amy Black, Bhavna Chauhan, Emma Ingram, Val Gow, and the rest of the dream team at Doubleday Canada. Thank you, all.

I'd like to give particular thanks to my editors, Sarah Adams and Jeramie Orton. Thank you for your hard work, good humour, and encouragement as we worked through *What Have You Done?* And Sarah gets the credit for coming up with a great title – again.

Thanks again to Jane Cavolina, my fabulous copy editor. You've spoiled me for any other copy editor, ever.

Thanks, always, to my agent, Helen Heller. You've been here from the beginning and are part of the dream team! Thanks also to Camilla and Jemma and everyone at the Marsh Agency for representing me worldwide and selling my books into so many foreign territories.

As always, any mistakes in the manuscript are mine.

I've dedicated this book to my readers, with thanks. Without you, I wouldn't be doing this. Your enthusiasm for my books is very much appreciated and makes me love what I do.

Thanks to all the bloggers, reviewers and podcasters who shout about books they love far and wide, and to the people who work so tirelessly to put on festivals for writers and readers all over the world. Thanks to libraries, everywhere, for all they do to promote reading and to redress inequality of opportunity.

And lastly, thanks to my family, who have learned to live with my sometimes frantic schedule. Sadly, our cat, Poppy, who kept me company through so many books, passed away during the writing of this one. We miss her. Special thanks to Manuel, always, for all the technical and other support. I couldn't do it without you.

Shari Lapena is the internationally bestselling author of the thrillers *The Couple Next Door*, *A Stranger in the House*, *An Unwanted Guest*, *Someone We Know*, *The End of Her*, *Not a Happy Family* and *Everyone Here is Lying*, which have all been *Sunday Times* and *New York Times* bestsellers. Her books have been sold in forty territories around the world. She lives in Toronto.

Facebook: ShariLapena
Twitter: @sharilapena
Instagram: sharilapena